THE DEVIL'S BARGAIN

Stella RIMINGTON

THE DEVIL'S BARGAIN

BLOOMSBURY PUBLISHING
LONDON · OXFORD · NEW YORK · NEW DELHI · SYDNEY

BLOOMSBURY PUBLISHING
Bloomsbury Publishing Plc
50 Bedford Square, London, WC1B 3DP, UK
29 Earlsfort Terrace, Dublin 2, Ireland

BLOOMSBURY, BLOOMSBURY PUBLISHING and the Diana logo are
trademarks of Bloomsbury Publishing Plc

First published in Great Britain 2022

A catalogue record for this book is available from the British Library

ISBN: HB: 978-1-5266-1293-9; TPB: 978-1-5266-1294-6;
EBOOK: 978-1-5266-1290-8; EPDF: 978-1-5266-5149-5

2 4 6 8 10 9 7 5 3 1

Typeset by Integra Software Services Pvt. Ltd.
Printed and bound in Great Britain by CPI Group (UK) Ltd, Croydon CR0 4YY

To find out more about our authors and books visit www.bloomsbury.com
and sign up for our newsletters

PROLOGUE

A cold wind was blowing spray in Harry Bristow's face as he waited in the gloom on the quayside. He wiped it away with his gloved hand, then clapped both hands together and stamped his feet in a futile effort to keep warm. He could hear the water slapping against the hull of the *Bogdana*, the Bulgarian freighter that was the reason he was there.

The ship had tied up several hours ago and, as soon as the gangplank was down, Harry had gone on board with the port customs officer, whose job it was to check the manifest and the cargo. Harry's interest, as the port's Special Branch officer, lay in the crew – and in particular those who wished to go ashore. In these Cold War days a sharp eye was kept on Soviet and East European sailors. They were allowed to land but not to stay and Harry's job was to make sure that those who got off the ship got back on again before it sailed.

It was all quite routine and friendly. They had gathered in the captain's cabin – the captain, an old sea dog who spoke a heavily accented English, and the First Officer, a much younger and altogether smoother character who was fluent. All four men had met before on the *Bogdana*'s previous visits and all knew the routine. First the toasts, drunk from small glasses – a sweet, fiery liqueur accompanied by juicy orange segments. Then the conversation: weather, family, football (all of them favoured Liverpool to win the Cup) – never politics. Then the captain produced the manifest, which he and the customs officer went through while the First Officer gave Harry the crew list, with ticks against the names of those who wanted to go ashore. As usual the First Officer's own name was ticked – he always went ashore, though Harry couldn't think why anyone would want to spend a cold wet evening in Heysham. Igor something unpronounceable was his name.

This must be their fourth meeting, thought Harry. The first time was on Harry's first day on duty at the harbour, shortly after he had been transferred to Special Branch from uniform. The next time he came Igor had remembered that Harry had a son and he had given Harry a Bulgarian flag for the boy. Young Charlie had been thrilled with it – no one else in his class had anything from behind the Iron Curtain. The third time they'd encountered each other Igor had given Harry a little box with a pair of pretty earrings inside for his wife. Harry knew he shouldn't have accepted it, but by the time he had opened the box Igor had gone ashore; when he came back it would have seemed rude to return them, especially as they were nothing valuable, just tiny pieces of red glass in some sort of metal setting. His wife did tell him later that a friend of hers had said that they were real rubies in gold, but he didn't believe it.

Now, waiting on the quayside, Harry peeled back his glove to look at his watch. It was nearly six o'clock. They had finished unloading the cargo more than an hour ago and they must be about ready to come ashore. They had to be back by midnight to sail on the two a.m. tide. As he strolled over to the gangplank the first crew members appeared, wearing identical pea jackets and boots. He checked their passports one by one, putting a cross against their names on the list. None of them spoke much English.

They moved off as a group, heading for town. They had all disappeared from sight when Igor came down. He had spruced himself up – under his raincoat he wore a blue blazer, and a white shirt open at the neck. He'd changed from boots to polished black leather slip-on shoes. He was handsome, as tall as Harry, with a head of thick blond hair and blue eyes. High cheekbones were the only Slavic hint in his face; otherwise he looked more like a local insurance salesman than the First Officer on a Bulgarian freighter.

'Evening, Igor,' Harry said. The foreigner grinned broadly and handed over what seemed to be a sheaf of newspapers with his passport lying on top. Harry looked at him questioningly. 'Thought you might be interested,' said Igor as Harry handed back his passport. 'By the way, I might not be back tonight. But don't worry – the skipper's OK with it. He'll pick me up at the next port.' And Igor winked as he sauntered off, leaving Harry speechless, clutching the newspapers.

Looking at his list, Harry saw that no one else was expected. He stood there for a minute, wondering what to do. Should he report Igor straightaway? But what if he did come back tonight? He'd only said he *might* not. If he did come back with the others after all, then Harry would look stupid and would have caused a big stink for nothing. Perhaps Igor was joking – pulling Harry's leg. Well, he thought, I'll know for sure when they come back at midnight. If he's not with them, I'll do something then, and tucking the newspapers into the side pocket of his waterproof, he retreated to the all-night café on the dockside from where he could keep an eye on the *Bogdana* while staying dry and warm.

Ordering coffee and toast at the counter, Harry looked around to see if there was anyone he knew, someone he could while away the time with until the Bulgarians came back to the ship. There wasn't; the place was almost empty: just a couple of harbour workers in the corner, talking about the football, and a table of seamen – Portuguese, he guessed, though they could have been anything as he couldn't understand a word of what they were saying.

The exchange with Igor had left him feeling uneasy. He pulled the folded newspapers out of his pocket to see what they were and why Igor had given them to him. It was then he realised that what he had was not a sheaf of newspapers at all; it was one thick newspaper folded round a stiff white envelope. A cold wave of shock washed over him as he hastily covered the envelope up, looking round quickly to see if anyone was watching. But no one at the other tables was taking the slightest bit of notice. Easing the envelope out from the folds of the newspaper, he opened it and withdrew the contents.

His hand held a wad of banknotes – twenties and fifties. He was breathing heavily now, gasping almost. He had never seen a fifty-pound note before and for a moment he wondered if they were real. He riffled quickly through the notes, mentally calculating as he went. There were at least sixty or seventy of them, though he wasn't going to count them out on the table like a cashier in a bank. He returned the notes to the envelope, before shoving it back into the pocket of his coat. There must be at least three grand in that envelope. Jesus. What was he to do? He felt his pulse racing and, quite improbably, he had to wipe a drop of sweat from one cheek, even though it was anything but hot in this half-empty café.

He knew he should report it straightaway – if you wanted a classic example of a bribe, this was a humdinger. And for a moment he resolved to do just that after his shift ended. But then he remembered the earlier gifts – his son's Bulgarian flag was innocuous enough, but what about the little red stones? Were they really rubies? Probably, he thought with a sickening lurch in his stomach, understanding suddenly that he had been set up. If he turned Igor in, he knew what Igor could say about him.

His toast was cold by now, as well as his coffee, and he felt too agitated to stay sitting there. He stood up, and for a crazed half second was tempted to leave one of the fifty-pound notes as a tip – or indeed all the contents of the envelope. But that would be madness. He left fifty pence instead and strode out of the café.

He walked round the harbour, past the big ferry scheduled to leave at the crack of dawn for the Isle of Man, busy now with men loading cargo and refuelling the enormous under-deck fuel tanks. He turned and came back again, still pondering his dilemma.

He knew the right thing to do – there wasn't any question in his mind. Hand over the envelope, explain he'd thought the rubies had seemed mere bits of glass, and throw himself on the mercy of his superiors. Mercy? In the bleak overhead lights of the harbour it didn't seem likely. And what about Igor? It was clear now that he wasn't coming back to the ship. But where had he gone and what was he doing? It must be important to him if it was worth that much money. Surely it wasn't just a girlfriend. He should certainly report it. It might be a matter of national security and it was his job to protect that. But could he report Igor without the presents coming out? No. It would all come out.

He found himself once more at the bottom of the *Bogdana*'s gangway, ready to count its crew back when they returned from their jaunt into town. He was still thinking about this new predicament. His wife, Gina, was pregnant and had left her job in the supermarket. They had planned ahead and could just about get by without her wages, but it would be a close-run thing. Three grand would make the difference between scraping by and living decently. But how would he explain the sudden change in fortune to her? He didn't know. Perhaps he should say he'd had an unexpected rise in pay – a promotion – even though he'd already told her it would be at least another two years before his rank was reviewed.

Yes, a surprise promotion – that's what he would say. But why would he have got a lump sum? Back pay? Seemed unlikely, but it would have to do. Gina was so proud of his move to Special Branch, but she was straight as a die; he could never tell her the truth of how he'd got this windfall. Even if he spent it bit by bit, Gina would notice – she was like a hawk when it came to watching their money. And he could never tell anyone else. Only he would know, he decided. Except for Igor.

He wouldn't tell anyone about Igor's unauthorised stay, either. Pray God he made his way back to the ship when it docked in the next port – not that Harry would ever know one way or the other. That would be his secret too. As he saw the group of Bulgarians come out of the shadow along the harbour, heading towards him and the gangway, Harry felt utterly alone. Well, alone except for one companion: his conscience.

The man headed straight for the minicab office just outside the port gates. There was a driver inside waiting for custom and he asked to be taken to the centre of the town. The journey took only a few minutes. The driver was keen for a chat and was curious why his passenger was on his own and why he hadn't walked the short distance. But the passenger didn't seem to speak English and the driver got only a smile in response to his questions. The passenger got out in the main street and the minicab drove off.

Not long after, in a dark row of terraced houses, the same man knocked on a door. No light came on in the hall but after a short delay the door opened. A stocky figure stood in the doorway holding out a bulky envelope, which jingled slightly as the man took it. Without a word, he turned and walked away, and the door closed behind him.

A hundred yards along the street, he stopped by a parked Vauxhall Cavalier – newish but dirty enough to blend in with the other cars. He opened the envelope, extracted a key, and unlocked the car door. Within seconds he was on his way, and in ten minutes he reached the M6, heading south for Liverpool. The man Harry Bristow thought of as Igor was certain he wasn't being followed.

T HE SUN WAS SHINING on the windows of Robinson's Kitchens in the Royal Albert Dock area of Liverpool, bouncing off the taps and sinks and shiny surfaces of the displays inside the shop. In a corner of the showroom Peter Robinson, as the owner of the business now called himself, was engaged in earnest conversation about tiles with a well-dressed young woman. He was arranging and rearranging samples of different colours for her, while she stood back, pondering the effect. At the back of the shop in a small office invisible from the street, a journalist from the *Liverpool Echo* was waiting to interview Peter Robinson for a lifestyle piece in the weekend edition of the paper. Robinson was standing for a seat on the city council and, as he was young, successful, good-looking and unmarried, there was a great deal of interest in him.

At last the customer was satisfied and, with a handshake and a dazzling smile, Robinson left her with an assistant to be shown out while he went back to the office, where the young journalist had set up her tape recorder in the centre of the table.

'I'm so sorry to keep you waiting,' said Robinson. 'That customer finds it very difficult to make up her mind. But I want her to be happy with the result, so I never try to hurry her.'

'Oh yes,' replied the journalist, already bowled over by the Robinson charm. 'You're known to go the extra mile to make your customers happy.'

'Let's get some coffee before we start,' said Robinson, ushering her out into the showroom where coffee was always to be found, filling the shop with its alluring smell.

'Now, tell me how I can help you?' he said when they were sitting down in the office.

'I'd like to start by asking you about your background,' she began. 'I know you're not from this part of the country. So tell me a bit about your early life; where were you born?'

An image of a flat in a grey block just outside Moscow flashed in Pyotr Romanov's mind. It was a block reserved for senior diplomats and KGB officers, so the flats were comparatively spacious and well maintained. He had lived there until he was five when his father was working in the Foreign Affairs Ministry. Then they had moved to London to the Soviet ambassador's residence in Kensington. Pyotr Romanov pushed those thoughts to the back of his mind and replaced them with the cover story carefully worked out in Kazikov's office so many years ago, when the Cold War was still raging and the KGB was still firmly in place.

Peter Robinson now replied, 'I'm a bit of a nomad, to be honest, which makes finding myself a home here even more important than might usually be the case. My father was in the oil business and my parents moved around a lot, so it wouldn't be accurate to name any one place as where I grew up. We did live in Canada for five years and that's probably the longest we were anywhere.'

'Your parents are British, though?'

'Actually, both my parents have passed away.'

'Oh. I'm so sorry.'

'It was quite a long time ago. But yes, they were British – and like most of us they were mongrels. I'd be hard-pressed to cite all the different blood that runs through my veins, but I know my father was half-Scots, part Welsh. My mother had some French blood she was very proud of, but otherwise was English – as far as I know. To be honest, neither was very family-oriented, and because we moved around so much I never got to know my relations – not even my grandparents, which is rather sad.'

'I suppose you must have gone to school abroad. What about university?'

'No. Like a lot of entrepreneurs, I didn't go to university – unless we're counting the University of Life! It's not something I'm proud of – I'd love to think that one day I could do a degree.'

'Between your life as a businessman and your new political career, it's hard to see how you'd ever have the time.'

'You're right, but I suppose everyone has to have a dream – even if it's unrealistic.' He gave a rueful smile.

'Why have you chosen Liverpool to build your business in?'

'I found myself in Liverpool by chance, really, and I loved it. It seems to have such possibilities. You see, when I was eighteen I decided to leave home – my parents were in Canada at the time – and I came to England. But I did it in a very roundabout way. I didn't have much money, so you might say I worked my way here. I worked on freighters, stopped off in the States for a bit, then I went on to South America and eventually wound up here in Liverpool – and this is where I decided to stay. I had had enough of travelling by that time.'

'And the kitchens business? Why choose that? It seems a long step from your background. I don't suppose your parents had luxury kitchens.'

Robinson relaxed a little – they were getting on to safer ground. So far his replies had been a tissue of lies and make-believe. The next bit would be largely true. Kazikov had left it to him to establish himself in British society however he could. The only help he could offer from his office in Moscow was an ample supply of cash.

'No. They certainly didn't. That was another bit of luck. I got a job as general dogsbody in a small ironmongery business. Not much more than a corner shop, really – long gone now. I gradually realised the growing interest in kitchens as people began to get more prosperous and wanted to improve their lifestyle. Kitchens are now becoming so much more than a place to cook. Then I moved to Manchester for a couple of years as an apprentice in a designer firm and came back here to open my first shop. I was lucky to benefit from a substantial legacy when my parents died. I had no idea they had saved any money.' As he said this, an image of Kazikov flashed into his mind, sitting behind his desk high up in the Lubyanka Building, issuing instructions to young Pyotr Romanov about the role he was to play. For the business purposes of Peter Robinson, now well established in the UK, Kazikov had effectively acted as a parent, and fortunately one with deep pockets.

'And now, I think I am right in saying, you have three shops in Liverpool and another planned for the Wirral. Will you find the time for a political career too?'

Politics of course was the point of it all. He had not come here just to run a successful kitchen business. Within three months of his arrival in Liverpool he had joined not just one but both of the major parties, though this rapidly became only one after he saw which way the tide was flowing – and before anyone noticed this cynical duplication of membership. He had given money, attended meetings, spoken his calm and reasonable piece each time there was a debate. Without any obvious sign of exertion, he found himself first nominated and then elected to a seat on the local council. His carefully judged, moderate positions were suddenly welcome among an otherwise divided vote, and he was now the favourite for election to the city council.

To the journalist's question he replied, 'You're right – I don't have the time. But I'd like to think Liverpool has room for people like me who come here and fall in love with this great city.' He smiled and looked at his watch. 'I like to think of Liverpool as a foster parent,' he said. 'But now, if you will excuse me, I have a meeting to attend.'

'Of course. Thank you so much for your time,' she said, now entirely captivated by the man and his story.

After she had gone he sat for a moment, thinking. There was one thing missing in the life of Peter Robinson and it wasn't the absence of a university degree. He had a mission in his life, one he confided to no one, and local politics was not its end but merely the means to it. The task he had been given in that office in the Lubyanka was to penetrate the highest circles of British political life, not only to acquire the most secret military, diplomatic and intelligence information, but to get a deep understanding from the heart of government of how things worked in Britain. Kazikov's aim was no less than to have the knowledge which would enable him to influence the course of the country – in fact to operate it like a puppet.

But circumstances had changed. The Soviet Union had collapsed. The KGB that had despatched Romanov on his mission was no more. He had heard nothing from Kazikov and could only assume he had retired or died or even been killed by whoever was in charge. He had heard nothing for more than a year from the small support team who had provided his money when he first arrived.

The last time he had tried to make contact, calling from a phone box miles away from Liverpool, the number was unobtainable. The silence wouldn't last forever, Romanov told himself, but he found the absence of any contact at all unnerving. Already the West was taking advantage of the break-up of the Soviet Union, luring the former members of the Warsaw Pact with promises and membership of NATO.

He felt angry and helpless, marooned as he was in the wrong place while his country went through a trauma. All he could do was listen to various radio stations and watch the news on television and try to interpret what was going on. His loyalties were firm. Russia was strong; hadn't the war proved that beyond doubt? The Germans had reached the outskirts of Moscow, Stalin had almost been forced to flee, yet the line had held firm, the pushback began, and Russia had emerged the victor. He was confident the same would be true now. He would continue on his own. He was sure that when things settled down again in Russia he would be contacted and the progress he would by then have made in infiltrating Britain would be of great value, and more than compensate for the uncertainty he felt now.

2

'I'LL NAIL THAT BASTARD one day,' muttered Harry Bristow to his junior colleague as they walked down the garden path of an immaculate semi in a suburb of Liverpool. The bastard referred to was standing at the door watching them leave. He was strongly suspected of being a senior commander in the Provisional IRA. The problem was that so far nothing could be pinned on him, and it made Harry furious to see him standing there complacently, probably laughing at him.

Much of Harry's work since he moved to Deputy Head of Special Branch in Liverpool a couple of years ago was involved with Northern Ireland. Though there was nominally a peace process, members and supporters of all the para-military groups lived in the city, and he and his team were constantly required to follow up leads from MI5 or the police in Northern Ireland; it was usually pretty frustrating work. Organised crime and drug running were also rife, giving Harry and his team more than they could handle.

Harry's career had prospered in the past years. He had had several promotions since his days in Heysham and on taking up his present job in Liverpool had become Detective Chief Inspector. Unfortunately for him his private life had not been so successful. It all started to go wrong after he met that bloody man Igor at Heysham docks and decided to keep his mouth shut and pocket the three thousand pounds. He hadn't been able to think of a credible lie to explain where it had come from by the time he got home so he had shoved it in his sock drawer, right at the back, and left it there. Inevitably, he supposed now recalling it, Gina had found the stash and naturally wanted to know what it was doing there. Caught off guard and with nothing prepared to say, he had blurted out that he had won it on the football pools. Of course she didn't believe him, and when he couldn't come up with anything more plausible she became convinced that he had done something criminal or at the very least disreputable. She refused to have anything to do with the money, even when another baby was born, conceived in an attempted reconciliation. So instead of making their lives easier or providing them with some luxuries, it became a burden and a source of argument and trouble. Harry did nothing with the money; it stayed there, in the drawer in its envelope. But it was always in both their minds, coming between them. Harry knew that Gina took it out occasionally and counted it to make sure he hadn't spent any of it, which meant that Harry could never forget it or overcome his feeling of guilt.

So when the promotion to his first job in Liverpool came up he seized it. He knew Gina would not want to move; she had her job back in the supermarket and their son was settled at school and his younger sister at nursery. Even though Liverpool was no more than two hours' drive from their home in Heysham, the new busier job and erratic working hours inevitably meant he saw less of his wife and their kids; gradually he grew apart from Gina, almost without realising it.

Then one day, when he was in the office talking about the football with another young detective, the receptionist came in and said he had an urgent phone call. His first reaction was that something had happened to Gina or one of the kids. He took the call in a conference room that was rarely used; later he would remember how someone had filled a vase with flowers that must have died weeks ago.

'Hello,' he said nervously.

'Is that Mr Bristow?' The voice was formal, a man's. Was it a doctor from the hospital?

'Yes, that's me. What's happened?'

'Nothing yet, Mr Bristow. My name is Staverton and I'm a solicitor. I'm phoning on behalf of your wife Gina.'

'Is she all right?' If something terrible had happened, why was a solicitor calling, instead of a hospital or the Manchester police?

'She's fine, Mr Bristow. I saw her not much more than an hour ago. She asked me to ring you. You will receive notice by post, of course, but she wanted me to introduce myself and to ask for the name of your own solicitor.'

'What? I don't have a solicitor.'

'I think it would be in your interests to retain one right away.'

'Why? What is this about?' Any relief he felt that Gina and the kids were OK was disappearing as he tried to take in what this man was saying.

'Hasn't Mrs Bristow talked to you? It was my clear impression that she had informed you of her plans.'

'What plans? To do what?'

'I'm sorry, Mr Bristow. I thought you knew already. I did not expect to have to impart the news myself. Very well. It's my unfortunate duty to say that it is your wife's intention to divorce you.'

'Divorce me? Why?'

'I'm afraid you'll have to ask your wife that question. I'm sorry to be the one to bring bad tidings.'

And soon enough Harry discovered that he had been largely replaced in the whole family's affections by an accountant so bland that Harry couldn't summon the smallest bit of dislike for him. Gradually, in fact, Harry actually welcomed seeing less of Gina, since she had become for him the personification of his true constant companion – his guilt.

That had been several years before, and now Harry could not complain about his circumstances. He was well regarded at work and, as Liverpool Special Branch was almost notoriously convivial, he had plenty of opportunity for socialising and could find female company when he wanted to. Once Gina had remarried, the deduction of alimony from his monthly income stopped, which made a big difference – he had bought a small house and a second-hand BMW, and could afford the odd meal in a good restaurant.

But he wouldn't have said he was living life to the full, and often, just as he felt things were going well, he would think of Igor, those many years ago, and the banknotes, still in his sock drawer, and the fact he had failed to turn them – or Igor – in. And at those moments, deep down, Harry felt a fraud.

'Drop me off in Bold Street,' he said to his colleague as they drove back into the centre of Liverpool. 'I need to go to Boots.'

He got out of the car a few buildings away from the chemist, where he needed to collect sleeping pills his doctor had prescribed. Since the *Bogdana* he had never slept well, and with so much on at work right now he had finally gone to the doctor to do something about it.

As he was walking past a branch of a bank, a grand Victorian building with columns and pilasters and an etched-glass window that had somehow survived the 1940s blitz, a man came down its steps – he looked familiar. He wore a suit and tie, which didn't fit with Harry's vague memory of him, and polished black leather slip-on shoes, which did. Suddenly in Harry's mind the man was walking down a ship's gangway, and when the man turned to the young woman beside him and grinned, Harry remembered him. It was Igor. His nemesis. Harry turned away quickly to avoid eye contact, and waited until the couple had walked off down the street. Then he went into the bank.

There were only two cashiers on duty, and he struck lucky in his first choice, a thin balding man in his fifties. Pulling out his police warrant card, Harry showed it to the cashier whose owl-like eyes widened. 'A man just left the bank. I think I know him, but I can't remember his name.'

'Oh, that's Councillor Robinson,' the man said, eager to help. 'Peter Robinson. Owner of Robinson's Kitchens. I don't know the lady, but he's a customer of ours.'

Harry's voice was shaking with shock as he thanked the man, and his legs were trembling so much that he had to hold the handrail to get safely down the steps outside. He sat for a short time on a street bench as he absorbed what had just happened. After a few moments he pulled himself together and went to collect his prescription, but all the time his mind was churning over what he had just seen, wondering if his memory was playing tricks on him and working out what he could do to learn more about Mr Robinson.

When he had finished with his errand it occurred to Harry that he was very close to the offices of the *Liverpool*

Echo and he knew from past experience that they had a well-indexed set of back copies of the paper. Some time ago he had taken the trouble to cultivate the archivist there and he decided to go along and see what he could learn about Peter Robinson.

'Ah,' said the archivist, a young-looking woman who was in her first job after qualifying at the university and hadn't yet learned discretion. 'I think he's lovely. So attractive and he's going places too. I suppose you're interested in him because he's on the city council.'

Harry smiled but didn't comment, waiting while she consulted her indexes and produced the archive's back issues, extracted and filed into Manila envelopes of clippings. He found several articles about Robinson, from which he learned that his father had been in the oil industry, which accounted for several years spent as a boy in Canada. He had left home at the age of eighteen, supposedly, and worked his way slowly by sea to England, stopping off in various countries en route – very convenient if you wanted to cover your traces, thought Harry – before pitching up in England seven years later when he was still a youthful twenty-five.

He had no doubt any more that Robinson was the Igor he had encountered on the *Bogdana*. What he couldn't fathom was why the man had gone to such lengths to disguise his identity – or invent one that would be near-impossible to expose – just to run a kitchen firm. Why was he here at all?

There could only be one reason, Harry eventually concluded. Robinson was a spy, working for Russia, he supposed. But doing what? Designing kitchens for the nouveau riche? What good would that do? True, he was on the city council, though even that seemed a derisory objective for one with such a complicated cover story. There must be more to this than he could see, he thought, as he thanked the archivist and left.

Harry went back to his house and stayed awake all night worrying about what to do. He knew what he ought to do – what he should have done years ago – which was to report the whole story to his boss, the Head of Special Branch. But then the whole story would come out. There would be an investigation by MI5. They would want to know why he hadn't reported straightaway that Igor had not come back to the *Bogdana* before she sailed. The presents, the ruby earrings and the money would all be exposed. They would find out even if he tried to keep that bit secret. He assumed Gina still had the earrings, and out of his guilt he had kept, though never spent, the envelope full of cash. He would be disgraced, lose his job certainly, possibly go to prison. He would never be able to work in the police again.

He tossed and turned in his bed all night and by the morning he had decided. He would say nothing. What was the point of ruining his whole life to expose a local councillor as a Russian agent? He could hear the snorts of laughter already; it would seem preposterous. Why would the Russians want to know what was going on in Liverpool City Council? And anyway the Cold War was over, wasn't it?

Yet, somewhere in the back of his mind, a doubt lurked. What if it was something else? Something more serious. Sabotage of some kind? Even terrorism or murder? He knew, though he tried to dismiss the thought, that the Russians would not have gone to all this trouble for nothing. And even if the Cold War was over, Robinson was a foreign agent and it was his duty to report him.

But no, Harry would keep his knowledge to himself and keep a close eye on Mr Robinson. He told himself that if he discovered Robinson was up to no good, then he would report him. But not until then.

3

MANON TYLER WAS GAZING out of her office window so she didn't hear either the tap on the door or her boss come into the room. She got a shock when she turned round and saw him standing in front of her desk. 'You looked a million miles away,' he said with a smile. 'Or was it four thousand?'

Ben Fleishman was a bear of a man – a teddy bear, really, a roly-poly figure who wore unflattering sweaters that did nothing to disguise his pot belly, and glasses with lenses the size of binoculars. He was famously easy-going, though woe betide the junior who mistook his amiability for weakness, or his lack of pretension for stupidity. Fortunately, Manon had never made either mistake, and now she realised with a pang how much she was going to miss the man who managed to be both her boss and her friend.

He said now, 'I hope you're getting a break before you go over.'

'I am. I'm spending two weeks in New Hampshire on Lake Winnipesaukee. My parents have a cabin there.' How grim that sounded – to go on vacation in your late twenties with your parents. It meant there was no partner in her life, and she sighed inwardly. Maybe going to England would change things, after the hapless line of losers she'd dated in the last few years. She knew she was attractive to men, but unfortunately they were always the wrong sort of men.

'You seem very well organised,' he said, then added with a smile, 'for you, that is.' He pointed at her desk, which he had nicknamed the Battle of the Bulge, since it was usually covered with a mountain of files and papers. Now it was completely clear, and a stack of neatly labelled box files stood on the floor awaiting collection, with not a stray paper in sight.

Fleishman said, 'I'm sure you're going to like England. But you've lived there before, haven't you?'

'Yes. I spent a year there when I was in college. The Junior Year Abroad programme. But not in London – I was at Bristol University. I loved it.'

'I think you'll love London too. The Embassy's right near Hyde Park.'

'I'm sharing an apartment in South Kensington with a girl from State. She's in the ambassador's office. I figure I can cycle to work. I've heard that Londoners are great cyclists.'

'Sounds good,' he said and paused for a moment, as if considering whether to say something else. Then he added, 'And about Rickles…'

She looked at him, curious. Rickles was the section head in London and would be her manager there. She had yet to meet him.

Fleishman hesitated, as if unsure how much to say. 'He can be a little intense. Sometimes he gets a bee in his bonnet. When he does, just let it alone. There's never any point arguing when he's like that.'

'Oh?' One of the nice things about Fleishman was that he was always tolerant of dissenting views. He encouraged debate and was disappointed when he found total agreement from his juniors.

'Yes. He's very sharp – you'll find that a change after my plodding ways.' He smiled. 'But as I say, sometimes a bit intense. Don't worry – I'm sure you'll be fine. And if anything really gets to you, don't hesitate to pick up the phone.'

'Thanks, Ben,' she replied, though she was a little troubled by what he'd just said. He was clearly warning her about Rickles. She didn't think she could ask him to explain more – he had obviously found it hard enough as it was.

'Anyway,' he continued, sounding relieved, 'do you know many people in London?'

'Not a soul – no, that's not quite true. I had a friend at Bristol and I've kept up with her since then. I saw her in New York a year ago; she'd just been through a bad divorce and took some time off. I've let her know I'm coming to London and she's keen to meet up again.'

'Excellent. I've never found the English easy to get to know, so it's good if you already know somebody there. I don't want you working all the time just because you haven't got anything better to do.'

'Don't worry; I'll make sure of that. I'm definitely going to join a gym because I want to keep up my training.'

Fleishman laughed. 'Don't talk to me about training and gyms,' he said, patting his spare tyre. 'I'll pop by tomorrow to say goodbye.' He turned to go, then suddenly stopped. 'Oh, I nearly forgot – you are coming to the talk this afternoon?'

She hesitated since she had been hoping just to relax for a change, knowing she was all good to go, and for once feeling absolutely no pressure. A rare thing at the agency. 'I wasn't planning to,' she said.

'You should. You won't have many chances to hear a former KGB general talk about the KGB in the Cold War. Especially since there isn't a KGB any more.'

'OK. It does sound interesting. I'll be there.'

The deputy director was finishing his introduction at the lectern on the small stage at the front of the auditorium when Manon slipped into an aisle seat at the back. The room was almost full, and she noticed the director sitting in the first row. There was a table on one side of the stage, where a grey-haired man sat in an armchair. His face was deeply lined but his eyes were bright and constantly on the move, taking in the members of the audience.

Like everyone else in the CIA, Manon had heard about the former KGB general, who had come to live in the USA after the collapse of the Soviet Union when the KGB went into meltdown. Unlike defectors during the Cold War who had escaped to the West in dramatic circumstances, smuggled out in the boot of a car or turning up at the American Embassy in Istanbul with nothing but a backpack full of classified documents, he had come quite openly as the representative of one of the new Russian companies which had sprung up after Yeltsin took power. He was completely out of sympathy with the new Russia as well as with the new security and intelligence services of his native country. He had become a visiting lecturer at Georgetown University where he attracted large audiences to his talks on recent Russian history.

This was the first time he had lectured to agency staff and there was a lot of excitement about it. It was expected that in this secure and professional environment he would be much more frank about his espionage work than he was in public lectures. After all, he had been Head of Intelligence against the West in the closing years of the Cold War.

All this was of little immediate importance to Manon, who had spent the last two years on the Middle Eastern desk, and in her new assignment in London would be working closely with the Brits on the same subject. Russia was way down her list of interests, professional or personal, and now her mild curiosity vied with impatience for the talk to end so she could go home and finish her packing.

The deputy director finally wound up his rather long-winded introduction. 'It's a pleasure now to hand over to our distinguished guest, Dimitri Kazikov, former general of the Soviet Union's KGB, now an expert on recent Russian history and a valued associate of ours in the agency.'

There was polite applause while the man in the armchair stood up and walked across to the lectern, switching places with the deputy director, who went to sit at the table. The Russian wore a tweed jacket, a shirt and tie, flannels and polished brogues. He could have been German or English, thought Manon, a successful businessman or a senior polit-ician. Yet for all the cosmopolitan nature of his attire, there was something military in his bearing, and when he began to speak it was with that air of authority found in high-ranking officers.

He spoke in low clear tones, accented but not difficult to understand. He had no notes. 'I thank you for your welcome, and am grateful that so many of you have come to hear me. I am very flattered of course, but please do not think it will go to my head. If a senior officer from the agency would change places and be speaking in the Lubyanka, I can assure you he would have just as big an audience.'

There was a ripple of laughter at this, everyone relieved that not only was he a comprehensible speaker of English, but he had a sense of humour too.

'As you all know, for several years before the break-up of the Soviet Union I was Head of Foreign Intelligence in the KGB. The *late* KGB, as you will also know. I would like to talk a little about the situation that led to the break-up of the Soviet Union and the consequent collapse of the KGB. Then I will say something about the present structure of the Russian Intelligence Services and perhaps try to forecast where the country and the intelligence services might be heading.'

And for the next thirty minutes Kazikov gave his view of the state of the Soviet Union and of the KGB in the 1980s; of Gorbachev's attempted reforms; of the failed coup against him and the personalities involved. He went on to talk about the restructuring of the KGB into the SVR and the FSB, which had been accomplished in the Yeltsin years before the millennium. Manon, whose entire career so far had been in counter-terrorism, found some of this a little hard to grasp and her mind drifted away to her imminent transfer to London. She was a bit concerned about what Fleishman had said about her future boss. It was clearly a warning and she hoped that she would be able to keep out of his way in the smaller team in the Embassy there.

At this point Kazikov's voice broke through her reverie. He was saying that the KGB had been in trouble already – before the Berlin Wall came down; before the break-up of the Soviet Union. The factors that led to the upheavals started some time ago, and affected the KGB as much as any other part of Russian society. Morale throughout the previous decade and especially since the death of Andropov had been very low. 'This particularly affected my area of foreign intelligence. It became increasingly difficult to recruit Western sources. Put simply, if you have little faith in yourselves, why should anyone wish to work on your behalf? Especially if the people you are trying to recruit have to be worried that you may defect to the West and expose them.

'And so,' he went on, 'we decided to deploy illegals. We put over a dozen agents into America and Great Britain, documented with false identities, of different nationalities, targeted at various areas of interest to us: politics, the defence systems, business et cetera. Some proved of no value at all; some managed to establish themselves and become potentially of great value; some you and your British colleagues detected.

'But then the cataclysm I have already discussed occurred. The structures supporting the illegals collapsed. An illegal cannot function when there is no support and no longer any functioning institution to receive and assess his product. So, many of them came back home.'

He seemed to have a second thought at this point, and said, 'Though there was one agent in Europe who did not return. He was uniquely qualified to live in his adopted country without support and I suspect he preferred to stay rather than return to a country in confusion. But I know nothing of his fate after I left the scene.'

He went on for several minutes more, drawing lessons from his experiences for the benefit of his listeners. Manon had enjoyed listening to him more than she had expected, so when he finished to a large round of applause and the audience was invited to stay and have a drink with him, she found herself unwilling to leave. And taking a glass of wine she lingered on the outer edges of the circle of her colleagues surrounding Kazikov. Eventually the crowd seemed to shift and she was suddenly standing right in front of the Russian.

Before anyone else could interrupt she said quickly, 'I was very interested in what you had to say about illegals.'

'That is most kind,' he said with a little bow of his head.

'You mentioned an illegal placed in Europe.'

'Yes,' he said, nodding. 'I was concerned that if we put all our fruits in the American basket, then one defector could spoil them all. This one had the perfect background for working in Europe. Only I was aware of his true identity.'

Manon smiled and went on, 'Was he sent to Great Britain, by any chance? Do you think he might still be there? I'm interested because I am just about to go to London on a posting. I'd love to meet him.'

Kazikov considered this. 'It was indeed to Britain he was sent. In my opinion he is unlikely still to be there. And certainly he would not be active now. The KGB Residency in London suffered from the same sort of chaos as all the others. The illegal would not have had the necessary support; I think he would have returned home some time ago.'

'Was he an adult when he went to the UK?'

'Yes, of course; I did not use children. Now I remember, though, he had spent time in Britain as a boy, which meant his English was excellent.'

Others were hovering around them, keen to have their moment with Kazikov, but Manon ignored them. Then, out of the corner of her eye, she saw the deputy director heading their way and knew she had to get in her final question fast.

'You don't remember his name, do you?' she asked eagerly. 'Either his real name or his cover name?'

He stared at her silently for a moment. 'No, my dear,' he finally said, his voice soft but his steel-grey eyes focused icily on hers, almost daring her to challenge him. 'I'm afraid I don't.'

4

As luck would have it, Harry didn't have long to wait before he encountered Robinson again. Nine months after his chance sighting of the man outside the bank, one of the city's MPs died of a heart attack while opening a supermarket in his constituency. There was intense interest in who would be chosen to stand for what was a very safe seat.

Harry noted right away that this was the constituency where Robinson was a councillor and that he was being spoken of as a possible choice as Parliamentary candidate, though he was by no means the favourite. Then, ten days before the selection committee was to meet to make its choice, a photograph of the front runner appeared in a local but widely circulated free newspaper, showing him leaving a massage parlour at midnight. Suddenly Robinson's chances improved. At the selection meeting his nearest rival had a coughing fit, and Robinson spoke clearly, simply and well. Twenty minutes later he was declared the official candidate of his party.

Robinson's selection coincided with Harry's next promotion, which made him a chief superintendent at an unusually young age. It didn't seem to make much difference to his duties, but it did increase his social obligations. Among them was a civic dinner, which his boss made clear he didn't want to attend, and he expected Harry to go in his place. Harry reluctantly bought a dinner suit, realising that attending this sort of affair was likely to be part of his job from now on.

A little grumpily he turned up on the night of the dinner at St George's Hall, where in spite of himself he was impressed by the splendour of the scene, with the light of the huge chandeliers glittering on the tables. He joined the queue of guests waiting to be introduced to the hosts but as he got nearer to the head of the line he saw to his dismay that he was about to be welcomed not only by the Lord Mayor and the Lady Mayoress, but also, third in the hosts' party, by Peter Robinson, there in his capacity as Parliamentary candidate.

Harry had no time to compose himself before the toast-master was shouting out, 'Chief Superintendent Harry Bristow.' His hand was sweating as he greeted the Mayor and Mayoress and then he was face to face with Igor. Robinson turned from the previous guest to Harry with a smile that seemed to freeze in position. It was not the cocky grin that Harry remembered from the gangway of the *Bogdana*. Robinson's eyes had opened wide and Harry was suddenly sure the man remembered him. It was obvious.

On the spur of the moment, without thinking what he was doing, Harry said, 'I think we've met before.'

'Really? I'm afraid I don't remember. Where was that?'

'Not in Liverpool,' Harry said slowly, realising as he spoke, with rising panic, that he was on a path taking him to an unknown destination.

'I don't think I've met you before,' said Robinson politely but firmly, turning towards the next guest.

'It was on the *Bogdana*.' Harry couldn't stop now. This was the man who had ruined his marriage and taken away his peace of mind.

For the very briefest of moments, Robinson's eyes narrowed and his smile disappeared. 'I don't know it,' he said curtly, and he turned decisively away, forcing Harry to move on.

As the by-election approached, Robinson stayed well ahead of the competition and, with a week left, it was clear he was going to win the seat easily. Each time a story appeared in the press, Harry found himself flinching. He was having sleepless nights; this was serious, and he cursed himself for his indecision and his stupidity. He told himself that he didn't need to wait till he understood what the Russians were up to – whatever it was, it had to be stopped now. The local council was one thing; a Member of Parliament quite another. Ensconced in Westminster, Robinson would be in a position to do real damage, especially because it was becoming clear he had a winning way with the electorate. Given who he was, that made him very dangerous.

Harry had been hard at work, compiling as much information as he could about the man. There were a few disparities he had gleaned from combing the official records available to him – the Land Registry, Companies House, the DVLA in Swansea – and Robinson had made the odd small mistake: his place of birth differed in two of these records, and his middle name was not spelled exactly the same. It also proved impossible to find any record of his first entering the country as a young man, though admittedly Home Office records were erratic. The usual chain of passports was impossible to follow, since Robinson had claimed the original one had been stolen during a holiday he had taken in Ireland.

For Harry, all of this confirmed his suspicions, which now became total conviction. But reviewing his dossier of information, he realised how difficult it would be to demonstrate irrefutably that Robinson wasn't who he said he was. Much less prove he was a Russian spy.

The only way he could do that, Harry knew, was to come completely clean about his own contacts with the man, from the time years before when 'Igor' had first landed seventy miles north of Liverpool, at Heysham. He didn't have a choice, so Harry decided he would make an appointment the next day with the Head of Merseyside Special Branch, his ultimate boss. He knew that Robinson would soon be in a powerful position, and had to be stopped; Harry knew too that for his own peace of mind, he had now finally come to the point where he must confess and atone for what he had done and failed to do in the past.

But confessing and atoning proved easier said than done. Each time Harry gritted his teeth and got ready to come clean something held him back. Was there not some way he could incriminate the Russian – if he was a Russian – without revealing his own role in letting the man stay in the country? Was it really necessary to confess to the bribes Robinson had offered, and Harry had too easily accepted? Time moved on, terrifyingly quickly, and the by-election loomed, yet still Harry did nothing.

The post usually arrived while Harry was halfway through his skimpy breakfast of coffee and a solitary piece of toast, eaten hastily in the kitchen of the little terraced house he'd bought after Gina remarried and the alimony payments stopped. But this morning, two days before voters went to the polls, the post was already there when Harry came downstairs. Bending to collect it, Harry found the usual flyer from the local pizza chain, a letter from the bank (who never wrote with *good* news), and a circular from an estate agent.

But there was also something unusual – a large A4-sized envelope which he looked at with curiosity. His name and address had been written in block capitals with a felt-tip pen, which meant this was not another piece of junk mail.

He was intrigued but also cautious. This looked a bit odd; a company would have used a typed label; his ex-wife wouldn't have used block capitals and he would have recognised her handwriting; his son never wrote. But if not family or friend, then was it a foe? It would be difficult for anyone unknown to Harry to find out his address; he was very careful about giving it out. But he had been working on a Real IRA cell for months; could they have discovered his address and sent a letter bomb or some other device?

He took the envelope, gently squeezed it, and felt reassured. There was nothing bulky inside, nothing that smelled strange or felt like a trigger. He toyed with the idea of taking it into police HQ to be X-rayed. But finally he decided to open it.

Carrying the envelope into the kitchen, he carefully slit it open with a steak knife where it had been sealed with Sellotape at the flap end. Reaching inside, he gently drew out two contact sheets of photographs and a plain folded sheet of paper.

The paper had a message on it, in the same block capitals:

FANCY MEETING YOU HERE. LOTS TO DISCUSS – LET'S BE IN TOUCH SOON. THOUGHT YOU MIGHT ENJOY THE ATTACHED...

The contact sheets each held a series of small thumbnail photos. The first one showed two men facing each other at the bottom of a ship's gangway – the photos had been taken from the ship's deck and looked down on the figures. Harry recognised himself, taking something from the other man, who had his back to the camera. No need to see his face, thought Harry – he knew immediately it was Igor, now Peter Robinson.

The next pictures were taken after this: Igor had walked away towards town and Harry was opening a little box; then he held up two drop earrings. In the final photos, he was looking around, shiftily, then putting the box in his pocket.

Harry had had no doubt after the encounter at the civic dinner that Peter Robinson and Igor were one and the same man, but he hadn't been entirely sure what Robinson was up to. In a corner of his mind he had allowed himself to think that it was just possible that Robinson was acting entirely on his own – that he had fled Bulgaria or Russia and come to England as an illegal immigrant, then succeeded beyond his wildest dreams in building a new career and a new life. But not any more. These photographs put that beyond doubt. Especially when Harry examined the second contact sheet, which was even worse from Harry's point of view than the first.

Again the first shots were of the gangway, but this time the other man was handing Harry a sheaf of newspaper, which Harry tucked away in his coat. The subsequent frames showed Harry alone at a table in a café – it was the café in Heysham harbour, he knew. One frame showed him reach in his pocket, the next showed his hand holding an envelope, the subsequent ones showed him looking down as he surreptitiously riffled through the banknotes on the table.

They had caught him out bang to rights – and without incriminating Peter Robinson in any way. There was no provable link between the figure with his back to the camera and the candidate for Parliament – none at all. But Harry's own presence was impossible to explain away. Oh, there might not be evidence enough for a court, and Harry might avoid a prison sentence. But his career would be over, and even the fallback of running security for a department store would be impossible once word got round that he had taken bribes.

So much for his plans for redemption. He'd been played like a fish on the line, and he felt as foolish as he felt guilty for his naivety. Now there was nothing he could do but keep his mouth shut and wait to hear again from Peter Robinson.

Two days later, Peter Robinson won the Parliamentary seat with a ten thousand majority. In his brief acceptance speech, Robinson declared with a broad confident smile, 'A new era begins for my constituency. Just as a new era begins for me.'

5

I T WAS TEN O'CLOCK on the morning after the by-election. Louise Donovan was sitting on a plastic chair drinking instant coffee out of a paper cup. Her normally bouncy, copper-red hair was flat and dull and her freckles stood out against her pale face. The campaign office, a vacant shop in a busy high street, was a scene of devastation – the trestle tables and the floor were covered with posters, flyers, rosettes, used coffee cups, and champagne bottles still containing the dregs of wine, all fizz long gone.

Louise had left at three thirty to stagger back to her room in the nearby Travelodge and now she had a throbbing headache not helped by the near-certainty that no one else would turn up for hours and she was going to be left to clear up the mess by herself. She knew Peter Robinson was up and about as she had heard him on Radio Liverpool just after eight o'clock when she first woke, but he wasn't likely to show since he probably hadn't been to bed at all.

She sat for another ten minutes thinking over the events of the previous day and Peter Robinson's stunning victory – he had increased the majority by three thousand. She wasn't surprised; she had met him the previous year when she had been sent up by party HQ for strategy discussions with the party group on the council and they had had lunch together.

She had found him charismatic and charming. Quite a change from the men she worked with at party HQ, who were either humourless policy wonks fresh from the universities, wearing black T-shirts and jeans, their intense eyes fixed firmly on a constituency and a career in politics; or older cynical types living on comfortable salaries who called her 'dear'. Louise was looking neither for a career in politics – she worked on election strategy, which was more project management than politics – nor for a man.

On the man front she'd had a more than ample dose. One night she'd picked up her husband Gerald's phone and found a text message from a number she immediately recognised – that of her oldest friend, Catherine. It was an intimate message, one which her husband would doubtless have erased along with all the others that he must have been receiving from Louise's best friend. When she had confronted him with her discovery, he hadn't even bothered to try and deny the obvious conclusion she had drawn. And within twenty-four hours he had moved out; two weeks later he and Catherine were living together. In virtually the blink of an eye, Louise had lost her 'partner for life' and her closest confidante.

But Louise was not one to curl up and weep when things went wrong. After a few weeks, her 'mourning' ended during a visit home when her father, a down-to-earth country solicitor who was used to dealing with tragedies among the farming community, told her unceremoniously that she was well out of it – adding that he had never liked Gerald, whom he thought from the beginning was a self-opinionated, unreliable fraud. He hadn't said anything before because he could see his daughter was obsessed with the man.

After that dose of cold water it didn't take long for her to pick herself up. She was, like her father, a qualified solicitor and worked in a south-coast town, but her first degree had been in politics and economics, and she decided to try and find work in the area of her earlier interest. She had seen this political-party job advertised, applied and a little to her surprise got the post. Even though the pay was a fraction of what she had been earning, she was enjoying it more than she had ever done writing wills and conveyancing contracts.

She had been sent up to Liverpool to help with the final week of the Robinson campaign. It had been exhausting but exciting, though as it turned out she had been a bit of a dogsbody. Now it looked as though there was more dogsbodying to do, as this place had to be cleaned up and cleared by the following evening – when the short lease ran out. In any case, Louise wanted to get back to London now the job was done. She liked living in the city, though it could be lonely, since she was new to it and had few friends there. But she had recently heard from an American friend named Manon, a girl she had met at university in Bristol, who was being posted to the US Embassy in London. Louise was looking forward to Manon's arrival in the UK since she imagined that Manon would not know many English people and would be lonely too.

People were beginning to drift in and the great clear-up began in earnest. Louise found herself looking over and over again at the face of Peter Robinson as she picked up the discarded flyers and posters. At some point in the late morning things began to improve – the tables were folded up and stacked, the floor cleared and black bags filled with cups and bottles. When more constituency helpers arrived in cars to take away the junk, Louise sat down and closed her eyes for a brief rest. She must have dozed off, and when she opened her eyes again she found herself staring at the face she had been seeing all morning. It wasn't flat on the floor but floating in front of her eyes. What's more, it spoke.

'You poor thing,' it said. 'You must be exhausted. Have you had any lunch?'

Later she would remember her forty-eight hours in Liverpool as a blur. She had planned to leave that evening, but within half an hour of going to lunch with Peter Robinson she sensed she would be staying longer. In retrospect, she saw she must have met other people from the local party – there had been an older man in a cardigan called Storrs, the constituency chairman, with a haranguing way of talking about 'keeping closely in touch with the constituency roots', whatever that meant – and presumably she had done her best to act the part of the authoritative representative of party HQ. But actually what later stuck in her mind was the sheer magnetism of the new MP and her growing realisation, as they finished their shared bottle of Chablis over lunch, that he – a man; a young-ish good-looking man – seemed as interested in her as she was beginning to be in him.

They had swapped life stories by the time their main courses had arrived, and his seemed so utterly exotic (if only very briefly told), with time spent seemingly everywhere, from Alberta to Rome, that she felt embarrassed by the humdrum nature of her own upbringing – Home Counties, middle-class girls' school, university, etc., etc. But she didn't feel this way for long, since he moved the subject quickly to politics, where they discovered a similar pattern of views: progressive on social issues, firm on foreign ones, each sceptical that the end of Communism would mean real change in Russia. He had a wide knowledge of the world abroad but a boy's innocent enthralment as well – he seemed astonished that she had been inside 10 Downing Street and twice attended a reception there. She gradually understood that for all his international travel and sophistication, he was still in many ways utterly provincial – and London to him seemed to be a Mecca or mountain that he was slightly scared of trying to scale. It gave her confidence to know that she could not only reassure him that the ascent could be made, but help him with the climbing too.

After a dreary meeting in the late afternoon with the local party officials there had been another tête-à-tête with Robinson, and then a slightly awkward moment where he hesitated, before suggesting, rather shyly, that since there still seemed so much to talk about would she, could she not consider staying on overnight? There was a nice hotel, not unreasonably priced, he said in a voice that started naturally enough, then trailed off... Until she said that it sounded a great idea, and actually she hated getting back too late, and anyway party HQ owed her for working most of the previous night and she would phone and say she wouldn't be in the next day.

This time – it being late afternoon – they went for a walk and he showed her some of the city's sights. They had ended up at the Albert Docks where he proudly showed her Robinson's Kitchens showroom, by then closed, and they'd sat on bar stools inside the shop drinking gin and tonic from a secret cache in a fridge in a kitchen display. Then they had a leisurely dinner in a nearby restaurant next door to the hotel where Robinson assured her she could get a room. Though by then neither seriously thought she would be resting her head there that night.

And instead she spent the night with him in his house – it was nothing grand but perfectly comfortable, though oddly devoid of personal touches. Later, when she thought about it all, she recognised that she not only barely knew this man, but the great majority of their conversation had been either about politics or about her. Yes, he had told her amusing stories about the passport nightmare of travelling from Israel to Jordan, and the time he had almost stepped on an alligator in – where had it been? The Florida Keys? Central America? But she realised, as she lay contentedly at three in the morning in his bed while he slept and she pondered this quick affair, that she didn't even know if his parents were alive, or where they lived, or whether he had siblings or – she suddenly felt anxious – he had ever had a wife. He was a mystery as far as that kind of information went, yet somehow he had been so attentive, and gentle, and already really rather loving, that it didn't seem to matter.

What mattered now was whether she would see him again. Was this just a one-night stand? When he came to London, would she see him or have to accept that what had just happened here in Liverpool wasn't going to happen anywhere else?

Apparently not. For at breakfast he couldn't have been more cheerful or thoughtful and by the time she caught her train she not only knew what day he planned to move to London, and the address of the flat he was renting there, but she had his landline and his mobile phone as well. Plus she had to promise to call him that night and let him know she had arrived back safely. And as the train travelled south through the Midlands, she received not one, not two, but three texts from him, each more affectionate than the last. Why he was so keen seemed inexplicable to Louise, but wonderful, quite wonderful, just the same.

6

S o far so good, thought Peter Robinson as he stood by the window of his Thames-side flat. If he looked to his right he could see the Houses of Parliament across the water; practically straight ahead was Thames House, the headquarters of MI5, and to his left, just a little further along his side of the river, was Vauxhall Cross, HQ of MI6. All his targets were within his reach.

For a moment he felt a rush of power – everything was going exactly to plan – but it was quickly followed by a wave of worry. He was afraid his life was becoming too complicated to manage alone with no support from those who had sent him here. His kitchen business in Liverpool, set up with the money Kazikov initially provided, had been successful beyond his dreams. But all Kazikov's cash had been used up now and he was dependent on the continuing success of the business to maintain the lifestyle he needed if he were going to progress in London and remain respected in Liverpool. He had put in a manager to keep the business going but it was still taking more of his time than he wanted to give to it.

His Parliamentary career had started well; he had taken his seat right away and within ten days he'd given a maiden speech – on support for the regions of the North – which had gone down well, pleasing the party, and pleasing his constituency since it had stressed how much more the government in

Westminster should be doing. He had also added a few bits about the importance of a strong defence industry, mentioning a local aerospace firm by name – all this part of his objective to get on to the Defence Select Committee one day. What was the odd expression he'd been taught, years before at the language school outside Leningrad, where the instructors had forced them to learn dozens of idioms? *Softly, softly, catchee monkey.* Yes, that was it. He smiled at the memory of those sayings – he had never heard any of them actually used by an Englishman. Where had the instructors got their ideas of how British people spoke?

He could also feel pleased that he had managed to acquire a well-placed girlfriend. Until now he had steered clear of any serious female involvement, regarding it as a risk rather than an advantage. There had been casual girlfriends but nothing of any duration. But now the balance had changed. The minute he'd seen Louise that day at the constituency office he'd realised that she was just what he needed. She had landed in his lap like a Christmas present, and he had followed up that encounter in Liverpool assiduously. She was too good an asset to let her get away; luckily he found her quite attractive so keeping her happy was not unpleasant at all. Through her work at party HQ she was incredibly well connected – there wasn't an MP on their side of the House she didn't know about, including the Party Leader and the Shadow Cabinet. What's more, she seemed as eager to help his career as to pursue her own.

But while congratulating himself on everything that was going right, at the heart of it all was a negative: the lack of support, the lack of any contact, the lack of anyone to praise him for how well he was doing. Were they just keeping quiet until he attained his objective or – and this was the source of occasional near-panic – was no one there at all any more? No one to whom he could pass the information he was working so hard to obtain. Was this whole enterprise no longer of any value? That was the thought that kept him awake at night.

There was another, more immediate anxiety too – the reappearance of Harry Bristow. It had been a staggering surprise when he had turned from the previous guest to find himself face to face with the young policeman, Harry from Heysham docks. He had recognised him straightaway and, even if he hadn't, Harry had recognised him. He had often wondered, in the years since he had arrived and stayed on in the UK, what had become of the young officer who had fallen so effortlessly for Igor's 'gifts'. But not for a million years had he expected him to show up again in his life – his *new* life, as Robinson not Romanov, as 'Peter' not the 'Igor' Harry had known.

Now was the time he could use backup from his support team; they would be able to deal with the threat Harry posed. They would make sure he had an 'accident' – or frame him for some crime and see him put away for a good few years. But as things stood, he would have to take care of the Bristow problem himself. Not in a classic 'KGB manner' – to do anything violent would risk jeopardising what had been a remarkably smooth operation so far. He hoped he had kept Harry's mouth shut for the time being by sending him the photographs his KGB support team had taken from the *Bogdana*, but he needed something else to neutralise Detective Chief Superintendent Bristow for good. He sat down at his desk, drew out a pair of thin cotton gloves from a drawer, and started to write on a piece of blank A4 paper.

He had just finished and was surveying his handiwork when his mobile rang. 'Hello darling,' he said, answering.

'I'm glad I've caught you. Are you busy right now?'

'Terribly. I'm looking out of the window. The tide's coming in.'

She laughed – another point in her favour; he didn't think he could have gone out with someone who didn't have a sense of humour. 'Listen, I completely forgot but I've been invited to a drinks party in the House of Lords. It's being given by Lord Chesborough.'

'That's nice,' he said mildly, but clocking this carefully. Chesborough was the defence spokesman for the government in the Lords. A great supporter of NATO, and anti-Russian. The enemy, in other words, but right in the target area.

'Yes, yes, but the point is it says "and partner". That means I can take you with me,' she said. 'Unless you'd rather watch the tide go out.'

7

H ARRY BRISTOW WAS SITTING in the waiting room
of the medical centre in police headquarters in Liverpool,
sipping nervously at a glass of water.

He was dreading what was coming, but for the first time in
months the terrible grinding anxiety and indecision had gone.
He had decided what he was going to do.

Harry had been in a bad state ever since he had received
the envelope of photographs in the post. But the stress had
really begun weeks before that on the night he encountered
Igor at the mayoral dinner at St George's Hall. He had lost
count of the times he had resolved to go to his boss and tell
him the story of Igor, now Peter Robinson. Morning after
morning he had left home utterly determined to come clean.
But something always got in the way – an urgent operational
requirement; his boss was on leave; whatever it was, it just
never seemed the right moment.

Then the photographs had arrived. Now it became much,
much more difficult. The photographs were dreadful – he
looked so shifty, so greedy, so corrupt. His feeling of stress
had turned to full-blown anxiety. He couldn't sleep. He
would go to bed feeling sick, with a tight band of tension
pressing on his diaphragm. He would toss and turn, then
finally switch on his bedside radio to try to distract his
mind. He would fall asleep then suddenly wake up after an

hour or so, hot and sweaty and still anxious. And so it would continue all night until the light began to show through his curtains and he would get up feeling exhausted, red-eyed and aching. It was the same, night after night, while he waited for something to happen; either for himself to summon up the courage to go to his boss with the photographs, which as time went on he realised he was not going to do, or for Igor to make a move.

But what would that move be? He didn't know, and not knowing made it worse. Would he get a call to go to the boss's office where he would find the photographs laid out on the desk? Would the photographs appear in the papers? Was he going to be run over, beaten up, physically attacked? He didn't know and that was wrecking him.

Of course, before long his colleagues began to notice there was something wrong. He looked awful; he was bad-tempered, indecisive – quite unlike the man who had been promoted on merit so young. People started asking him if he was OK and eventually his physical state came to attention higher up the chain of command and he was summoned for a medical. He explained to the doctors that he thought he was suffering from a delayed reaction to his marriage breaking up and losing contact with his children, and though they were puzzled about why this had suddenly emerged as a problem and in such an acute form after such a long time, they accepted it, gave him sleeping pills and told him to come back in a month.

Then it had happened; the thing he had been dreading. He came downstairs a little later than normal one morning because he had not fallen asleep until five o'clock and had woken up late. There on the doormat, on top of the other post, was an envelope. He knew immediately who it was from by the black capital letters in which his name was written, and at the sight of it his pulse raced. He picked up the envelope and turned it over and over in his hands, pressing it and feeling it, looking for some clue as to what might be inside. It was a smaller envelope than the previous one and he finally concluded that it could only be some sort of letter. It was postmarked London.

He sat down at the kitchen table and slit the envelope open quickly with a knife, extracting the one sheet of paper it contained. The message was short and simple, written in the same black block capitals.

BE BY YOUR PHONE FROM 8 P.M. ON
WEDNESDAY, THURSDAY AND FRIDAY

There was no signature but there was no doubt it was from Igor. The day was Wednesday and Harry spent it at home, unable to face going to work. By seven o'clock he was sitting, waiting for the call. It didn't come, and at eleven thirty he finally went to bed for another sleepless night, this one spent listening for the phone. On Thursday by eight he was back in place, waiting once more. He had come home early saying he was unwell, which was obviously true as he was grey, sweating and weak. His colleagues wanted Harry to see the doctor again and, in spite of his insistence that he was fine, an appointment was made for him for the following day.

Finally, at nine o'clock the phone rang. It was Peter Robinson.

'Good evening, Harry,' he said, speaking clearly, with no introduction and no attempt to disguise his voice. 'I hope you enjoyed the photographs. You were sensible to keep them to yourself. Now listen. I have a job for you. I advise you to accept my offer as I don't think you are going to keep your present position much longer.'

He went on to instruct Harry that he was to resign from the police, using whatever reason he chose, and move to London where he would be provided with accommodation and a decent living wage. He was to set things in train straightaway and he would be phoned at the same time one evening during the following week, when Robinson expected to hear that things were in hand. Harry would then be given further instructions.

All this was fresh in Harry's mind as he sat that Friday morning waiting to see the doctor again. During the night he had come to a conclusion. He had no doubt that he must obey Peter Robinson's instructions. The threat behind his words had been very clear. If he did not, something would happen to destroy his career and possibly destroy him as well. He had decided he would apply for early retirement immediately on medical grounds. Given the state he was in, he was certain it would be granted – today's appointment should lead to a final sign-off from his police duties. He would be able to leave the force with a pension and with his reputation undamaged. The only dishonour would be in his own mind where the knowledge of his betrayal of his country, himself and everyone he cared for would never go away.

But as he sat there in the waiting room, listening for his name to be called, he made a resolution, a promise to himself, that even though his police career was about to end, he would still do his best to expose the man who had ruined his peace of mind. Though these heroic thoughts were quickly followed by

44

the humbling admission that he would only expose Robinson if he could at the same time save his own skin.

'I said, "Mr Bristow?"' asked an impatient voice.

Harry looked up, startled, and saw the doctor waiting in the doorway of the consulting room. 'Sorry,' he said, rising to his feet. 'I was miles away.'

8

'AT LEAST IT ISN'T raining,' said Manon Tyler to herself as she hurried out of the American Embassy in London. She was late for her lunch date with her old friend Louise. It was all the fault of Rickles, her new boss. She'd been warned about him by Ben Fleishman, her boss at the agency's Langley headquarters, and though Ben hadn't been specific she had got the message and it had turned out to be true. Rickles was a fusser, a nagger and a worrier. A couple of days ago he had told her to prepare a briefing note for the ambassador's forthcoming meeting at the Foreign Office on the threat of violence from right-wing extremists in Britain. The only relatively recent material she had been able to find was a six-month-old paper from a Joint Intelligence Committee meeting that the Head of Station had attended. To bring it up to date she had had to read innumerable news reports and magazine articles; it had taken hours. She thought it was all a waste of time since presumably the ambassador was going to the meeting to be briefed on the situation by British officials, who would have access to much more authoritative sources. She had just finished it in time to put it on Rickles's desk before grabbing her coat and dashing out.

She'd already learned that the place to find a taxi was South Audley Street just to the side of the Embassy, but naturally today there was not a single black cab showing its yellow light.

At last she spotted one and, joy of joys, the driver saw her and stopped. She flopped down on the back seat of the cab and looked at her watch – five minutes late already and she still had to get to the restaurant. She was panting and perspiring; she had been so looking forward to this lunch and now she was worried that Louise would have grown tired of waiting and would leave before she got there.

Calm down, she told herself, I'm sure Louise won't mind. When she eventually arrived at the restaurant twenty minutes late, Louise was immediately visible, her copper-red hair glinting under the lights. She was sitting at a table against the wall with a mirror behind her and a bottle of water in front of her, calmly doing the crossword puzzle in the *Guardian*.

'I'm so sorry I'm late,' said Manon, pushing her hair out of her eyes.

'Don't worry,' replied Louise, getting up and kissing her on the cheek. 'Everyone's always late in London. That is unless they're early. It's impossible to be on time, what with the traffic, the demos, the strikes. What about a glass of wine?' She waved at a passing waiter. 'It's lovely to see you. How are you settling down?'

'Quite well really, thanks,' said Manon. 'I'm sharing a nice flat in South Kensington with another girl from the Embassy. She's been here three or four years and she knows everything and everybody. She's in the ambassador's office.' And Manon, now comfortably settled with a glass of wine, talked on happily about how her flatmate had told her that the newly arrived ambassador was proving a bit of a nightmare. He had apparently built a vast empire of fast-food franchises in the Midwest (where he was known as the 'King of the Takeaway Pie'), but he was proving less adept at diplomacy, causing a bit of a stir in his first week on the job by referring to the Queen as 'one heck of a gal'. Other gaffes had followed, which required a lot of fancy footwork by his office and everyone else in the Embassy.

'What about your job?' asked Louise, who knew that Manon had applied to join the CIA in her final year at college – the year after she had studied in England and they had first met.

'I'm an analyst,' said Manon. 'I can't tell you too much about it, but basically I do research and write papers on current topics – whatever's needed, really. I'm an expert on everything and nothing.' She laughed. 'It would be great if it weren't for my boss. But the less said about him the better. And anyway, I want to hear about you,' she said. 'I haven't seen you since that week in New York, when you were waiting for your divorce to come through. But you look great now. So how are things?'

'Much better, thanks, though it's taken me most of the time since I last saw you to sort myself out. I think I told you that the first thing I was going to do was get a new job. I couldn't have gone on working there with my ex and that woman in the same office. So I just resigned, with nothing else planned. But after a bit I suppose I just started to recover and I saw this job in London advertised and I applied and got it.'

'So you've gone into politics? Somehow I never saw you as particularly political.'

'No. I'm not really political, in the sense you mean. I'm working for a political party but really I'm more of an analyst like you than a politician. I do election strategy. Don't ask me what it is exactly, but part of it is I help local parties work out how to get their candidate elected. I've just been doing that, actually, up in Liverpool. They had a by-election in one of the constituencies because their MP died and I went up to help them get their man in.'

'That sounds fascinating. Did he win?'

'Oh yes. No problem about that. He was a great candidate.' Louise paused. 'Actually, we got quite close. He's taken up his seat now so he's living down here during the week. We've been seeing quite a lot of each other.' She stopped, blushing slightly.

'Oh. Lucky you,' said Manon slightly enviously. 'I'd like to meet a nice, eligible – I take it he's eligible – Member of Parliament. Have you got any more up your sleeve? Has he got a friend?'

Louise grinned. 'He seems to be eligible. He hasn't admitted to any wives or children. I think he's been too busy growing his business. He owns a chain of upmarket kitchen-design shops in Liverpool and around. He built the business from scratch by himself. He doesn't have any family here or anywhere else, as far as I've gathered. He lived in some remote part of Canada till he was eighteen, when, he told me, he decided he was going to come to England. He worked his way doing all sorts of weird jobs in strange places, then ended up in Liverpool. I think he must have borrowed the cash to start his company. Anyway, he's obviously a very good businessman, but then he went into local politics, got on the council and is now an MP.'

'Wow,' said Manon, impressed. 'He sounds like quite a guy. That's more like an American rags-to-riches story than an English one. What's his name? I'll look out for news of his rise in politics.'

'He's called Peter Robinson and I'm not sure if he is English, actually,' said Louise, laughing. 'His parents were, he told me.

49

But he might be Canadian – he was born there. Must be one or the other or he couldn't be an MP.'

They chatted on while they ate a leisurely lunch, then Manon looked at her watch. 'Oh, God. It's nearly three. I must get back or Rickles will be on the warpath. Here's my share,' and she put some money on the table. 'Do you mind if I leave you to pay the check?'

'Who on earth is Rickles?' asked Louise, helping Manon to gather up her things.

'He's the boss I was complaining about. My section head. I think he imagines he's running a boot camp. I'm hoping one day I'll work out how to deal with him but at the moment I'm under the heel of the boot.'

'You shouldn't put up with it,' said Louise.

'What can I do?'

'Ask to be transferred to another section.'

'I can't. This one is my specialty. Anyway, I must go. Let's do this again very soon and look out for a nice MP for me.' And with a kiss on Louise's cheek she left the restaurant.

In the taxi back to the Embassy Manon thought about what Louise had said. She was right – why should she have to put up with Rickles? He was a bully. Why shouldn't she apply for a transfer? She had always worked on terrorism but that didn't mean she always had to. There was a big counter-espionage team, even though the Cold War was over; its section head was reputedly brilliant and great to work for. She pondered this as the taxi chugged through the traffic. She had been fascinated by that talk she had attended just before she left Langley by that old Russian general, with his story of the collapse of the KGB and the illegals – hadn't he said there was one still in Britain? It all seemed so much more romantic than terrorism.

She found Rickles standing impatiently in the doorway of the office she shared with several other analysts. He was probably the same height as her old boss Ben Fleishman, but he was lean and bony – he jogged each lunchtime in Hyde Park and in the mornings too before he came to work. She found his sharp figure an accurate reflection of his temperament – mean, jagged and ungenerous. She was missing Fleishman, who was the opposite on every count.

As she appeared Rickles looked none too casually at his watch. She could see he was holding her paper on the threat of violence in Britain from right-wing fanatics and it was covered with scrawls. She said, 'I had lunch with someone from Party Central Office. Useful contact, I think.'

'It's not your job to cultivate sources,' he said scornfully. 'Now. You'll need to have another look at this. It won't do. There's not nearly enough detail here. You must be able to produce something fuller than this – and I'll need it by lunchtime tomorrow.' And he dropped Manon's paper on her desk and went out, leaving her deflated and furious, and more determined than ever to get free of his clutches as soon as she could.

9

B ORIS DENISOV SETTLED HIMSELF comfortably into his large swivel chair and looked around his spacious Lubyanka office. He was pleased; pleased with himself for the way he had managed to ride the storms and earthquakes that had struck Russia and in particular the KGB in the last few years.

Gorbachev's declaration of his policies of glasnost and perestroika in the mid-1980s had begun the troubles which had become a full-scale crisis when the then head of the KGB, the drunken Kryuchkov, had played a leading role in the short-lived coup against Gorbachev in the summer of 1991. Denisov had been in his first posting after training school. Suddenly all around him was in chaos – both in the KGB and in the whole country. The KGB had finally been split up and the parts organised and reorganised several times in a few years. Many of his former colleagues had taken the opportunity to get out, and some of them had got very rich, and some (often the same men) were now leading criminal gangs – many bad things had been done.

One of those who had got out was General Kazikov, whose former office now belonged to Denisov. Kazikov had been Head of the KGB's First Chief Directorate, the arm responsible for foreign intelligence – spying operations abroad. Under the latest reforms that activity had been hived off and was now a separate service, the SVR, with its own headquarters – no longer in the Lubyanka at all.

Kazikov had left the KGB in 1991 as the Soviet Union fell apart and Yeltsin had started large-scale privatisations. He had found a job in an oil company, gone to the USA as its representative and just stayed there. Now he was a US citizen.

Well, good for him, thought Denisov – except that he had heard recently that Kazikov had been giving lectures on the KGB at the CIA HQ in Maryland. He'd better watch his step. No part of the Russian intelligence services, whatever they were called and however they were organised, would tolerate traitors. He wondered whether Kazikov had become rich. If Denisov was honest with himself he had to admit that it might have been better, better for his family perhaps, if instead of staying in the service he had left to join the bonanza so many of his former colleagues had enjoyed. Then he too would now be wealthy.

It was ironic, he thought, that many of those who had prospered in the new world order had been mediocrities in the KGB, whereas he, one of the top students in his years at the KGB training school, was still getting by on a government salary. True, he was now a general in the Internal Security Service – the youngest in the rank – with medals and a pleasant apartment; his family was comfortable and his daughters were being well educated abroad. But he was not rich by any standards.

His musings stopped suddenly when there was a knock on the door. 'Come in,' he said, cross to have his thoughts disturbed.

The gaunt figure of Simonov, the Chief Archivist, appeared in the doorway. Many people described Denisov as imposing: he was tall and straight-backed, well built and fit-looking. Simonov was even taller, but no one would dream of calling him imposing. As a young man he had been a gifted student of linguistics, with a bright academic future ahead of him. But during his national service in the army he had been cruelly bullied, and after one exceptionally bad hazing session he had been left with a cracked spine and severe internal injuries. His treatment at the military hospital had been incompetent – the doctors were under orders to make light of his injuries – and eventually he had been discharged from the army, a cripple unable to digest more than a very limited diet.

Though Simonov suffered from extreme anxiety after all this, his mental and analytical skills were otherwise undiminished. As part of the cover-up a post had been found for him in the KGB archives, though it seemed to some that there was more than enough in the files in the Lubyanka to make an anxious individual even more so. However, the job had suited him and now he was the Chief Archivist, and with his team had been responsible for ensuring that the old First Chief Directorate files went to the new premises of its successor organisation, the SVR. Denisov had now commissioned Simonov to clean up and weed the remainder to ensure that nothing survived that could damage the modern service.

'I am sorry to disturb you, General,' said Simonov, 'but I have found something rather strange and I wonder what you would like me to do about it.'

'Really? I have been entirely happy with your supervision of this… review, Simonov.' He wanted files destroyed but without any trace of his involvement. Otherwise there would doubtless one day be a file about the files.

'Thank you, sir. Normally, I would have proceeded on my own authority, but in this case I felt certain you would want to be aware.'

Denisov tried to suppress his irritation. 'Well,' he said, 'what is it?'

'We have found a small safe which is not only locked but sealed with the personal seal of General Kazikov. The seal has a date: December 1991 – the very month that General Kazikov left the service. Would you like me to send it unopened to the SVR or would you prefer us to have it opened so you can check the contents?'

Denisov thought about this for a moment then replied, 'A small safe, you say?' Simonov nodded. 'Have it brought up here just as it is. Then get a technician to open it. I will personally examine the contents before deciding what to do with them.'

An hour later the safe sat open on a side table in Denisov's office. The archivist and the technician had gone and Denisov was reaching inside to remove the contents – a thin file in a red folder. He opened the cover to find himself staring at a photograph of a face he knew well – Pyotr Romanov. He had been the star student in Denisov's intake at the KGB training school and Denisov had always been jealous of him. He had disappeared from the course during the final year and never reappeared. The rumour was that he had been sent on some mission so secret that no one knew what it was. Now, after all these years, Denisov was about to find out what had happened to him.

The document he was looking at was a photocopy of a British passport in the name of Peter Robinson, issued in Canada, but its identifying photograph was of Romanov. So Romanov had been sent somewhere under cover. It must have been a particularly secret operation to have needed this level of security. Denisov turned to the next document which was a cable from naval intelligence, addressed 'Personal for General Kazikov'. It reported that the cargo was safely delivered. Next came a sheet of cheap-looking writing paper that had been folded, probably in an envelope, though the envelope was not there. It was handwritten in English and read, 'Job done. No problem.' There was no signature or date. The final sheet in the file was again in English but written by Kazikov himself, thought Denisov, who recognised the handwriting and also knew that Kazikov was fluent in the language. It appeared to be the draft of a notice, which read:

> The engagement is announced between Patrick Roberts, son of Charles and Anna Roberts of Norwich, and Sarah Emily Smythe, daughter of Dr and Mrs Ian Smythe of Oxford.

Underneath was written in Russian:

> Place in *The Times* of London on a Wednesday. Meet the following Friday 11.00 Islip Church.

Stapled at the bottom was a small photograph of a church.

The final page was a list of four British banks with account details. Against each account was written '£500,000'.

Denisov closed the file and sat back to consider what he had read. It was quite clear that Kazikov had sent Romanov into England documented as a British citizen. He had been inserted by sea with the help of naval intelligence, probably with the assistance of one of the former satellite states of the Soviet Union to disguise the role played by Russia.

There was no clue in the file as to what Romanov was there to do, but he had certainly been provided with very considerable funds. It seemed that Kazikov had intended to run the case personally. The engagement notice was obviously the emergency contact arrangement, but there was no way of knowing whether it had ever been used. Why had Kazikov sealed the file and archived it when he left? There were only two explanations. One was that Romanov was dead. The other, even more chilling, was that rather than hand the operation over to someone else, Kazikov had abandoned Romanov to fend for himself.

Denisov knew what he should do. Running illegals operations in target countries was no part of his responsibilities; he should immediately send the file to the Head of the SVR and let him decide what action to take. Finding Romanov would not be easy. The likelihood was that if he were still in England he had long ago ceased doing whatever his task was, disillusioned with his abandonment by the old regime. He had probably taken the money and was now sipping cocktails on the balcony of a Swiss ski chalet. Even if he was still in England he would almost certainly have stopped looking at Wednesday copies of the London *Times* to check for the engagement notice. If he didn't respond to *The Times* notice there might be some other way of finding him through his cover name – though there would be rather a lot of Peter Robinsons in England.

Denisov knew that all this was not his business, but he couldn't let the idea go. It occurred to him that there was an opportunity here for him to do something. On his appointment as Head of Internal Security he had received an invitation from the Head of Counter Terrorism Command at the Metropolitan Police in London to a couple of days of talks on the terrorist threat. He had accepted and was due to visit London in two weeks' time. As he sat there, in Kazikov's office with Kazikov's file open in front of him, he made his decision. He would use the day he had set aside to visit his daughter, on a postgraduate year in Oxford, to try to raise Peter Robinson.

10

'THE BEST THINGS COME out of the blue' had been one of Manon's mother's favourite sayings, though in Manon's experience, you couldn't rely on the 'best things' showing up at all. They certainly hadn't in this job, where Rickles, her boss, was growing more and more demanding and unpleasant. It was becoming obvious that, for whatever reason, he had taken a personal dislike to her and had picked her out as a target for bullying. Every morning during the week she had to fight the impulse to stay in bed and phone in sick. Her colleagues in the section had noticed it too and were trying to counter it with friendliness and camaraderie but nothing could offset the sinking feeling whenever Rickles loomed in the doorway of her office. For the first time, Manon was starting to consider whether she was really cut out for a career in the agency. It seemed depressingly clear that Rickles was wondering the same thing.

Then everything changed. She was having lunch in the canteen with her colleague Millie, a self-styled 'local yokel' – Millie was English and had grown up in south London. Millie was always good for a laugh, with her hilarious accounts of her very active social life, and Manon was finding her company a welcome distraction from the effects of a particularly grim ten minutes she had just spent with Rickles. It was as Millie was elaborating on the disastrous conclusion to her latest date

(Millie seemed to have an endless succession of suitors) that a voice from behind Manon said, 'Can an old man join you gals? You seem to be having a whale of a time.'

And to her surprise she realised that the man sitting down with his lunch tray was Jeffry Wilberforce, the Head of Station and their ultimate boss. She had shaken his hand on her arrival from the States, but otherwise their acquaintance had been limited to polite nods when they passed each other in the corridor. Wilberforce was a tall, rangy man, who still spoke in the curious twang of someone who had grown up on a ranch in the Texas Hill Country. Soft-spoken, he nonetheless projected an air of quiet authority, and he was a highly experienced intelligence officer, specialising in counter-intelligence, with particular expertise in Russia and the former Soviet territories – or the '-Stans' as they were known informally.

Though Wilberforce was well known for being accessible to his staff, Manon still felt a little as if two parlourmaids were being joined for tea by the Lord of the Manor, and as he politely introduced himself (as if they didn't already know who he was) she sensed the awkward dialogue that she thought lay ahead – *who are you exactly?*, *which department do you work in?*, etc., etc. But to her surprise it turned out he already knew both their names, where they each worked, and even what they did there. Before Manon could explain she was a recent arrival, he asked her how she was liking England, joking that she should be polite about the weather in front of the native Millie.

He proved an easy conversationalist, and made them laugh as he described some gizmo that had been recently installed – 'it's a new videoconferencing package called CUSeeMe,' he explained. 'Though, if you ask me, it should be called C-Nothing, since that's all I could make out. Every time you move there's a delay – so if you raise your hand, then several seconds later on the split screen you see your hand move. It's very distracting – I spent most of the meeting watching my fingers twitch instead of listening to what was being said. The tech guys swear it's the bee's knees, and it's supposed to be the latest, most secure version, but it will have to get a lot better before it's going to be any real use. It's not half as good as a face-to-face meeting, so I guess I'll be flying to the States for a few years yet.'

'Do you go there very often?' asked Millie.

He shrugged. 'Twice a year, maybe. It depends what's going on. Langley prefers to come here.' He added with a sly smile, 'Especially during Wimbledon.'

'Have you been back lately?' Manon asked.

'I was back last month – you were probably still there. I had meetings with a Russian who used to be a senior officer in the KGB. He hasn't exactly defected, but he's left Russia and moved to the States. He was giving a talk, but there were some informal meetings as well and I had a few things I wanted to ask him.'

'Was that Kazikov?' asked Manon.

Wilberforce looked at her in surprise. 'Yes, it was. How do you know about him?'

'I went to the talk. It was fascinating, I thought.'

'Oh no!' Millie suddenly exclaimed, looking at her watch. 'Got to go.' She blushed at her mini-outburst. 'Please excuse me. My meeting's about to start.'

Manon wondered if she should go too, but as she started to get up from the table in the wake of Millie's departure, Wilberforce held up a hand. 'Can you stay for a minute?'

'Yes, of course,' she said, sitting down again.

'How long have you been with the agency?'

'Three and a half years.'

'Hmm. And all of that time in counter-terrorism?'

'Yes, and focused on the Middle East.'

'Well, HR are the ones to give career advice, I suppose, but it's sometimes good to make a change. My grandma used to say, "Swap the loaf before the bread goes stale."' He grinned at Manon. 'Texas wisdom, for what it's worth. But tell me, does counter-intelligence interest you at all?'

Manon thought for a moment. 'If you'd asked me six months ago, I would have had to say no. But actually, after listening to Kazikov, I realised I'm very interested in it.'

Wilberforce was nodding. 'Good. The thing is, there's an opening in CI, the unit run by David Saunders. He and I have both heard good things about you, so maybe you should have a look at the job description; it'll be posted by HR any day now. It's an analyst's position, but there's sometimes a chance to get involved in the field. What would you think about that?'

'That would be great,' said Manon, excited by the prospect of not being entirely desk-bound. But then she hesitated, and Wilberforce looked at her curiously, sensing a question. 'The thing is,' she said, 'I don't have any training or experience. Just an interest.'

'It's the interest that matters,' said Wilberforce. He was smiling. 'The rest they can teach you. I think you'd like Saunders. Nice guy – tough when he needs to be, but fair. And good at bringing people along.'

'You come highly recommended,' said David Saunders ten days later. He was the Head of Counter Intelligence, a short and balding man, with a friendly smile but astute eyes. His office was down the corridor from Wilberforce, and over-looked Grosvenor Square.

'I do?' said Manon. Was Rickles so keen to get rid of her that he had praised her to another department head in the hopes he'd poach her?

'You do,' Saunders said emphatically. 'I talked to your old boss Fleishman. He recommended you "without reservation". Believe me, that's high praise coming from him.' He could see the surprise on her face, because he added, 'There didn't seem much point asking your manager here. You've barely got started, after all.'

Perhaps she was not the only one who found Rickles difficult. Saunders went on, 'So, what do you know about counter-intelligence?'

'Very little,' she said honestly. 'But I'm a quick learner, I think, and I am very interested in the whole area.'

They were sitting in armchairs on either side of a low table by the window. On the wall opposite Manon hung a brightly coloured painting of an orangutan. To her enquiry, Saunders had explained proudly that it had been done by his daughter, a fine-arts student at the Slade.

'That sounds good to me,' he said now. 'I'd have been concerned if you said anything else. Better keen and green, my old boss used to say. There will be a lot to learn, but I can promise you it won't be boring. You will start as an analyst with your present rank, but there's the possibility of promotion if things go well, and when there are operations going on we may want you to do some fieldwork on occasion. We are not a large department, so unlike life at Langley, we all have to pitch in sometimes. Does that sound OK?'

'Absolutely.'

'Good.'

They talked for another half hour, Saunders leading her through bewilderingly diverse topics, most related to her present work – what did she think would happen inside Iran? How reliable was intelligence coming from the Saudis? Would the Americans pull out from Afghanistan anytime soon? Others definitely were not – was she following British politics? Had she been to the British Museum? She sensed all of the questions had a purpose, even if it was only to get a better sense of her as a person.

'Wilberforce mentioned you heard Kazikov speak at Langley,' he said at one point. When she nodded he asked, 'What did you make of him?'

'I liked his talk very much – most of it was new to me.'

'He's a bit of an odd fish, or maybe it's just that he's living in a kind of no man's land. He's not a defector, even if his old pals at the KGB probably consider him a traitor. But he's never let us formally debrief him; everything is done on an informal basis. Meetings with him are always a kind of seminar, and if he doesn't like a question we ask him, then he just ignores it, or else talks completely off the point. And of course he's still free to come and go anywhere he likes – though he's never been back to Russia and spends most of his time in America now. After all those years fighting the Cold War, he must find it rather strange. Especially since it isn't very clear what will happen in Russia. I'm sure he doesn't want to burn his boats there – otherwise he would have been more co-operative with us.'

'That explains a lot,' said Manon, remembering her one-on-one encounter with the man. 'Most of what he had to say was historical – the view of the Cold War from the other side, in effect. But I had the sense he knew much more than he was willing to say. There was one thing—' She stopped, not sure if she should go on.

'Yes? What was that?' said Saunders encouragingly.

She shrugged her shoulders. 'It's probably nothing. But he mentioned after his talk that he had personally placed an illegal here in the UK – all the others were in the States, and they were all blown. So Kazikov made sure knowledge of this one was kept to the absolute minimum number of people – even the KGB Resident in the London Embassy didn't know about him.'

'And did he say what happened to this illegal?'

'That's what intrigued me. Kazikov didn't know. He said he assumed he would have just given up – gone back to Russia or gone somewhere else when everything melted down in the Soviet Union. I just thought that sounded very cold-blooded. He sent the man here and then, when trouble came and Kazikov left and went to the States, the illegal just got dumped. It made me wonder if he was still here. If he'd managed to get a job, perhaps, and settle down. It must have been very frightening just suddenly realising no one cared about you any more and you were on your own.'

Saunders smiled. 'You have to be tough to be an illegal and able to look after yourself. But the trouble is, in those circumstances, you have no purpose – if you have no one to pass your information to. Did Kazikov say what this guy's target area was?'

'No. He just clammed up when I asked him questions. After his talk I managed to speak with him for a moment – I told him I was about to come over here so I was intrigued by his account of this UK illegal. I asked him what name the man was using.'

'The cover name? Or his real Russian name?'

'Both.'

'And?'

'He said he didn't remember.' She sighed. 'And that I just don't believe. Maybe he could have forgotten the cover name, but not the man's real name. And actually, I felt certain he knew them both.'

'Wow. You certainly put him on the spot,' said Saunders, laughing. 'I'm not at all surprised he wouldn't tell you. To an old spy, some things are just too secret to reveal – ever. He'll take that information to his grave.'

Saunders leaned back in his chair. 'My guess would be that this illegal has given up long ago. Too much has changed in his home country for him to proceed with his mission, whatever it was. But I tell you what,' he said with a grin. 'Assuming you're going to take the job I'm about to offer you, maybe you can sit in if Kazikov comes to give a talk here, and ask him again.'

11

T HERE WAS NOTHING REALLY that Harry Bristow could complain about, but the easy circumstances of his new life in London didn't lessen his guilt, and some days only seemed to increase it. The offer Robinson had made him had been generous – needlessly so. By that time Harry had accepted that he was never going to summon up the nerve to confess what he had done, so Peter Robinson was not at any risk from him. But Robinson could not know that, so he had set out to buy Harry's silence.

'You'll be on the books of my company,' Robinson had announced, when they'd met in a park on the outskirts of Liverpool. They'd sat on a bench just outside a small playground, full of loud, tiny children and their mothers. 'You'll have the same take-home pay as a top-class chauffeur and you'll live rent-free. I have a flat in Marsham Street in Westminster. It's a good investment for me, and you get to live in the centre of London.'

So Harry became a chauffeur. He didn't have to wear a uniform or a cap and he was quite well off with his pay and his police pension and a free flat. But at the end of the day, what was he? Chauffeur to a spy. No wonder he lay awake some nights, asking himself how he could have got himself into this position; what harm was Robinson planning to do to the country? He often had to get up and walk round the flat, make a cup of tea, listen to the radio, until the sound drove out the noise in his head and he could sleep. Sometimes it was so bad that he would go out and pound the streets until it got light and other people started to appear; only then did he grow calm enough to go back to bed for a couple of hours.

His duties were straightforward and gave him plenty of time to brood over his situation. He didn't miss Liverpool much but he did miss the respect his previous position had afforded him, and also its sense of purpose.

Now and again he felt his old instincts reappear – one afternoon, as he was waiting in the front seat for his passenger, he saw a kid snatch a lady's handbag, and within seconds he was out of the car and had the kid pinned to the pavement, squealing in surprise.

But normally the job was fairly routine. At nine thirty each morning he would cross the river in the black BMW saloon, and wait outside one of the new luxury blocks of flats that dotted the South Bank. A few minutes later Peter Robinson, MP, would emerge and get into the back seat, then Harry would recross the river and drop him outside the Houses of Parliament. Some mornings he dropped him closer to Victoria, where Robinson had taken an office in a small block as the London HQ of his kitchens business. He had installed a manager to run the business day to day up in Liverpool, but he still directed its affairs overall from London.

Most of the time Harry was free for the rest of the day, though sometimes Robinson would need ferrying to a lunch appointment, meeting or a dinner. Occasionally Robinson went out with his girlfriend to a restaurant or the theatre in the evenings, but he was no night owl, and Harry would usually be home himself by eleven. Most Fridays in the early afternoon Harry drove his boss to Liverpool where on Saturdays he held surgeries for his constituents. Often these only lasted till lunchtime and Robinson would spend the rest of the day in meetings with his manager or on constituency business, or else have Harry drive him back to London.

Robinson seemed utterly uninterested in Harry's private life or what he did in his spare time. Conversation between them was limited to arrangements for the day, details of timing and locations. He never made small talk, or remarked on the weather, or enquired after Harry's health. Nor did he encourage any of the usual exchanges that go on between an employer and his driver. At their meeting in the park, when he offered Harry the job, Robinson had made it clear what sort of relationship this would be.

'You know some things about me,' he said, 'and I know things about you. That means we can have a deal that works for both of us.'

Harry tried to push it further. 'Why are you here? What are you hoping to do?' he had asked, though in his heart he knew at least part of the answer – this man was a spy for a foreign power.

But Robinson barely acknowledged the question. He'd looked at Harry with expressionless eyes and said, 'To serve my constituents to the very best of my ability. With the help of people like you.'

The one bright spot in Harry's life was the arrival of his son Charlie in the London area. The boy had been accepted for the Metropolitan Police and was training at the police college in Hendon. They hadn't seen much of each other since the divorce, though Harry had notified his former wife of his move to London. He didn't want to be the first one to make an approach, not when his son was choosing to go into his father's old profession, which Harry had disgraced. But then a letter arrived at his flat from his son, asking if they could meet one weekend. Harry was surprised at how pleased he was that the boy wanted to see him.

Two weeks later, on a Saturday when Robinson stayed in London and told Harry he didn't need him or the car, Harry drove the BMW to the college. As he approached he saw his son waiting at the barrier gate. He seemed to have grown – he must be an inch taller than Harry now, and he looked good with his hair cut short. Harry pulled over and parked, then got out of the car. He restrained his impulse to give his son a hug and shook hands instead. 'Long time,' he said mildly.

Charlie shrugged. 'Two years,' he said, then his voice softened slightly. 'I guess we've both been busy.'

They walked to a nearby café.

At first Harry found it hard to make conversation. Eventually he asked, 'How's your mother?'

'Fine, Dad,' Charlie said shortly. He added quickly, 'She sent her best.'

I bet she did, thought Harry, though without the animus he might have had in the past. His son's response suggested he wasn't sure how his dad felt about Gina marrying again, and Harry had to check the impulse to explain that actually this was fine with him. Better to keep things separate, he decided, though he realised there was a gulf between father and son that wasn't going to be easy to bridge.

'And Gwen?' he asked. His daughter and Charlie's little sister. Harry realised he didn't even know if his children got along with each other.

'She's doing great,' said Charlie. 'She's in year ten.'

'Of course,' said Harry dutifully, though he hadn't known in fact – it seemed to him that she had just started secondary school. But then, he hadn't seen his daughter for almost two years.

Fortunately, conversation proved easier when they talked about Charlie's own course at the police college – how it was going, what Charlie wanted to do when he finished. Obviously, to be a policeman in the Met, but Charlie was slower to answer when Harry asked what area of policing interested him most.

Eventually he said rather shyly, 'I'd like to do what you did, Dad. I was always so proud to have a dad who was a detective. I used to imagine you investigating – searching for evidence, linking it together, coming to a conclusion then giving evidence in court. And when I found out you were in Special Branch, investigating spies and terrorists, I thought that was amazing. So I'd like to do the same thing as you one day.'

As he listened to his son talking, Harry's eyes started to fill with tears, which he brusquely brushed away. He had never known how much this boy admired him and now, when he had betrayed everything that his son thought he was, he was agonised.

'Don't be sad, Dad,' said Charlie. 'We can meet a lot more when I start work in the Met. I can tell you how it's going and you'll be able to advise me. And you can tell me about your new job – what is it exactly that you do now?'

'Private security,' Harry said vaguely. 'Rich people get paranoid, and pay people like me to keep their fear at bay.'

Charlie laughed. 'Well, they must be paying you pretty well if that BMW comes with the post.'

He looked at his watch then said, 'Must go. Thanks for coming to see me, Dad. It's been great to talk. Please come again soon.'

As he drove back to London, Harry's mind went over and over his situation, searching for some way out of the lie he was living; some way of exposing Robinson without having to sacrifice himself and let everyone know his shame. It would help if he had some sense of what Robinson was up to. OK, he was an MP now, and from the occasional mention of the man in the papers Harry knew he was trying to become something of a defence expert. Harry could imagine how, if Robinson could get into the heart of things, this might help his masters – Russians? It must be; he couldn't believe it was the Chinese. But it all seemed too opaque to see any easy way – or any difficult way, for that matter – to find out exactly what was going on. Especially given his present position as driver, and no longer a Special Branch officer.

It was then that Harry started to take notes – a sort of journal, really, but one confined to entries about Robinson: where he'd gone and what he'd said, and in particular noting the rare occasions when Robinson spoke in Russian on the phone. There were obvious limits to what Harry put down, since most of the time he was either not actually driving the MP, or there was nothing to report – Robinson was never going to confide in Harry, even about the most innocent of his activities. But over the course of a free weekend, when Robinson took the train back to his constituency, Harry wrote lengthier accounts of how he had first met the Russian when the latter was just another junior officer on the *Bogdana*, and how he had encountered him again in Liverpool. In writing the story down, Harry was at pains to tell the whole truth: from the original bribes he accepted from Officer Romanov, both small and big, to the blackmail that forced him to become the now Peter Robinson's chauffeur. He included the photos Robinson had sent him along with his threatening messages, and also newspaper clippings which traced the progress of Robinson through the ranks of British society and British politics. Gradually he built up an impressive dossier on the man which was as complete as Harry could make it, and he supplemented it with the new notes he jotted each day about Robinson's doings. He was very careful not to leave any of the material lying around, and stored it in a locked steel box designed for a bank vault; Harry kept his under a loose floorboard in his flat. He didn't know what use his journal and these papers would ever have, but he wanted there to be some evidence that could one day expose Robinson for what he was, even if that exposed Harry too.

He also considered contacting an old colleague who was now working in London, but that wasn't an option if his own involvement with the MP was not to come out. He liked Robinson's girlfriend Louise, and they got along increasingly well. But she was Robinson's girlfriend, after all, which meant the last thing Harry thought he could do prudently was confide in her.

Then one afternoon in the week after he had seen Charlie, he was driving her back to the party HQ where she worked, not far from his own place in Marsham Street. Suddenly she asked, 'Harry, have you always been a driver?'

'No. I'm new on the job, to tell you the truth.'

'Really? You're a very good driver. I find London traffic terrifying.'

'You just have to stay calm, miss, especially in traffic. People only have prangs when they do something silly. I always say, there's no point getting agitated.'

'I'll try and take your advice, Harry, and I wish you would call me Louise.'

'All right, Louise,' he said, and grinned at her in the mirror. 'What did you do before this job? You're not a Londoner, from the sound of it.'

'No, I'm from Lancashire originally. Then I lived in Liverpool.'

'And?'

'And what, miss? I mean Louise.'

'What did you do up there?'

Before he could think to make anything up, he said, 'I was a copper.'

'You were?' She sounded surprised.

Harry was still getting used to the fact that chauffeurs were low in the society pecking order, virtually invisible. Slightly peeved, he said, 'Yes, I was eighteen years in the force.' He paused, still irked. 'Chief superintendent.'

In the mirror her eyes widened as she nodded. Then she laughed. 'Well that's reassuring.'

It was his turn to be surprised, though he sensed there was a new intimacy between them. 'Why's that?'

'It means Peter must be completely respectable, don't you think?' She was laughing again now. 'Who would hire an ex-senior police officer if they weren't entirely above board?'

'Y OU SEEM CHIRPY TODAY,' said Louise Donovan after they had been shown to their table.

'Yes, I'm feeling pretty upbeat,' agreed Manon. 'I've had some good news.' And it was nice to have someone to share it with, and even nicer to do it in the pleasant surroundings of this rather smart bistro just off Piccadilly. Lunch for Manon was usually either a snack in the Embassy canteen or a sandwich from the nearby Pret eaten at her desk.

'Don't tell me – your ogre of a boss has been transferred. Preferably to Timbuctoo.'

Manon laughed. 'Nice thought. But not quite that extreme, and I'm the one being transferred.'

'Oh no! Not back to the States?' asked Louise, sounding disappointed.

'No; just to a different department. New boss; same pay,' Manon said, making a face. 'But more interesting work. Two out of three seems pretty good to me.'

'That's great. I'd order champagne but that might not go down well with your new boss – and anyway I can't afford it!'

'Another time, and then the treat's on me. But enough about me – let's discuss the important things. How goes it with the new man in your life?'

'Good, thank you. So far, anyway. There must be faults somewhere, but I haven't found anything serious yet.'

'Is he still a mystery man?'

'Pretty much, though bits and pieces of the life story are emerging gradually.' Louise paused, then added, 'He's just a bit reserved. I think it's because now that he's an MP he's a public figure, but he doesn't want to share too much of himself.'

'He'll be lucky if he can get away with that for long. Isn't this the land of the tabloids? They love people's private lives.'

'Yes. They're dreadful. I think he wants to protect me from any possible embarrassment as well as himself.'

'That sounds rather gallant. Is that what Peter's like?'

Louise seemed to suppress a sigh. 'Don't get me wrong – he's not some knight in shining armour. Just a very nice man – kind, thoughtful, gentle, caring but also sometimes quite reserved.'

Manon had been glad to see Louise apparently so happy in this new relationship, but now she felt some doubt creeping in. She herself could never have a relationship with someone who kept their cards so close to their chest. 'Well at least he's not bad-tempered,' she said. 'I once went out with a guy who used to fly off the handle quite unexpectedly. Most of the time he was lovely but then something would happen and he would go berserk.'

'Oh no. He's not like that. He can be very direct with people – almost rude sometimes – but I've never seen him angry.' Louise paused for a moment. 'Though actually that's not true. He went to some meeting out of town a few days ago and ever since he's been a bit snappy. Harry – that's his driver – started to tell me about it, and Peter practically bit his head off.'

'Where did they go?'

Louise shrugged. 'I don't know. Harry mentioned something about the traffic on the M40, but then Peter shut him up.'

Their food came and there was a pause in the conversation while they ate, until Louise put her knife and fork down. 'Yummy,' she said. 'How are you fixed for time?'

'I'm OK. My new boss is pretty relaxed. If he thinks you're committed, then he leaves you alone to get on with it. Why? Do you have plans?'

Louise looked at her watch. 'It's just that if you want to meet my mystery man, he should be coming along in about a quarter of an hour. We're both going to a conference in Westminster and he said he'd pick me up here.'

And in fact, Peter Robinson arrived just a couple of minutes later. Manon was facing the restaurant entrance, and saw a man come in – tall, well dressed, looking around the room as the head waiter approached. It was obviously Robinson; he spotted Louise and strode over, brushing past the waiter without a word. Rude, thought Manon.

He stopped behind Louise and put a hand on her shoulder. 'Found you,' he said.

Louise jumped slightly at this sudden touch, then laughed. 'You gave me a shock.'

'Good. I wouldn't want to be boring.'

'This is my friend Manon,' she said. Robinson nodded at Manon, and looked at her, holding her gaze for what seemed an inordinately long time. It wasn't creepy in any kind of sexual way, but something about his cool appraisal made Manon feel extremely self-conscious.

'We were about to have coffee,' said Louise. 'Have we got time?'

'Of course,' he said, and sat down next to her.

'Manon is the friend from the States I was telling you about. She works at the Embassy.'

He nodded politely, seeming slightly bored, then something clicked and his expression changed. As he looked intently at her, Manon saw why Louise had been attracted to him. He was not extravagantly handsome – always less appealing in a man than people thought – but he had deep-set blue eyes, high cheekbones and a strong chin. The effect was of resoluteness, and a kind of male strength that was not to be confused with pointless machismo. 'What do you do at the Embassy?' he asked Manon.

She fell back on her standard line. 'I'm an analyst,' she said. 'Specialising in the oil and gas industry mainly.'

He nodded thoughtfully, but it was a temporary acceptance; he went on questioning her. 'Why are you based here if you're focused on oil and gas? Wouldn't it make more sense for you to be in Washington? Or in the Middle East even?'

Manon was slightly taken aback by his aggressive tone, but she knew her cover story and had ready answers. At this point the waiter appeared with a tray of coffee so she took the opportunity to postpone her reply until they had all helped themselves. Then she said, 'Yes. We have people all over the world working on the same subject.'

She finished stirring her coffee and continued, 'I think the view is that it's useful to have people based in various places to get a rounded picture. London holds the headquarters of some of the largest oil and gas companies in the world – and of course the City of London.'

'Hmm,' said Robinson, apparently losing interest.

Then he suddenly said, 'But you're part of the State Department, yes? Or is it the Defense Department? Or another department altogether?'

'State,' Manon said simply, and gave him a charming smile.

At this point Louise intervened. 'Peter, she's barely got here. Let her get her feet under the desk, won't you?'

Manon laughed. 'That's OK. I ask a lot of questions in my work so I don't mind answering some.'

The bill came and Manon tried to pay it but to her embarrassment Robinson took it firmly out of her hand. 'Can we give you a lift?' said Louise.

'Thanks, but I'll be fine,' replied Manon. Robinson said nothing.

Outside they stood on the pavement as a BMW glided down the street and pulled up in front of them. The driver got out and opened the rear passenger door. Louise kissed Manon goodbye on the cheek and got in, sliding along the seat to leave room for Robinson. But before he got in too, he turned to Manon, saying, 'Are you sure we can't give you a lift? Grosvenor Square isn't out of our way.'

It would save her a taxi fare and probably some time as well. But something made her resist. 'Thanks, but I've got shopping to do.'

'Well maybe you can join us some time for dinner. Your work sounds fascinating; I'd love to hear more about it.'

I bet you would, thought Manon, a little surprised by her own cynicism. What she wanted to know was why he was taking such an interest.

T HE NEWS OF THE impending arrival of Boris Denisov of the Russian FSB aroused emotions in three very different parts of London. In the Russian Embassy in Kensington Palace Gardens, Sergei Ivanov, the SVR Resident – Head of the SVR Station – was furious. At his morning meeting on the day he heard about it, he asked his senior team, 'Did any of you know these meetings with the British were planned?'

Heads were shaken all round the table.

'We should have been invited to send a representative. It would have been an ideal opportunity to talent-spot the opposition. And what's this about Denisov having a daughter at Oxford? Did we know that?'

Again heads were shaken.

'Apparently he's intending to visit her after the talks and he's turned down the British side's offer of transport. Says he wants to go on the train and experience a bit of British life,' Ivanov sneered. 'Well, I hope he enjoys it. There will probably be a strike. But I am not happy about any of this. I think we should have been consulted and we certainly should be involved. Find out everything about the plans for this visit, including his outing to Oxford.'

In Westminster on the Wednesday of the week of Denisov's visit, Peter Robinson was sitting on one of the green benches in the House of Commons, but his mind was not on the debate. He had scanned his copy of *The Times* that morning only to find himself completely thrown by an engagement notice in the Announcements. It had become almost a fetish of his to look at the Births, Marriages and Deaths columns every Wednesday. He had been doing it for more than a decade, ever since losing touch with his support team, but he never dreamed that after all this time the call to a meeting would appear.

And now that it had, he wasn't at all sure that he wanted to be contacted; he felt he was doing very well on his own. Someone from Moscow interfering might mess up everything, and possibly compromise his security. He knew, of course, that now he was getting very close to his target position in the centre of political life, he needed a contact to pass his information to. So finally, in spite of all his doubts, he let his curiosity overcome his caution and decided he would go to the meeting.

In the American Embassy in Grosvenor Square the Head of the CIA Station, Jeffry Wilberforce, had been kept in touch with the arrangements for Denisov's visit by MI5. He had been invited to send a representative to the meetings, both those with the police and the intelligence services. He was very surprised to learn from reading the briefing notes that Denisov had turned down the offer of a car and driver to take him to Oxford to see his daughter on the Thursday of his visit, and that he had chosen instead to go by train. Wilberforce wondered why the British had acquiesced. There would be massive embarrassment if anything happened to him on the journey. He noted it had been a police decision to agree to the request and he supposed they would find a discreet way of keeping an eye on him. Interesting, he mused, that Denisov had sent his daughter to Oxford. He wondered if the man could be a secret Anglophile and, if so, whether that might make him a suitable target for an approach.

On the Thursday morning of his visit to London Denisov emerged from his hotel at eight thirty.

'Taxi, sir?' enquired the doorman. Denisov nodded and the doorman let out a piercing whistle. 'Where to?' he asked as a cab drew up.

'Paddington station.'

The doorman repeated the destination to the driver.

'OK, guv. Climb in,' and the taxi drove off. The doorman watched it go then looked at his watch.

At Paddington, Denisov paid the driver and walked swiftly into the station, matching his pace to that of the hurrying crowd, trying to look as though he was just another passenger. He had dressed in a short black leather jacket, worn over a sweatshirt, and black jeans. He also had a small backpack. In the few days he had been in London he had been observing the street style and now, looking around, he thought he had judged his appearance rather well.

He stood on the concourse, apparently waiting for someone, but actually watching closely as another man bought a ticket from a machine, and then Denisov went to a different machine and successfully acquired a day return to Oxford. Passing the departure board, he saw that his train, the 9.35 to Oxford, was already at the platform so he went through the barrier and got on.

The train was quite full already and more people were piling in.

He had chosen his seat, one of the aisle seats at a table for four, because he thought it would give him a good view of the other occupants of the carriage, but in fact the height of the seat backs made it difficult to see anyone except those immediately around him. Just as the train was about to depart a young man wearing a cycle helmet and carrying a folding bicycle got on and sat at the table across the aisle. 'Sorry,' he said, as he knocked Denisov's legs with the bike. Denisov didn't reply and waited, slightly on edge, wondering if more was going to be said. But the young man simply took off his helmet and grinned at a little girl who with her mother was sitting at his table.

Denisov spent the next forty minutes or so looking out of the window and thinking how much more pleasant it must be to live in one of the small brick houses with little gardens, which filled the suburbs of London, rather than in the tall blocks crammed together in the outskirts of Moscow.

When Didcot Parkway, the stop before Oxford, was announced, the woman at the other table started getting her things together and packing away the little girl's toys, ready to get off. Denisov too stood up and then suddenly the bicycle owner moved and it became apparent that they were all disembarking here.

Denisov stood on the platform for a moment while the crowd of passengers began to clear, then he went out through the front of the station in search of the taxi rank. There was a small queue for taxis, including the woman and the little girl and the helpful bicycle owner, who was carrying one of their bags in his free hand. After mother and daughter had been safely despatched in their taxi, the cyclist stayed to unfold his bike and Denisov lost sight of him as he arrived at the head of the queue.

'Could you take me to Islip?' he asked the driver, not sure how to pronounce the word.

'Where?' asked the man, frowning.

'I S L I P,' said Denisov, spelling it out.

'Oh. *Islip*.' Light dawned on the driver's face. 'That's thirty miles or so from here. You should have stayed on the train to Oxford. It's much closer.'

'Oh dear,' said Denisov, looking surprised. 'Well, now I am here, will you take me?'

'Sorry, guv. No can do. It'll take half an hour to get there – and the same back. I knock off in twenty minutes. But hang on,' he said, seeing Denisov's disappointment. 'I think I know who will.' He got out of his car, looked back down the line of taxis, and yelled at the top of his voice, 'Alf! Gent wants to go to Islip. Can you take him?'

A faint 'OK' came back and a taxi left the line and drew up beside Denisov. So much for counter-surveillance, thought Denisov ruefully. He sat sideways in his seat so he could see if anyone was following them, but he saw nothing to alarm him.

'This is Islip, guv,' said the driver half an hour later, as the car turned off the main road into a village of honey-coloured cottages and winding streets. 'Where do you want me to drop you?'

Denisov looked out of the car window and saw, over the roofs of the cottages, the tower of the church that was his destination.

'This will do fine here,' he said, 'thank you very much,' and handing the driver a generous tip he walked off. Another turn brought him to a triangle of grass dominated by an old tree, and behind it he recognised, from the picture in the file back in the Lubyanka, the village church.

Denisov's eye was drawn to a car tucked in beside the wall of an ancient thatched cottage. He could see no one inside but he felt very exposed as he approached the gate into the churchyard. He paused and looked back and noticed several other cars parked on a small patch of the road. As far as he could tell, there was no one in any of them. The occasional vehicle passed along the street but otherwise there was no one around.

The total absence of people was eerie, as if the place had been cleared for his arrival. He wondered if it had been this way when Kazikov or one of his people had chosen it as a meeting place.

He pushed open the gate to the churchyard, where the gravestones were scattered among old trees, the grass speckled with bluebells. In the church porch a blue mat lay over the tiles bearing the message in gold 'Welcome to St Nicholas Church'. Denisov smiled to himself thinking how unwelcome he would be if his reason for being there were known.

He turned the ring handle on the old wooden door of the church and pushed cautiously. He jumped as the door let out a cacophony of creaks and rattles, announcing his arrival to anyone in earshot. He stood in the doorway, taking in the scene. The church was small and unmodernised. Rows of oak pews filled the nave and the side aisles, and beyond an arch was a choir, with a dark wooden organ at one side, its pipes painted gold. A sudden ray of sun lit up the inside of the building for a moment; Denisov saw it was empty. The time was ten to eleven. Closing the door behind him, he went and sat down in a pew in the darkest spot at the back of the nave to wait. A particularly loud rattle made him stiffen, his heart beating fast. But it was just a strong gust of wind shaking the church door.

He listened to the faint ticking of the clock on the tower as it moved towards eleven. Suddenly there was a loud creak and the door swung open. A tall, broad-shouldered man in a dark overcoat stood in the porch. He didn't notice Denisov sitting in the shadow. As he closed the door and came into the church, Denisov stood up and said quietly in Russian, 'Good morning, Romanov.'

The man's hand went to his pocket as he swung to face the voice. 'Who the hell are you?' he demanded.

THAT EVENING A LIVELY meeting was taking place in the SVR Residency in the Russian Embassy in London. The Resident himself was presiding.

'Yuri,' Sergei Ivanov said, turning to a stocky young man in a grey hoody and jeans. 'You begin. Tell me exactly what you did and what you saw.'

'I took the folding bike,' began Yuri, 'and waited where I could see the hotel entrance. He came out at eight thirty and took a taxi. I heard the doorman tell the driver to go to Paddington station so I cycled hard and got there first. I waited by the taxi drop-off place and when he arrived I followed him in. He got a ticket from a machine and I saw him get on the Oxford train, so I bought a ticket to Oxford and got on the train too. It was quite full but I managed to get a seat in the same carriage. I had to sit just opposite him or I wouldn't have been able to see him.

'He wasn't doing anything; just gazing out of the window. I thought he was going all the way to Oxford. But when the announcement was made for a station called Didcot Parkway, he stood up, ready to get off. I wasn't sure what to do, because I thought perhaps no one else would get off and if I followed him he would be suspicious; but luckily quite a few people disembarked, including a woman with a little girl and a lot of bags. I helped her, even though I had the bike in my other hand, so I think it looked quite natural. The woman wanted a taxi so I went with her to the taxi rank, keeping an eye out for Denisov who joined the queue behind us. I saw the woman and the kid into the taxi and then I hung around nearby, fiddling with my bike. I wasn't near enough to hear where Denisov wanted to go but it seemed to be a problem because the driver got out and shouted to another driver further back. He said something that sounded like "Gent wants to go to Eye Lip. Can you take him?" The other taxi came up and Denisov got in.

'I didn't think I had a hope of following them, and I didn't know where this place was, so I rang the others and told them what had happened and said I would take the next train to Oxford and meet them there.'

Mikhail took up the story. 'We had almost reached Oxford when Yuri rang. We didn't know where the place was, or even how to spell it, but we eventually found a place spelled "I S L I P" only a few miles from where we were. Yuri had given us the registration number of the taxi, so we decided to park up just outside the village and wait for the taxi to arrive.'

'Which it did,' said Alexei. 'It turned off the main road into the village and stopped and Denisov got out, paid the driver and set off walking. We drove into the village and passed him. There were a few other cars around so I don't think he would have noticed us particularly. We drove round a bend out of sight and I got out. I walked back and saw him go into an old church. I moved up a bit closer and hid in the churchyard – there were a lot of big trees. At first there was no one else around; it was dead as a morgue. Then, a little before eleven, a black BMW arrived and parked close by the churchyard wall. Two men got out. One was a big guy in a black overcoat and he went into the church. The other was his driver – he stood around for a bit, then got back in the car to wait. I took pictures but they aren't very clear because of the trees and the light. That's when I got a message to say Mikhail was parked nearby. There was still no one around and I don't think anyone saw me.'

At this point Mikhail broke in. 'I managed to find a place to park in another part of the village, near a shop. Then Alexei turned up. We weren't sure what to do next. We couldn't stay there, outside the shop, much longer. We didn't fit in – two blokes in a car just sitting there. We decided that as Denisov had no way of getting out of there except by taxi we would find the local taxi office and watch what happened. As it turned out, it was in the same line of buildings as the shop and just as we sat there an empty taxi left and we followed it. We were lucky because it stopped near the church and picked up Denisov. We drove out on a big road to Oxford, guessing that was where he was going and we were right. We saw the taxi behind us after a bit and let it get in front.

'And we followed it to Oxford,' continued Mikhail. 'The taxi dropped him off at the station. I don't know why, because that wasn't where he was going. Perhaps he didn't want the taxi driver to know.'

'So I got out and started to follow him on foot,' said Alexei.

'Thank God,' commented Mikhail. 'The street system there makes Moscow's look simple. If he'd stayed in the taxi I would almost certainly have lost him.'

Alexei picked up the story again. 'He walked towards the middle of town and I'm sure he didn't spot me – it was very busy on the street, with lots of people leaving the station.'

'And where was he going?'

'To one of the colleges. By good luck it's one of the closest to the station. They call it Nuffield – I asked someone. He said it was named after a car manufacturer.'

Ivanov said drily, 'I appreciate your research, Alexei, but what happened then?'

'He stopped at the porters' lodge and after a minute or two a young woman came down to meet him. His daughter.'

'How do you know for sure?'

'Well, I guess it was. I managed to get photos,' Alexei said. 'They left the college and went for coffee nearby. On Park End Street – there's a café. I didn't go in. I was worried he might have seen me in Islip. But I think these are clear enough.' He handed several pages of printer paper to the Resident, who looked at them closely. They showed Denisov from the side, walking in step and partially obscuring the view of a young woman. She had shoulder-length brown hair and a long straight nose.

Yuri now spoke up. 'Mikhail collected me at the station. We'd caught up with them by then – there's a car park just across from Nuffield. We took some photographs too.' He passed over his printouts, which had been taken surreptitiously from their car and showed Denisov and his daughter face on as they left the college. The Resident had seen mugshots of the daughter, taken for her passport application; the face in these photos was clearly the same.

He put down the photographs. 'Well,' he said, 'Denisov wasn't lying – he did go to Oxford to see his daughter. He was just, as the English like to say, being economical with the truth.'

That same evening in the CIA Station in Grosvenor Square, Jeffry Wilberforce was looking at two reports which had arrived on his desk. The first, from one of his officers who ran contacts in the main hotels in London, reported that Denisov had left his hotel at eight thirty in a taxi for Paddington. The second came from the porters' lodge at Nuffield College in Oxford where a number of foreign students, including Americans, were studying. It said that Denisov had arrived to meet his daughter just before one o'clock.

'I have to wonder,' said Wilberforce to Saunders, the Head of Counter Intelligence, 'why it took Denisov so long to get there. What do you think he was up to?'

15

THE RUSSIAN TEAM THAT had carried out the surveillance in Islip and Oxford at the Resident's direction assembled in London at the Embassy. Led by Yuri, they sat around a long table in a conference room on the top floor, while Ivanov the Resident waved the photograph they had taken of the black BMW that had brought Denisov's contact to the meeting in the Islip church.

'So what have we discovered about this?' he demanded impatiently.

Yuri spoke for the team. 'We checked the number plate and it turns out the car is registered in Liverpool. That was straightforward enough. What puzzled us was the small white mark on the windscreen. We had the photo enlarged, and it seems to be some sort of pass – it has a number and a pattern of squares with a crown on top. Alexei here has looked into it, and it seems that's the logo for the House of Commons.'

'I knew it,' crowed Ivanov. 'It proves the man is a British agent. It's his pass to their buildings.'

Inwardly Yuri sighed. The boss is really paranoid about Comrade Denisov, he thought, but kept it to himself – there was never any point arguing with Ivanov in front of other people. But why was Ivanov convinced Denisov was up to no good? If he had known more about Ivanov's own history, Yuri would have already known the answer to this question.

Before the collapse of the Soviet Union, Sergei Ivanov, now in charge of all Russian intelligence activity in London, had been only a middle-ranking officer in the KGB. He had not been among the star pupils at the training college and his was destined to be a mediocre career. But in the 1990s everything had changed and for Ivanov the influence of an uncle, who was good friends with someone in a position of power in the new regime, had got him a good job in the newly created SVR. His performance there was diligent and reliable, if not inspired, and he was too insignificant to make many enemies. This and a stroke of luck – a far superior candidate had suddenly resigned – had landed him the plum assignment in London.

In spite of his elevation, or possibly because of it, he deeply resented people like Boris Denisov – younger than him, marked out as stars from the beginning – who had grabbed the very top jobs. Though it was hard for him to admit, even to himself, he knew that Denisov had achieved his position by skill and competence rather than, as in his own case, by influence. This only made him resent Denisov more, and now that he had caught him doing something that looked suspicious, Ivanov was on to it like a hound after a rabbit. Happy to believe the worst, he concluded almost right away that Denisov was a traitor, working for the British, and that he had come to London to meet his controller, the man who had turned up at Islip church.

Yuri was not convinced. He knew more than Ivanov about British intelligence, and as he had told his team, 'I don't believe this contact who met Denisov is in the Secret Service of the UK. If he was he wouldn't be advertising it by having a sticker in his windscreen. I think it's more likely he works in government.'

He said now carefully to Ivanov, 'We wondered whether this contact was a Member of Parliament.' Before Ivanov could dismiss the idea, he added hastily, 'That would explain why he had that posh car *and* a driver.'

'Of course,' said Ivanov after a moment's pause, now acting as if this was his idea. 'I imagine many of the MPs are also employed by the security services here.'

Yuri nodded dutifully. 'Alexei,' he said, pointing to his team member at the end of the table, 'discovered that Liverpool – where the car is registered – has four of them. MPs,' he added helpfully, seeing Ivanov start to frown.

'But two are women,' piped up Alexei.

'Yes,' said Yuri. 'Which leaves two possible candidates. We have photographs from the press of them both. Here, have a look at this one,' he said to Ivanov, sliding his open laptop across the table to him.

Ivanov peered at the screen. 'Yeah… perhaps.'

'I am confident it's the same man we saw in Islip. His name is Peter Robinson. It was from a distance and the light wasn't that good, but I am sure. So is Mikhail,' Yuri added.

Mikhail was sitting next to Alexei. He said a little nervously, 'I am. Obviously it would be better if we could see a full-length picture, but it does look exactly like him.'

Ivanov grunted, but then seemed to accept the identification. 'I agree that it's the same man. He is obviously a spy as well as a Member of Parliament – as I said, it is a common practice in the West, for it allows the government to keep track of dissident politicians.'

Yuri suppressed a groan at this, then waited for his instructions. And Ivanov stood up as he delivered them. 'I think, therefore, the next step is for you and your team to go immediately to Liverpool to find out more about this man Robinson. Be careful there. Naturally, if you act indiscreetly and are discovered and identified by the British authorities, I will have to deny I know anything about you.'

Naturally, thought Yuri sourly, standing up himself since it was clear that Ivanov considered the meeting over.

The following day, a Friday, saw the three Russians in a street near Robinson's constituency office. They had added a technician to their numbers and were unpacking their gear into a small house that Alexei had spotted was empty – there was a large 'For Sale' board outside. It had taken little effort to break in through the back door.

After discovering that Peter Robinson held a surgery for his constituents most Saturday mornings, the Russian team spent the rest of the day photographing the various branches of Robinson's kitchen shops and planning their surveillance. On Saturday morning they were in place by eight thirty and at nine saw the BMW arrive and Peter Robinson go into the office. Yuri and Tomas, the technician, followed the BMW when it drove away. They stuck fairly close to it through busy shopping streets until after about twenty minutes it turned into the car park of a small apartment block in a quiet residential area. There it stopped, and the driver, identifiable as the driver from Islip, got out and let himself into the building.

'I could do it now,' said Tomas. 'I only need ten minutes.' But Yuri shook his head and drove on. 'It's too exposed. There'll be another chance.'

The chance came later in the day. The driver collected Robinson from the constituency office at five thirty. Followed by all four Russians in two cars, the BMW drove to a large hotel in the centre of Liverpool. There seemed to be some sort of event taking place; the hotel's car park across the street was packed, and a stream of smartly dressed people was crossing the road and going into the door marked 'Ballroom'.

Robinson got out at this entrance, and his driver pulled into the car park, driving slowly round, looking for a space. The two pursuing cars did the same and eventually all three cars were parked. By now it was pouring with rain. Alexei and Mikhail watched as the driver of the BMW got out and, opening an umbrella, huddled under it as he walked across to the hotel.

By now the car park was quiet; it seemed that everyone who was going to the event was inside. Alexei sent an all-clear signal with his headlights and Tomas, small bag in hand, cap on his head and coat collar pulled up, strolled over to the BMW. In seconds he had the door open and was sitting inside. In less than five minutes, Tomas was out again and walking back to his own car.

'Job done,' he reported as he got in. 'The only problem was I think I left the seat wet.'

'That's OK. His coat'll be wet when he comes back. Let's get out of here.'

That evening in their small house, the Russians celebrated as they heard snatches of conversation from the BMW after Robinson left the event at the hotel. By the morning, the house was empty and the Russian team was on its way back to London.

16

' I F YOU HAD A crystal ball what outside countries might you see playing a major part in determining the future of the Gulf region?'

The question from the seminar leader, Professor Rogofsky, hung in the air like a balloon waiting to be punctured by a reply. It was warm in the seminar room; its mullioned windows, overlooking on one side the college's quadrangle and on the other a busy bus-filled street, were firmly closed.

Nuffield was a college that looked old but was in fact comparatively modern. Built in the 1930s with an endowment from Lord Nuffield of Morris car fame, it taught only postgraduate students, and specialised in the social sciences, particularly politics and international relations.

It was only Manon's second day there – she had come up the week before to meet the professor and get his approval to attend the seminar – but she was already enjoying it, largely for his mild eccentricity. Though she was also discovering that he had the unnerving habit of suddenly calling on one of the eleven members of his seminar for their opinion. So far Manon had managed to keep a low profile, but now her luck ran out.

'Ms Tyler,' said the professor. 'You have joined us recently, and I am sure we would all be interested to know your view.'

Manon paused before replying, not because she didn't have a view – she had lots of them, in fact – but because she needed to gauge how knowledgeable she wanted to appear in front of this audience. Well, not all of the audience; there was only one student whose reactions would really matter.

She said finally, 'Potentially, Russia is a competitor with the oil states – since both sell natural gas to the European Community. The United States is more of a client than a driver of policy – though I can foresee a day when it is oil independent. The country I do see trying to have a larger role is China.'

'China?' This from a goateed student on the other side of the table. He had talked a good deal already, without the professor needing to call on him. His voice was sceptical, almost sarcastic, as if Manon had nominated Liechtenstein as a major player in the region.

Annoyed, Manon thought quickly about how best to deal with him. The last thing she wanted was to be conspicuous; that was not the role she was meant to play here.

Fortunately another student joined in with a comment – a young woman with a slight accent. She was the only other female in the group and, unlike the men, was smartly dressed, in dark trousers and a silk blouse. Over the back of her chair was casually thrown a beautiful grey suede jacket which Manon had already admired – and envied. 'It makes sense,' the woman now said. 'China has worldwide ambitions. And nowhere to go but up.'

The goateed student emphatically disagreed; soon the two of them were engaged in a hammer and tongs argument about China's future importance to the Gulf states. Manon found herself relaxing, and pleased that her 'rescuer' turned out to be the person she had been sent to get to know.

Just a week earlier she had been working at her desk in the Embassy when she was summoned to a meeting in her section head's office. Opening the door, she found to her surprise that Jeffry Wilberforce, the Head of Station, was there, sitting in one of the easy chairs around a low coffee table; Saunders, her manager, was sitting on the sofa against the wall. Out of the window at the far end of the room there was a fine view of the square, where the trees were in leaf now, and the tourists much in evidence.

Manon was intrigued to find no one else in the room, and wondered why she alone had been summoned to such a high-level meeting.

'Have a seat,' Wilberforce said in his dry hint-of-a-drawl voice. 'And don't look so nervous. First item of the agenda is to say we're all really pleased how you've begun this new post. Like a horse to water, I'd say.'

'Thank you,' she said, relieved at the praise.

Saunders was nodding. 'Very pleased indeed. So pleased, in fact, that we have something of a special assignment for you. Ordinarily, we'd wait to put you in the field until you'd got your feet a little wetter in the counter-intelligence pond, but this is something that really can't wait, and we think you're ready for it anyway.'

Relief was now replaced for Manon by curiosity. So far her work had been confined to paper – reading, analysing, the occasional bit of succinct writing (Saunders liked reports brief and to the point).

'I should say,' said Wilberforce, 'that if you're not happy with what we're asking you to do, then you must tell us right away.'

To demur was the last thing in Manon's mind, especially when Saunders leaned across and put a sheet of paper on the table. 'This is your target. She's Tatiana Denisov, a Russian currently studying at Nuffield College, Oxford.'

Manon picked up the piece of paper, which seemed to be a photocopy of an application form for postgraduate study at Oxford University. A passport-sized colour photograph of the applicant showed a woman with high cheekbones, blue deep-set eyes and straight brown hair. It was not a face one would easily forget, though it was striking rather than beautiful. The details on the form gave her age as twenty-four. She had a degree from Moscow State University and an address in Moscow.

'What is she studying in Oxford?'

'International Relations. She's doing an MPhil – that's a two-year course and she's in her second year.'

'OK,' said Manon slowly, taking this in. 'What is her interest to us?'

'Her father is a senior officer in the Russian Internal Security Service, the FSB. Recently he visited the United Kingdom at the invitation of the Metropolitan Police to discuss counter-terrorism. On his last day he went to visit his daughter. Oxford is an hour away by train, but he managed to take four hours getting there.'

'How was that?'

'We're not sure; there's a large gap in his travel itinerary that day and we don't know what he was doing – or where. But we have our suspicions, and they include the possibility that he was meeting someone.'

'But wouldn't you expect the SVR Residency at the Embassy to be doing that? Rather than a visitor from the internal security service? Especially one who was invited here by the police on an official visit?'

'The Brits keep a very sharp eye on what the Residency is doing,' said Saunders. 'So conceivably if they were worried about surveillance, they might have had Denisov make the meet.'

Manon was thinking hard about the implications of what Saunders was saying. 'You say you worry he was meeting an agent? Isn't there a chance that *he's* the agent?'

'You mean, he's working for the British?'

'Yes,' said Manon. 'I was thinking maybe MI5.'

Wilberforce butted in. 'You're right to raise that,' he said. 'But I've broached it with the DG there and at MI6 and they're both adamant that they've had no dealings with Denisov. They are as intrigued about this as we are.'

'Anyway,' said Saunders, 'whatever he was doing, that's not why we wanted to talk to you today. If Denisov were running someone here, it would be useful to know, but it would be even more useful if we could make contact with him ourselves. Naturally, it's a long shot, but if there were any chance of bringing him over to our side, he would be a terrific asset. With Russia in such upheaval these days, it would be immensely useful to have a high-up source in their domestic security agency.'

Manon nodded, but couldn't imagine what her role was supposed to be. Denisov presumably was now back in Moscow; what did they want her to do – fly there and make him an offer he couldn't refuse? Through the window she could see into the square, where a woman was walking with a small child, who was carrying a balloon by its string.

'So?' she asked hesitantly.

'So,' said Saunders with a trace of a smile, 'we have no direct way to get to Denisov. An approach in Moscow is out of the question, and we think he would have run a million miles away from even the slightest contact with us while he was visiting the UK. However, he seems to have a father's natural affection for his daughter, and she is still here and will be for another year. We thought – and I stress that it's still more an idea than a plan – that if we could somehow get close to her, opportunities might arise to make contact with her dad, or at the very least find out more about him.'

'And,' said Wilberforce, 'we thought if someone could join her year and her faculty and get to know her well, something might come of it.'

'I think I know who that "someone" is,' said Manon, smiling now. It did look to be a long shot, but this made the idea seem, almost perversely, even more attractive.

'We have some contacts at Nuffield,' Wilberforce said. 'Nothing formal; no one actually working for us. Just people, you might say, who are well disposed. It would be possible to have "someone"' – and he too smiled at the absurdity of this, since by now it was obvious it was Manon – 'placed at the college, who was finishing a degree that she'd started and never finished when she came to work at State. And now she's posted here at the Embassy she's being given study leave.'

'Would I have been at Oxford when I started this degree?' Manon asked, slightly alarmed. She had never set foot in the place, much less studied there.

'No, no,' said Saunders. 'We'd make your cover story as true to fact as possible. You would have started a graduate thesis back in the States – that's the story; we can talk about where this was – and now you're putting a toe back in the academic water. You wouldn't officially be a student at Oxford – that would only be credible if you started when the new academic year begins in fall. The idea is that you're thinking of going back to do a higher degree; that we – that is to say, the

Embassy – are willing to give you some time to explore the possibility, and that you're sitting in on one of the seminars to see if that's really what you want to do. That's the official agenda; the unofficial one is that the seminar is one Denisov's daughter attends and that you do your best to befriend her and see where that gets us.'

Suddenly there was silence in the room. Manon caught Saunders glance over at Wilberforce; both men were looking worried. Finally Saunders said, 'So, what do you think? I should tell you we thought you were uniquely qualified for this because Tatiana is attending a seminar focusing on the Middle East, Iran and the Gulf. With your background you'd be a very convincing student.'

Manon had about a hundred questions, but realised they could wait. Right now they wanted a reply. She took a deep breath and said, 'You can count me in.'

Saunders slapped his knee. 'I thought you'd do it.' He was beaming.

Manon beamed back. She felt flattered, and sensed she was supposed to. She looked out at the square again. The little girl must have let go of her balloon, for it was now floating high above her, well above the treetops. The girl was crying, and her mother was kneeling down to console her.

Manon turned to look at Wilberforce, who was also grinning. 'Great!' he exclaimed, and Manon could only pray that his was the voice of experience over hope.

17

HALFWAY THROUGH THE SEMINAR Professor Rogofsky called a fifteen-minute break for coffee and tea, served from two large urns brought in from the college dining hall. As a queue started to form, Manon moved towards it, trying to position herself carefully, dodging the goateed student when he tried to engage her in conversation – presumably more about why China wasn't going to figure in the Middle East. With a firm 'excuse me', she got past him and managed to join the queue just in front of the Russian woman Tatiana. The goateed student was directly behind Tatiana now, and looked keen to resume their argument.

Before he could say anything, Manon asked Tatiana, 'Is there always a break for coffee?'

Tatiana smiled and said, 'Yes. Three hours is too long without one, don't you think?'

'Absolutely.'

'Especially when things get heated,' said Tatiana, rolling her eyes meaningfully to indicate the goateed man behind her.

Manon grinned. 'It is a long time to concentrate,' she said. 'I'm not used to it, to tell you the truth.'

'You're new here, aren't you? I don't think I have seen you before. My name is Tatiana Denisov.'

'I'm Manon. Manon Tyler. And yes I've just joined the course.'

They got coffee, and stood by one of the windows. Outside the traffic was heavy, even in mid-afternoon. Manon said, 'Oxford isn't quite what I expected.'

'I know. It's more of a city than people realise.'

'Still, the college is very nice.'

'Yes. Compared to the university I attended in Moscow, this seems a paradise. Last I heard there was still snow on the ground there.' Tatiana smiled.

'Is that where you're from – Moscow?'

Tatiana nodded. 'And you?'

'I'm American.'

'You don't say,' said Tatiana in a parody of a Midwestern twang. They both laughed, and then from the head of the long table at the other end of the room, Professor Rogofsky rattled his spoon against his cup, and called out, 'I think we should reconvene, ladies and gentlemen. Sorry for the brevity of the break, but we have two more presentations to hear, and I don't want our discussion cut short.'

Manon looked at Tatiana and shrugged. 'Nice to have met you,' she said.

'Likewise, as you Americans say. But perhaps when we're finished you'd like to have coffee or a glass of wine.'

'That would be great,' said Manon, and took her place at the table again with a sense of satisfaction at how far she had got in a short time.

After the seminar finished she joined Tatiana and they walked down the stairs and out of the college. 'Where shall we go?' asked Manon. 'I'm afraid I don't know Oxford at all.'

'Follow me,' said Tatiana, 'and I'll introduce you to the delights of Park End Street's best wine bar. It must be the best, since it's the only one.'

They crossed the street and walked west, towards the station, which was just as well for Manon since she wanted to get back to London in time to call in at the Embassy to report on her progress.

Park End Street turned out to be a jumbled row of mainly Victorian buildings that housed everything from an auction-eer to a night club. Halfway down, Tatiana led the way into a small wine bar with stripped floorboards and pine tables. It was half empty at this time of day, though Tatiana said that later it would be heaving because they had good music groups playing there in the evenings.

Taking their glasses of wine to a little table by the front window, they talked a bit about the seminar, with Tatiana reassuring Manon that no one ever got through the whole of the reading list the professor handed out each week. Then they moved on to the subject of the other students, most of whom Tatiana seemed to find very serious and very dull, though she reserved most of her scorn for the goateed one who she thought was an idiot. She was fascinated by the professor, however – who, she told Manon with raised eyebrows, was said to be on wife number four.

This let Manon ask about student life at Oxford, and Tatiana sighed. The replies that followed almost seemed sad. No, there wasn't much social life. Yes, she had a boyfriend, but he was back in Russia, and lately he had not been very communicative – anyway, they hadn't ever vowed anything remotely like eternal love or (she hinted) fidelity. The Oxford men were either jejune, she went on, or grimly academic, and the women were anything but chic. She had not made many friends, and the other postgraduate student in her accommodation had become seriously ill the month before and retired to her parents' house in Northumberland.

She paused, then said, 'But what about you?'

Manon shrugged, then explained she was working at the American Embassy in London. She hoped she could leave it at that – and for the moment, at least, it turned out she could, as Tatiana didn't pursue it. Manon said, 'I do sympathise about the social life, you know. London's a wonderful city, but to be honest I can't really say I've made any friends there. The people at work are very nice but most of the other women working in the Embassy have families of their own. As for meeting men, I'm not keen on bars, frankly, and internet dating has never appealed.'

'I know,' said Tatiana. 'One night I looked at a dating website.' She shuddered at the memory, and Manon laughed.

Tatiana smiled and went on, 'But how can you work in London and be a graduate student here?'

'I can't really,' said Manon. 'I'm not a student – yet. I'm just attending the seminar. If I like Oxford, and they let me in, then I'll take extended leave and do the degree properly, starting in fall. Until then I'll come up for the seminar, and come the next day as well – to use the library.'

'You'll come twice every week?' asked Tatiana. She sounded pleased by the prospect. 'That's quite a lot of commuting.'

'I know,' said Manon with a sigh. 'I live in south London, which makes it even worse. I'm hoping I might find a room somewhere in Oxford where I could stay a night each week,' she added on the spur of the moment, hoping that Saunders and Wilberforce would approve the idea.

Tatiana said nothing, but seemed to take this in.

A week later, Manon was back for the seminar. The paper given this time was on the lasting impact of the Balfour Declaration. Manon was able to contribute to the discussion without incurring the wrath of the verbose student with the goatee – or anyone else for that matter.

At the break, she was delighted to find Tatiana come over to her to say hello, then propose meeting up again afterwards. They went to the same wine bar, which Tatiana jokingly suggested could become their 'local'.

Once they sat down with their glasses of wine, Tatiana said, 'You know, I've been thinking about what you said about finding a room here in Oxford when you come up for the seminar. I have an idea. My flatmate isn't coming back this term. If you didn't mind having her stuff all around, then I'm sure she wouldn't mind if you used her room. It's in Jericho and not very smart,' she added, 'but it would save you all that commuting time, wouldn't it?'

'Are you sure?' Manon asked, trying not to seem too keen. 'I wouldn't want to get in your way.'

'Hardly. I'd like the company. And if I didn't,' Tatiana said with a small laugh, 'it's only one night a week.'

'That would be wonderful.' Don't get ahead of yourself, girl, Manon thought sternly, and for a fleeting moment she wondered why this Russian woman was being so friendly. Was it conceivable that she was on a mission of her own, one which had her trying to recruit Manon? What if the agent her father might have met with and was controlling was someone from the CIA – like Rickles? she speculated, briefly revelling in the delicious possibility. Then she pulled herself together, dismissed these fantasies, and recognised the simple truth: the woman was lonely.

'I think we will be friends,' said Tatiana firmly.

'Me too,' said Manon, feeling a little guilty for her deceit.

18

PETER ROBINSON'S HOUSE IN Liverpool was a suburban villa that was nice enough, but modest for such a wealthy man. It was located on the edge of his constituency, and was looked after during the MP's absence in London by a housekeeper, an Irishwoman called Mrs O'Neal. She opened the door for Harry and there in the hall were three packing cartons neatly stacked.

'Would you like a hand with these?' asked Mrs O'Neal, who was not much over five feet tall and at least seventy years old.

'Thanks, I can manage,' replied Harry, smiling to himself. In fact the boxes turned out to be quite heavy and a bit of an effort to lift, even for him. The three cartons were closed and tightly taped up and he wondered what was in them until, as he dumped the last one in the boot of the BMW, it split in one corner, and Harry saw that it was full of books. No wonder the boxes weighed a ton, he thought.

Harry's life had settled into a comfortable routine, though this only served to worsen the inner turbulence he felt. Despite their constant proximity to each other, Robinson still made no effort to get to know Harry any better as time passed, and though this was a relief to Harry in many ways, it also meant his employer remained an enigma. He was up to no good, but exactly on whose behalf? And what was Robinson hoping to do – MPs were really only individually powerful if they became cabinet ministers, and as a first-term MP Robinson wasn't going to see that kind of promotion anytime soon.

His girlfriend Louise seemed nice and straightforward, and was always both friendly and polite to Harry, so he found it difficult to believe she was complicit in what he thought of as Robinson's subversion. She worked for the party and was well connected through her job, but he had overheard her once joking with Robinson that they were both 'rookies' in their respective posts, so presumably she was still relatively junior.

Harry had rented out his own house in Liverpool, so on the weekends when he drove Robinson up to Liverpool he stayed at a Premier Inn at Robinson's expense, before driving the MP down to London on Sunday or sometimes Monday morning. It was pretty dull in Liverpool for Harry; he usually ate in the hotel restaurant and spent the evening watching television in his room. He avoided his old haunts – the pubs and bars and restaurants he used to frequent – and the company they might provide. He didn't want to see any of his former colleagues and find himself forced to confess that he was now driving for a living. But on this particular trip, Robinson had told him he could go back to London the next day, since the MP was staying on through the weekend and would catch a train south on Monday. He had one chore for Harry, however, which was to collect the boxes from the house Robinson still retained in his constituency.

Harry was back in London late that evening, delayed by heavy traffic around Manchester. Arriving at Marsham Street, he left the boxes in the locked boot. Robinson had arranged for Louise to meet him at the MP's flat the following morning to let him in with his load. Crafty bugger, thought Harry, since he had been hoping Robinson might lend him a key so he could go in on his own. As with his house in Liverpool, Robinson was making sure Harry wouldn't have any opportunity to poke around.

In the morning Harry drove across the river, and parked with the concierge's agreement quite illegally in front of Robinson's building. As he took the lift with one of the boxes, he realised he had never been inside the flat, and when Louise opened the door he was struck by the sheer spaciousness of the living room. It was only sparsely furnished, with two white sofas strewn with colourful cushions, and a coffee table that was all chrome and glass. Along one wall fitted bookshelves stretched from floor to ceiling, though they were only half full – the reason, he assumed, for his bringing the boxes down from Liverpool.

There were recessed dimmer lights in the ceiling, switched off now as sunlight came in a dazzling wave from the full-height windows. When Harry's eyes adjusted, he saw the extraordinary view along the river. In the distance he could make out the skyscrapers of the City of London and among them, dwarfed now, the dome of St Paul's Cathedral; closer to him loomed the Gothic towers of the Houses of Parliament.

How different from the ordinary house where he had collected the boxes, thought Harry. Robinson was probably wise to live modestly in Liverpool – that way, no constituent could label him a fat cat – but this place was a different story altogether and indicated very considerable wealth. Had it all come from the kitchen business, Harry wondered, or was Robinson receiving funding from another source?

Louise came out from the kitchen, where she had been making coffee for them both. She was wearing jeans and a simple long-sleeved shirt. During the week she was always smartly turned out, and he was glad to see that she didn't feel the need now to dress as if on duty. She said, 'I hope you don't mind – there wasn't much milk. Two sugars, right?'

'That's perfect, and in a cup and saucer no less.'

She laughed. 'Nothing but the best for Mr R. I'd prefer a mug myself, but his kitchen doesn't run to anything that downmarket.'

He wasn't sure how to take this – was she being sarcastic? He took a sip from his cup. 'This is quite a place,' he said.

'You like it? It seems a bit bare to me, but I'm doing my best. All he needs now are a few pictures on the wall and some more books on the shelves, and then it might actually feel lived in.'

He wondered how often she was here, and whether her urge to make the place more homely was wishful thinking. Robinson always seemed nice enough to her when they sat in the back while Harry drove, but it was impossible to tell what he was like in private. He was encouraged enough to say, 'It probably needs a female touch.' Her eyebrows raised and he said quickly, 'Apologies. I must sound very old-fashioned.'

Fortunately she laughed. 'Not at all. Men in my experience are absolutely hopeless when it comes to setting up house. Those that aren't tend not to have girlfriends.' She laughed again. 'Whoops! I'm not being very PC either.'

Harry finished his coffee and put down the cup. 'I'll bring the other boxes up now if that's OK.'

'Of course. Can I give you a hand?'

'Nah. There's only two to come, but they're awfully heavy. More books, I think.'

He brought the next box up and found Louise on the phone, so returned downstairs for the third. It was the one with the split corner, so he handled it carefully, but just as he brought it into the flat it suddenly gave way, and books spilled out of one end all over the floor. 'Sorry,' he said, as she bent down to join him in picking them up. 'That one bust as I was putting it in yesterday.'

'It's not your fault. Peter must have overloaded it.'

He started to put the loose books in a pile, glancing at the titles as he handled each volume. There was a paperback life of Churchill, a single volume of Hansard, a second-hand edition of *Who's Who* and a copy of *The English Constitution* by Sir Walter Bagehot. He supposed this was the right sort of reading material for a young and aspiring MP.

'Should I put these on the shelves?' he said. Louise was kneeling now and didn't answer. He noticed she was holding a book and staring at its cover, almost transfixed.

'What's wrong?' he asked, hoping to God Robinson hadn't been thick enough to include pornography among this collection.

'This one's not in English,' she said after a moment. She held the book up, and he could see that its title was in peculiar letters – not in the alphabet he knew.

'What language is that?'

By now Louise had picked up a second book, and it too had strange letters on its cover. 'I think it's Russian,' she said. She lifted a third book, and ruffled its pages. 'This one has both.' She held it out to him.

He took the book from her. The cover said it was an edition of Pushkin's poems. Harry opened it and saw that on the left pages the text was in English; on the right-hand side the letters were all from a different alphabet.

'That's Cyrillic,' Louise said. 'The Russian alphabet. But why on earth does Peter have three books in Russian? He's from Canada. He told me he knew a little French, from a year he spent in school in Quebec. He never said he knew any other languages. And certainly not Russian.' She sounded mystified.

Harry brushed it off. Now was not the time for encouraging suspicion. 'Maybe he wants to learn Russian,' he said calmly.

'Yes,' said Louise, taking back the book and riffling its pages absent-mindedly. She suddenly looked up at Harry. 'Or maybe he knows it already.'

19

'THIS IS A COMPLETE waste of time,' muttered Yuri, pulling off his headphones and running his hands through his hair. 'He's a Member of Parliament and nothing else.'

The team in the SVR Residency had been taking it in turns to listen to the audio from the microphone in Peter Robinson's car, but so far, after a couple of weeks, they had heard nothing to persuade them that Robinson was anything other than what he appeared to be – a hard-working Member of Parliament with a thriving kitchen design company in the north of England. As for Ivanov's theory that Robinson was an undercover British Special Services officer who was running Denisov as his agent, they had been sure when he suggested it that it was rubbish and nothing had changed their minds. It was true, however, that they could find no explanation for the meeting in the church at Islip, which even Yuri, the most sceptical of the team, had to admit was mysterious.

Later that day, at a meeting with Ivanov, Yuri set out what they had learned so far.

'His driver's called Harry. We don't know his second name. He seems to have something to do with the police.'

'Aha,' chipped in Ivanov. 'That's interesting.'

Yuri continued, 'I think he may once have been in the police in Liverpool – that's where Robinson's kitchen business is. He has a son he talks to sometimes who is himself training for the police and there's a friend in London he once spoke to who seems to be in the Metropolitan Police. But that's all. It's just social chat. He never talks about Robinson.'

Ivanov said, 'We know the British Special Services work very closely with the police.'

Yuri ignored this and said, 'Robinson has a girlfriend called Louise. Harry and she are quite friendly. She works in Robinson's party headquarters and Harry often picks her up there and sometimes he takes her home to her flat in the evenings. Occasionally they talk about Robinson, but it's just superficial chat. I don't think she's known Robinson very long. Harry seems to have known him longer and she asks him questions about him but Harry doesn't say much. There's also a guy called Philip in Liverpool. Robinson phones him every morning on the way to the House of Commons and sometimes again later in the day. This Philip seems to be managing his kitchen business. Then there's the political agent in Liverpool. He often rings the car when Robinson's not there and Harry says he'll pass on a message.'

Yuri shrugged. 'That's more or less it. They seem to go up to Liverpool most weekends. Sometimes Louise goes with him, sometimes not. So it all looks very much as you would expect. Nothing suspicious.'

'Except that meeting in the church,' said Ivanov. 'We still don't know what that was all about. How does he know Denisov? Tell me that, please.'

But Yuri only shrugged again, and Ivanov ordered that they go on listening to the audio. He was sure, he said, that something would turn up.

And a week later, it did.

*

'Here. Come and listen to this,' shouted Mikhail to his colleagues. It was his turn to listen to the recording of the audio from Robinson's car.

'Don't say something's actually happened,' replied Yuri, getting up from his desk and sauntering across the room.

'Wait till you hear this.'

Yuri put on the headphones and Mikhail watched his face change as he listened.

'My God. He's speaking Russian,' exclaimed Yuri. 'Who is the woman?'

'I don't know; he's never talked to her before that I know of. But she's got to be Russian the way she speaks.'

'What about him? Where did he learn to speak Russian like that? He says her father gave him her number and he needs to meet her. He doesn't sound very pleased about it.'

'Neither does she,' said Mikhail who had the headphones back on. 'But they've agreed to meet at three thirty outside Nuffield. Whatever that is.'

'That's Oxford,' said Yuri. 'It's the same place Denisov went to, after he went to Islip.' Then, slowly, as it began to dawn on him, 'That woman must be Denisov's daughter. But why is Robinson meeting her and how come he speaks Russian like a native?' After a pause he leapt to his feet. 'Of course! It's because he *is* a native. He's not a British Special Services officer. He's a Russian! But what the hell's he doing here? And how did he get to be an MP? My God, this is big. We need to tell the boss.'

'I knew it,' exclaimed Ivanov, ignoring the sceptical looks of his team. 'Denisov's up to something.'

'Yes. But what?' asked Yuri, confident his boss didn't have any idea. 'He's clearly not British; he must be Russian. But what's he doing here and how does Denisov know him?'

'I don't know,' admitted Ivanov. 'But we have to find out.'

'Are you going to report it to Moscow?'

'Not yet. Let's get some answers first.'

A COUPLE OF WEEKS LATER, as Peter Robinson collected his mail in the House of Commons, he was surprised to see amongst the bundle a stiff white envelope marked 'Embassy of the Russian Federation'. For a moment his heart beat faster and then he saw that other MPs were holding similar envelopes. When, back in his office, he slit open the envelope, he found it contained nothing more sinister than an invitation to an evening reception at the Russian Embassy and a talk by the ambassador to celebrate Russia Day. He did not immediately put it on the pile of correspondence for his secretary to pick up and answer. He kept it separate while he thought about whether to go or not. Somehow, in a way he couldn't rationalise, he felt it would be a risk to enter the Embassy. But moments later the MP who shared his office came in and, noticing the envelope on the desk, said, 'I see you've got the Russians' invitation too. I always go to that. It's interesting to see what they want to tell us. And the food and drink's excellent – have you ever tasted Russian champagne?'

'No, never. I was just about to accept,' Robinson replied, taking the decision on the spur of the moment. 'I'll look forward to the champagne.' After all, he reflected, the risk of meeting anyone who recognised him was minimal. It would be interesting to be inside the Embassy again after so many years and see if it had changed much from his father's day as ambassador. He didn't recognise the name of the current ambassador, who had only been in London a short time and from newspaper reports was a businessman, not from the foreign service or from the KGB as so many of those in senior positions usually were. It was most unlikely, he reassured himself, that he would come across anyone he had known in Russia; if he did it was even more unlikely they would recognise Peter Robinson MP as Pyotr Romanov.

On the evening of the reception, Robinson and a couple of other MPs to whom he had offered a lift were driven by Harry Bristow to the top of Kensington Palace Gardens, where they got out of the car at the police guard post and, after showing their invitations, walked together to the Embassy. This suited Peter Robinson; to his own surprise, he was feeling nervous and he was glad to be just one of a group as they arrived at the entrance.

They handed in their invitation cards and were ushered into a large ballroom; one end was set out with chairs for the ambassador's speech, while at the other end waiters stood with trays of glasses of drinks. 'Try the champagne,' muttered Robinson's colleague in his ear before grabbing a glass for himself and drifting off, leaving Robinson momentarily alone to gaze up at the chandeliers and remember how enormous this room had seemed when as a little boy he was occasionally allowed inside. But though it seemed smaller now, it was brighter, somehow more elegant than in its Soviet days.

He walked over to a group of guests, where a fellow MP was talking to a senior civil servant from the Department of Trade whom he had had dealings with about a factory in Liverpool.

After a while they were joined by two Russians from the Embassy who introduced themselves as First Secretaries in the ambassador's office and invited them to sit down, explaining that the ambassador would be speaking in a few minutes. They shepherded them towards the chairs; in the general confusion, as everyone else also took their seats, Robinson found himself next to a Russian official on either side of him, a situation that made him feel very uncomfortable.

The ambassador was a middle-aged, slightly florid man who looked as if he enjoyed the good things of diplomatic life. He spoke for twenty minutes, but all Robinson could remember afterwards were a few platitudes about peace and friendship. His mind was simply in too much turmoil to concentrate. He was trying to understand his own reaction to being there in the Russian Embassy. He should have felt safe and secure. This was the London home of the government of the country he was supposed to be working for – his homeland.

But instead he felt he was in hostile territory. Was it because he was afraid someone might recognise him and blow his cover, or was it something else? Why had he resented Denisov when he turned up?

He had achieved the objective Kazikov had set him so long ago. No one would have thought he could do it, and he had done it on his own with no help from anyone. And now, after all these years of working alone, he was at last in a position to provide what Kazikov had wanted – high-grade intelligence from the centre of British political life. He was hoping before too long to be appointed to the Defence Select Committee – that was what he was working towards. But what was it all for now? He had to admit it – he didn't know the people in power back in Russia any more, or what they were trying to do. He didn't even feel any loyalty to them. As he sat there brooding, the ambassador finished his speech and left the platform. With a scraping of chairs the audience stood up and headed to the buffet at the other end of the room.

'Let me get you a drink,' said one of the Russians who had been sitting next to Robinson, as the other Russian steered him towards a small group standing to one side. Before he realised what was happening, he found himself hemmed in by a couple of burly, tough-looking Russians, and facing a short, dark-haired man with flushed cheeks. This man said in accented English, 'Good evening, Mr Robinson. I am Ivanov, Political Counsellor here at the Embassy.' He held out his hand, which Robinson shook warily.

Ivanov then continued in Russian, 'I am the Resident of the Sluzhba Vneshney Razvedki here in London. My colleague Denisov, of the Federalnaya Sluzhba Bezopasnosti, tells me he met you a few weeks ago. I would like to talk to you about your work here.'

Robinson's face was a frozen mask, gradually turning a greyish white as Ivanov spoke. There was a short silence then Robinson replied in English, 'I am afraid I do not speak Russian, Mr Ivanov.'

'Oh. I think you do, Mr Robinson,' Ivanov replied, still speaking in Russian. 'Like a native. In fact I think you are one of our countrymen and you are standing now on what is legally your home soil.'

Deeply agitated, Robinson suddenly threw one arm into the air just as a waiter was passing, and knocked the tray the man was carrying clean out of his hands. In the ensuing confusion of broken glass and spilled champagne, he pushed his way out of the group of Russians and joined some MPs who were talking to several senior police officers. He was right to think the Russians wouldn't want to make a scene and confront him there. He kept his eye on the door of the ballroom, and when he saw a small party gathering to leave, he joined them and walked in the middle of the group to the top of the road where the cars were waiting.

'I T'S NOTHING VERY SPECIAL,' said Tatiana, step-
ping into the room, 'but I hope you'll be comfortable.'

In fact the bedroom was surprisingly spacious, especially for
such a modest house. Jericho, less than a mile from Nuffield
College, consisted of a web of small streets lined by equally
small Victorian houses. Tatiana, who had read up on Oxford
before she joined the university, explained that they had been
built for printworkers at the Oxford University Press. Now
most of the residents were young professionals and it had
become rather trendy. 'I like living here,' she said. 'It's so near
the centre of town and it's got lots of shops and cafés and
pubs close by. There's even a local cinema.'

The house had two bedrooms upstairs; the one on loan to
Manon faced the street, which fortunately seemed relatively
quiet. It looked as though it had been tidied up, presumably by Tatiana; the desk in front of the window was clear
for her to do her supposed coursework. She would need to be
careful not to leave anything suspicious lying around, Manon
thought, noticing that the door had no lock.

'This is perfect but I must contribute to the rent,' she said.
'Tell me what you think is fair.'

Tatiana shook her head. 'I spoke to Lucy and she wouldn't
hear of it. She was just glad to know her room was proving useful; anyway, you're only here one night a week until

term ends. She said once she's back, you can take her out for dinner, and that will do nicely. Speaking of which, why don't you settle in and then come down and have supper? There are only eggs, but I could make an omelette if that suits you.'

'I've got a better idea. Why don't we go out somewhere? My treat. That can be my deposit on the rent.'

Tatiana looked pleased, and Manon realised again how lonely she seemed. They went to a nearby Italian restaurant which was full of young couples and a few students. Over prosecco, they chatted about the seminar – the goateed student had been particularly annoying in that day's class. When their food came, Tatiana stirred her bowl of steaming fettuccine with her fork. 'Mmm. That smell reminds me of Venice.'

Manon laughed. 'I've never been there, or anywhere in Italy for that matter, but they're both on my bucket list.'

'You must go,' said Tatiana. 'It's glorious.'

'Have you travelled much in Europe?'

'Quite a bit. My father's work meant we spent three years in London, and we used to go on holiday to the Continent.'

'Three years. That explains it.'

'Explains what?'

'I've been meaning to ask how you came to speak such excellent English. You're entirely fluent.'

'Thank you,' said Tatiana, who seemed flattered.

'Does your father still travel a lot?' Manon asked casually, keeping her eyes firmly fixed on her plate.

'Frankly, I don't really know. He and my mother no longer live together.' Tatiana was looking wistful. 'It was just one of those things. They say that the children don't always know what is really going on in a marriage. I certainly didn't – when my parents split up, it came as a complete surprise.'

'I am sorry.'

'No need. They're both alive and well, so it could be worse!'

'Has either remarried?'

Tatiana shook her head. 'No. And I doubt they ever will. I think it was one of those relationships where they couldn't live without each other, but they couldn't live together either.'

'You see them both, then?'

Tatiana looked thoughtful. 'For a while, I did not see my father. He's the one who left; not my mother. She is what you'd call old-school – through thick and thin, and rough and smooth, you still stay married. My father is more impulsive, though he would call it "decisive". So I suppose I blamed him, and we did not speak for several years in fact. But it's better now. We had a rapprochement before I came here, and he was in the UK just last month and came to see me.' She looked pleased by this.

'Was he here on business?'

'You could call it that. He works for the government.'

'That can't be easy these days,' said Manon. Go slowly, she told herself.

'It's not. Things could turn out well in Russia, or life could become a nightmare. After glasnost at first everyone hoped for change; now many of them have discovered that change isn't always for the better. They want to go back to the certainty of the old days.'

'You mean under the Communists?'

'Well, yes.' Tatiana put down her fork for a moment. 'You have to understand, to many people, especially the older ones, Communism is all they've ever known. Democracy is many things, but it is never predictable. And predictability is the one thing a Communist regime can provide, even if it's predictably awful.' She smiled and shrugged her shoulders. 'People working for the government – like my father – get very cynical. They seem incapable of hope, probably because their jobs have always been to extinguish hope – especially any hope for change. My father—' she started to say, then seemed to catch herself. She looked up brightly at Manon. 'Anyway, enough about my family. Tell me about yours.'

Two days later Manon sat in Saunders's office, reporting on her most recent visit to Oxford. Wilberforce would have joined them, Saunders explained, but he had been called suddenly back to Langley the day before. She was relieved the Head of Station wasn't there; she felt that what she had to relate was small beer.

She'd already cleared her accommodation arrangement with Saunders, who had congratulated her on managing to get so close to her target in such a short time. Now, as she described her evening with Tatiana at the restaurant, she felt rather embarrassed that she had so little to tell, but he seemed surprised with how far she had got and warned her not to move things along too fast. 'You must try to avoid appearing too friendly or she may get suspicious. Don't forget she sees you as an American diplomat, and her father is a Russian intelligence officer. She may well have been warned to look out for over-friendly Westerners.'

Manon nodded and went on, 'When we got back from the restaurant Tatiana had a call. On her mobile. We were in the sitting room chatting, but she went into the kitchen to take it – I couldn't hear much but I know she was speaking in Russian. When she came back in she seemed elated – but also kind of troubled; I don't know how else to describe it.

I'd picked up a magazine and didn't say anything, but after a bit she said it had been her father on the phone. I asked how he was, or something anodyne like that, and she said fine, but then she added, rather dramatically, that parents could be very demanding. I know she's close to her mother but this seemed to be about her dad.'

'And what did you say?'

'I said I agreed with her – and I made my mother out to be very intrusive. She said her mother was that way too, but nosy rather than demanding. Her father, on the other hand, seemed to think that even after five years' silence he could suddenly come back and count on her for help. I asked what kind of help, and she sort of waved it away – it had to do with his work, she said, but she wasn't more specific than that. I didn't think I should press her.'

Saunders was silent for a moment, considering this. Then he said, 'Good. You've done well. You need to win her trust first, and worry about getting information out of her later. If you don't do it in that order, you'll find you won't get anywhere.'

'HI MANON,' SAID TATIANA at the seminar's coffee break the following week. 'Do you have your key to the house with you?'

'Yes. Do you need it?'

'No. It's just that I'm not coming straight back tonight. I have to meet someone.'

'Oh, don't worry; I'll be fine. In fact, I could get some stuff at the Co-op on the way back and make some supper. Unless you're having dinner out.'

'God no. It shouldn't take more than half an hour.' Tatiana made a moue with her lips. 'I'm doing a favour for my father. It's someone he knows,' she sighed.

After the seminar, Manon briefly waited behind, ignoring the goateed student who was trying to chat her up, until Tatiana had left the room. Then she also left, going out of the main entrance to the college, only to find to her dismay no sign of the Russian. Instead of heading back to the house, she quickly went round the corner, peering up the street that climbed towards the middle of town. She spotted Tatiana halfway up and could see her clearly, looking smart in a short leather skirt and her enviable designer boots, with her brown hair tied up into a ponytail. She was carrying a small canvas bag over one shoulder, and in one hand held a large yellow envelope.

Manon set off rapidly, almost running, worried she would lose her. As she approached Queen Street she saw the entrance to an enormous shopping mall on her right, and her heart sank – she would never find Tatiana in there. But straight ahead of her, through a crowd of pedestrians, she glimpsed a flash of bright yellow, then made out the figure of Tatiana, stopping to window-shop in front of a women's boutique.

Manon hung back until Tatiana moved on, then followed from a distance of thirty yards or so – far enough away to take evasive action in case Tatiana suddenly stopped again. Losing her in the crowd of shoppers, Manon went and stood in the sheltered entrance to Marks and Spencer, watching the street. As she waited there she thought of what Saunders had said last time she reported to him – don't push it too fast; win her confidence before you try and get information. She felt fairly sure he would not approve of what she was doing. She also remembered what she had been told on her very first training course when she joined the agency: 'Surveillance is always carried out by specialised teams. It is almost impossible for one person covertly to follow another without being spotted or losing the target.'

But in spite of her inner voices, when the ponytailed figure suddenly emerged at Carfax, Manon set off in pursuit. She followed as Tatiana started to walk along the High, which stretched for almost a mile downhill to Magdalen Bridge. Crossing the street, Manon dodged a group of Chinese tourists, then waited for a double-decker bus to lumber by. Emerging, she looked ahead, but Tatiana had disappeared.

Manon started to run, feeling panicked, slowing down only to check inside the shops she passed. There was no sign of the Russian in any of them, but then she came to an opening that wasn't the entrance to a shop, but more a narrow alley; turning into it, she found herself in a vast covered market, with long avenues bisected at either end by two shorter aisles. There was still no sign of Tatiana, and Manon felt even more agitated now – she was far more worried about how she would find Tatiana in this colossal collection of little shops than she was about being seen herself.

Fleetingly she wondered if she should give up. Part of her knew she should; she was completely out of her depth and was disobeying her instructions to take it slowly. If Tatiana saw her it could blow the whole operation and Saunders and Wilberforce would feel let down and would never trust her in the field again.

But then she pictured their interest and excitement if she discovered what Tatiana had been asked by her father to do and who she was meeting. The prospect was too intriguing to miss. No, she couldn't give up, she decided, so she set out along one end of the market, staring down each aisle as she crossed it. Still no Tatiana – but then, she might be in any of the bewildering array of tiny retail outfits: cafés and coffee shops, an ice-cream stand, a sweater shop, a shoe shop, a greengrocers, a fishmongers, at least four butchers, a 'cookie' shop that smelled heavenly…

She had reached the far end of the market and was glancing at the French delicacies of the posh cheese shop when a voice behind her said, 'Manon! What are you doing here?'

It was Tatiana, her tone not altogether friendly.

'Oh,' Manon exclaimed. 'You gave me a shock.'

'I thought you were going to the house,' Tatiana said, almost accusingly.

'I was, but then I remembered a friend of mine in London has a birthday next week. I wanted to get her a present.'

Tatiana looked only slightly convinced, so Manon burbled on. 'I was thinking a sweater, perhaps.' She pointed to a stall along one side of the market. 'But I couldn't find anything I think she'd like there. So I thought maybe I'd get her some fancy soaps and leave it at that. I'll try a department store – if there is one round here.'

'Try Boswells. It's what the English would call quaint, but it has some lovely things. It's not far.' And it was while she was giving directions that Manon realised Tatiana was still carrying the yellow envelope. Was she intending to post it? If so, why had she come all this way? There were no post offices in the immediate vicinity, and very near the Jericho house there was a little newsagent's which also functioned as a post office. But then she remembered Tatiana was supposed to be meeting someone; perhaps her envelope was to be given to them. In which case she couldn't have met them yet and Manon hadn't missed the rendezvous.

As if in answer to these questions, when she walked out on to Market Street, following Tatiana's directions for the department store (which was all of two minutes' walk away), Manon saw a man striding ahead of her. He was well dressed in a navy blue suit and polished shoes, and what caught her attention was that he was carrying a yellow envelope like Tatiana's. As she watched him she noticed something about his gait that she had seen before – a fast walker, impatient, confident.

When he reached the corner of Cornmarket, he turned to look at the traffic and for the first time Manon could see his face. It was the new boyfriend of her old friend Louise – the recently elected Member of Parliament, Peter Robinson.

'**Y**OU DID *WHAT*?' WILBERFORCE was not happy.
'I followed her,' repeated Manon, looking scared.
'I know you told me to play it cool and try to win her confidence but Tatiana was acting strangely and I guessed she was doing something she didn't want anyone to know about. She said she was meeting someone for her father, so I thought it would help us if I could find out who it was. I'm sorry if I did the wrong thing but I did discover something important, I think.'

Saunders had joined Manon in Wilberforce's big corner office in the CIA Station deep within the Embassy. Now, seeing how upset Manon looked, he broke in. 'Tell us everything that happened.'

'Well,' Manon said, close to tears, 'I have to tell you right at the outset that she spotted me.' Wilberforce groaned. 'I had an excuse ready – it was in Oxford's covered market so I said I was shopping for a gift for a friend. But I'm not sure she believed it.'

Saunders's face was grim but he spoke gently. 'Is there some good news too?'

'Yes. I recognised the man she must have met.'

'Must have met? Didn't you see them meet?'

'Not exactly, and ordinarily it wouldn't have meant anything. But each of them was carrying an envelope – a yellow,

A4-sized mailing envelope. They were identical, and that seemed odd.'

Wilberforce and Saunders exchanged puzzled frowns; they didn't know what she was talking about.

Manon added, 'But that's not all. The man is someone I know – well, not know really, but someone I've met before. He's an MP named Peter Robinson, and he's the boyfriend of a friend of mine. It seemed more than a coincidence. And his constituency is up north, so what would he be doing in Oxford?'

'Manon,' said Saunders, breaking into the flow of words, 'please go back to the beginning and tell us exactly what happened. We are not angry. Quite the opposite. It sounds as if you have discovered something very important.'

So Manon told them the story of the day, beginning with Tatiana telling her at the seminar that she had to meet someone as a favour to her father. She related how she had followed Tatiana to the covered market, how Tatiana had been carrying a yellow envelope, how she had lost her and then bumped into her. She said that Tatiana seemed suspicious and she was not sure whether her explanation convinced her. Finally she described how she had just caught a glimpse of a man walking away from the market and noticed that he was carrying an identical yellow envelope. 'But Tatiana still had hers,' she said. 'I thought that from behind the man looked like someone I had seen before, and then he got to a crossing and he turned to look at the traffic and I saw his face and I did recognise him. It was the MP Peter Robinson who I'd met before, as I just told you.'

'And you think he had been meeting Tatiana?' asked Wilberforce.

'It was the envelopes,' replied Manon. 'Like I say, they were identical.'

Saunders turned to Wilberforce. 'Could have been a brush contact?'

'Brush?' asked Manon.

'Yes,' said Wilberforce. '"Brush" as in "brushing past". One person wants to pass something to another but they don't want to risk being seen together so both carry an identical container – a briefcase or bag or a large envelope. They arrange to be in a crowded place at a fixed time and they literally brush past each other and make the swap. When you come out of the crowd then to any observer nothing's changed, since what you're carrying looks to be the same thing as before.'

'I get it,' said Manon. 'In this case they chose a rather obvious container and it was just their bad luck that I happened to see Robinson and recognise him. I did wonder why, if she'd been meeting Robinson, they hadn't gone somewhere to talk.'

'Because it wasn't about talk – it was about one giving the other something. Probably a document, given the envelopes.'

Wilberforce leaned back in his chair, tugging absent-mindedly at the knot in his tie. Then he said, 'How sure are you that the guy you saw was this MP? Could you have made a mistake?'

'No. I'm certain it was Peter Robinson.'

Wilberforce looked at Saunders. 'We'll need to tell the Brits about this before we can go any further.' Saunders nodded and Wilberforce continued, 'Well done, Manon. You may have uncovered something really significant. Let's hope Tatiana doesn't take fright after seeing you there.'

They were silent for a minute, then Manon said, 'The thing is, I'm not sure she's entirely signed up for whatever she's being asked to do. She said she doesn't like getting involved in her father's business. He came to see her, then he phoned her, and she complained to me that he wanted her to do a favour for him. I think it must have been meeting Robinson – or should I say "brushing" him? – on her father's behalf.'

Wilberforce was looking thoughtful now. 'That would make sense.'

Manon felt encouraged and went on, 'She seems to trust me. Maybe I can work on her a bit and try to find out.'

Wilberforce shook his head. 'No. I think you should just wait and see what she's willing to tell you. You said yourself she wasn't happy finding you in the market. If you try to pump her, she might get even more suspicious. What do you think, Dave?'

'I agree. Don't push it – and this time it's an order,' Saunders said to Manon, though he added a smile. 'You've done really good work, but I don't want you to get impulsive again and jeopardise things. There's not much we can prove at this point, and we don't want Robinson scared off. Or Tatiana, for that matter. And we also don't want to put you in harm's way.'

Wilberforce nodded in agreement.

'Understood,' said Manon, holding her hands up in mock-surrender. 'I'll wait for her to make the next move.'

Wilberforce smiled. 'I have a feeling you may not have to wait very long.' Then he said more seriously, 'You mentioned that this MP is the boyfriend of someone you know.'

'Yes, my friend Louise. She works at the headquarters of Robinson's party. She's some sort of strategist. Used to be a lawyer. I think she met him in Liverpool when she was helping with his election. She hasn't known him long.'

Again, Saunders and Wilberforce exchanged looks. This time Manon was confident it was not because they were disapproving but interested.

'Do you know her well?' Wilberforce asked.

'Pretty well – we're old friends. I met her when I was here on my Junior Year Abroad in college. I saw her when she visited the States a couple of years ago – she was having a hard time, going through a messy divorce. When I knew I was coming over I let her know, though to be honest I wasn't sure how much we'd see of each other. But we get along really well and I see her quite often.'

'And Robinson? Does she talk about him a lot?'

'Yes, she does, and at first I think she hoped that he was "the one". Now I'm not so sure that she's so sure, if you get what I mean.'

'You said you met him,' said Saunders. 'What did you think?'

'Well, it was only briefly – he showed up for coffee when Louise and I had lunch at a restaurant. I can't say I cottoned to him, but it was only the one time, so I may not be being fair.'

Wilberforce leaned forward. 'Forget "fair", Manon. I want to know what you felt. This isn't court, and it's important to know your impressions of the man.'

Somehow this reproof didn't bother Manon at all; she realised she was learning a lot from these two. She said, 'I don't know how to specify it, but I just found him a little creepy. And arrogant.'

'Creepy?' This from Saunders. 'Was he coming on to you?'

'No, no. He wasn't creepy that way. On the contrary – he seemed a kind of cold fish. But he was very interested in my job – I told him I worked at the Embassy as an analyst in oil and gas. Usually that's enough to steer people off the topic, but he wanted to know a lot of details. And he didn't seem that warm when he spoke with Louise. I had the feeling she was the mandatory girlfriend, if you know what I mean. And a useful one; she knows the party people really well because of her job, and receives the kind of invitations – to Number Ten for example – that a new MP probably doesn't get.'

Saunders spoke again. 'Do you think she feels there's anything dodgy about our friend Mr Robinson?'

'Hard to tell. She's a generous soul and she wouldn't say anything unless she was sure about it.'

'If she did know, would she care?' asked Wilberforce.

'Absolutely. She's nobody's patsy, and she's completely straight. I can't see her ever covering for anybody if she thought they were crooked.'

Wilberforce nodded, satisfied. 'Good. Then, with Louise, I'd like you to get as close as you can. Unlike with Tatiana, I want you to try and winkle out anything she has to say about the MP. Is that OK? I don't want to make things awkward for you.'

'That'll be fine,' said Manon resolutely. 'I'm seeing her tomorrow night, in fact.'

'I was thinking,' interjected Saunders, 'that maybe you could have lunch with her and see if she can get Robinson to come along.'

'Really?'

'Yes. She should understand it – friends do like to introduce each other to their partners. You could even say you'd like to meet him properly.'

'And then?' asked Manon, curious about where this plan was heading.

Wilberforce chuckled. 'Hold on, Dave. I know what you're thinking, but before we get involved with this MP we need to keep our hands clean with the Brits. Russian intelligence officers and their daughters are fair game, but meddling with a Member of Parliament, however dodgy we may think he is, is a hot potato. We don't want a diplomatic storm round our heads. Let's just go cautiously.'

H ARRY HAD HESITATED FOR days, unable to decide whether to accept the invitation to his son's passing-out ceremony at the Hendon Police College. He was torn between pride in his son's achievements and a deep shame at his own betrayal of the standards of the police service that had promoted him, given him a good career and an honourable retirement. His whole life ever since that fateful evening on the dockside at Heysham had been a fraud. It was always in the back of his mind but, increasingly, now that he saw his son and heard from him, it came to the forefront.

What particularly made him squirm was that Charlie had chosen to join the police out of admiration for his father and a desire to follow in his footsteps. That was an agony for him. But he had finally accepted the invitation because he knew that Charlie would be deeply disappointed if he wasn't there.

The day of the ceremony was fine and clear. Robinson had gone by train to his Liverpool constituency, so Harry had the use of the BMW, and the big car glided easily through the Saturday-morning traffic on the A1. The car park at the college was filling up and a crowd of smartly dressed families and friends was making its way to the parade ground when Harry drove in. A stage had been set up faced by rows of seats for the audience. A brass band was playing light music, and the atmosphere was happy and festive.

As he stood, looking around, he heard a voice calling, 'Harry,' and he saw his ex-wife Gina and his daughter waving from a row of seats very near the front. He went over to join them and was relieved to see that his replacement, her second husband, was not with them. His daughter had grown up since he'd last seen her; she was fifteen now and halfway through her GCSEs. She looked lovely in a flowery summer dress and a straw sun hat.

He was rather surprised to find that there were seats reserved for all three of them. 'How did you manage this?' he asked Gina but she just smiled and said, 'Ways and means,' so he didn't pursue it further. When the audience had all found seats, the band stopped playing and everyone stood up as the Metropolitan Police Commissioner, the Mayor and the Home Secretary walked on to the platform, followed by a small group – some in uniform, some not. Then the band struck up a military tune and the graduates marched smartly on to the parade ground, wearing dress uniform and helmets, forming a sea of navy blue and silver, the badges on their helmets gleaming in the sun.

Harry felt a sudden surge of emotion and Gina fished in her handbag for her handkerchief. After a further display of marching, the parade came to a halt and the graduates formed into ranks to be inspected by the Commissioner and the Home Secretary. Then it was time for the special awards. A handful of young men and women marched from their places in the ranks and grouped by the steps leading to the platform. Harry was delighted to see that Charlie was one of them. He looked at Gina. 'You didn't tell me,' he whispered.

'Wait and see,' she replied.

After some opening remarks by the Commissioner the first prizewinner went up to receive his medal. Charlie was the last in line and, when only he was left, the Commissioner announced, 'The Sword of Honour for the outstanding student goes to Charles Bristow.' Harry hardly saw Charlie go up to collect his award; he was overwhelmed by immense pride – a pride that turned to immense shame as he thought of his own career and the deceit at its heart.

Finally, the ceremony was over, and Charlie came to find them in the crowd. Everyone was taking photographs of everyone else; Charlie introduced Harry to several of his mates, all of whom to his embarrassment seemed to know that he had been a senior police officer – even that he had been in Special Branch. Seeing them, fresh with ambition and optimism and integrity, made his spirits sink even further. He had to escape; he made an excuse that he must get back to London, said goodbye to Gina and his daughter (promising the latter that he would be in touch and see her again soon), but he found his exit interrupted by his son.

'Thanks for coming, Dad. It meant a lot to me.'

'It meant everything to me, son. I can't tell you how proud I am of you. Sword of Honour – who'd have thought it when you were a scrawny little boy.' Charlie laughed, and Harry said, earnestly now, 'It's just terrific.'

'I could never have done it without you, Dad. I had the best role model a kid could hope for.'

'I don't know about that. I wasn't there a lot of the time.'

'I do. I followed your career all the way through. Let's meet up soon, OK? I'm not quite sure where I'll be posted, but I'll have a few days off before I start. I'd like to spend some of them with you.'

'That would be great,' Harry said. He went to shake hands, but Charlie enveloped him with both arms and gave him a big hug. Harry had to force himself not to shrug him off. If only the boy knew that he couldn't have had a worse role model than his father – who right now felt the most dishonest man in the world.

It was on the drive back into the centre of London that Harry made his decision. There had been vows before – to come clean about Robinson, whatever the result – but this time he would not be deterred. The issue now was not whether to reveal what he knew about Peter Robinson but how to do it.

As he drove he reviewed the various options. His mind turned to Louise. What exactly did she know? he wondered. Or perhaps it was more what had she sensed? He felt sure it was more than she had let on. After her comment about the Russian books, she hadn't said anything further and he hadn't felt able then to pursue the topic. He could now, and he resolved to do it the next time he saw her alone.

ON THE FOLLOWING MONDAY Louise woke up to the sound of water pouring down the drainpipe outside her bedroom window. She looked out to see the pavement gleaming with rain and a couple of pigeons cowering on the windowsill of the house across the road. Typical summer, she thought – it was beautiful yesterday and now look at it. Thank goodness she didn't have to go into work till half past eleven. She was giving a presentation at a group meeting and she would have time for a leisurely breakfast and to look through her notes. Perhaps the rain would have stopped before she had to go out.

She was dressed and sipping her second cup of coffee in the kitchen when the phone rang.

'Hello.'

'Good morning, Louise. It's Harry here, Harry the driver. I'm sorry to disturb you so early but I need to talk to you. There's something I need to tell you.'

He sounded strange. His voice was shaky, and he seemed to be panting as though he'd been running and was out of breath.

'What's the matter, Harry? Has something happened to Peter?'

'No. He's still in Liverpool. Not coming back till tomorrow. But he's what I want to talk to you about. I've got to tell you something. It's urgent. I should have told you sooner.'

'Well, do you want to come round now?' She was intrigued. 'I don't have to go out until later.'

'Yes. Thank you. I'll be there in half an hour if that's all right.' And he rang off.

Precisely half an hour later the door answerphone rang and on the screen she saw Harry, coat collar turned up, rain dripping off his hair. When she opened her door to let him in she was shocked by his appearance. His eyes were red-rimmed and his face was grey and crumpled-looking.

'Come in, Harry, you poor thing. Put your coat in the bathroom.' And she fussed around him, worried about what on earth he was going to say. She sat him down at the kitchen table and poured him a cup of coffee, then sat down herself and waited.

'It's about Peter Robinson,' he said. 'I should have told someone sooner but I couldn't do it. Now I know I have to. I'm sorry to burden you with it.'

He stopped and put his elbows on the table and his head in his hands.

'Whatever is it, Harry? It can't be that bad. Just tell me what it is and we'll sort it out together.' But her voice sounded uncertain – she was beginning to fear what was coming.

And then he started to tell her his story. He told her about the docks and the *Bogdana* and the bribes, small at first and then the money. How he had turned a blind eye and let Igor disappear into the country without reporting it. He told her how he had kept the money and lied to his wife about where it had come from. Then he told her how he had seen Igor again, years later, coming out of the bank; how he had confronted him at the mayoral banquet and about the photographs and the pressure and finally how he had left the police and become Robinson's driver.

As she listened Louise's face changed. At first she looked interested and concerned, but now her mouth was slightly open, the colour had gone from her cheeks and her eyes were round and unblinking.

When Harry stopped speaking she said, 'I don't understand. He told me he had come here from Canada, that he'd worked his way here. He said his parents were British. So was that all lies?' She was trying to absorb what he had told her and make sense of it. Harry said nothing, waiting for her to take it in.

'It's incredible. I can't believe it. But I *do* believe it, Harry,' she added, hastily. 'It explains so much about him that I've been wondering about. But what do you think he's doing? Why is he here and who's behind him?' Her mind was racing as she took in the implications of what she had learned. 'And *who* is he?' she said finally.

'He's some sort of a spy,' replied Harry. 'Though I don't know what he's doing or who he's working for. But I think he's still doing something. I drove him last month to a small village near Oxford and he met a man in the church. I wasn't supposed to see what was going on. He told me to wait in a neighbouring pub, but I didn't want to talk to anybody, so I hung around the car. That's when I saw a man head into the church after Robinson. They were inside for an hour or so; there were some other men sniffing around too but I don't know who they were.'

There had been a gradual change in Harry as he was telling his story, as though the telling had lifted at least part of the burden off his shoulders. But it had landed firmly on Louise's; she now looked frightened and upset.

'He can't be working for the Bulgarians,' she said. 'Now the Cold War's over they're on our side. They would have told him to come home. I think it's the Russians. Do you remember those Russian books in his flat?'

'Yes. I think you're right. And I've heard him speaking in what I think is Russian to some woman – and it wasn't an overseas call. So she's here in the UK somewhere.'

Now it was Louise who had her head in her hands. 'We've got to do something, Harry. Peter or Igor or whoever he is might be doing the country a lot of damage. We don't know. Now you've told me all this I can't just do nothing.'

'I know. And you're right. I can't keep quiet any longer and I know that I've got to expose him whatever it costs me. But I can't bear to go to the police. I've tried over and over again to do it but I can't. It's just too shaming. That's why I've told you. Now you know the story I have to do something. I've written it all down,' Harry said. 'Every detail I can remember. It's in a notebook in my flat.'

And he went on to tell her exactly where he had hidden the journal, in a locked box under the floorboards beneath a cabinet in the corner of his sitting room. 'I've got a few more things to add to bring it up to date, then I want you to have it for safekeeping while we decide what to do.'

He reached into his jacket pocket and pulled out some keys on a ring. 'I want you to have these. That's the electronic fob that lets you into the building. It's flat number 35; that's the key of the flat door and the little key unlocks the box with the notebook in it. If anything happens to me, go quickly to the flat and get the notebook and give it to someone who can do something about it.'

'Oh Harry,' said Louise, now looking seriously scared. 'Do you think you're in danger?'

'I think I would be if he knew I was planning to tell my story.'

Louise got up to make some more coffee. Standing at the worktop with her back to Harry, she said slowly, 'I have a very good friend. She's American – works at the Embassy here – and I'm pretty sure she's with the CIA. I would like to tell her the story. She'll know how to handle it – what to do. She will be very discreet and sensible and make sure it gets to the right people. Can I do that, Harry?'

Harry didn't pause for a moment's thought. 'Yes,' he said and she could hear the relief in his voice. 'Please will you do that.'

She turned round to look at him and it was as though he'd arrived with a virus which had suddenly disappeared, leaving him all better and feeling well. He was standing up straight and colour had come back into his cheeks. 'Let's have that cup of coffee, then I'll drive you to work,' he said.

'WELL, MANON,' SAID WILBERFORCE, 'when I asked you to keep close to your friend Louise and find out more about this MP Peter Robinson, I certainly didn't expect you to come back so soon with a story like this. Let me just sum up what you've told us, to make sure we have it straight.' He had got up from his desk and was standing by the window that looked out into Grosvenor Square, where a thin drizzle was spoiling the start of the weekend.

It was nine o'clock on Saturday morning. Wilberforce had come straight from Heathrow after an overnight flight from Washington; he had been in meetings at Langley for most of the week. The jacket of his smart blue suit was hanging over the back of a chair along with his tie, and he looked tired and rather crumpled. Saunders, sitting on the small sofa, had been intending to go to his son's football match and was wearing an oversized jumper, light corduroy trousers and trainers.

Manon, on the other hand, had dressed for work and looked cool and composed in a light brown leather skirt and a short tweed jacket. In fact she looked a lot calmer than she felt. She was well aware that she had broken into her bosses' weekend to tell them a story that sounded pretty far-fetched.

Wilberforce went on, 'So we've talked about your friend Louise before. She's the girlfriend of Peter Robinson, the MP you thought you saw in Oxford after he'd swapped envelopes with Tatiana Denisov. I remember when we talked about this we asked you to try to meet Robinson and find out more about him. But now it seems that his driver has told Louise a highly coloured story about Robinson not being British at all but some sort of East European or possibly a Russian.'

'Yes, though "highly coloured" makes it sound as if you think he's making it up. Louise was sure he was telling the truth. He's written the whole thing down in a journal and he's going to give it to her. So we'll be able to check the facts and the dates.'

Wilberforce nodded. 'If this is all true, the most remarkable thing is not how he got into the country. I can imagine a young policeman struggling to get by accepting a bribe and then being too scared to admit it. What I can't understand is how Robinson established himself in Liverpool – you say he has a very successful kitchen business there – and then in local politics. I suppose he must have had financial backing, but how did he adapt himself to the local culture? I wonder if he has lived here before.' He paused, gazing out of the window. 'I'm not meaning to say I don't believe what the driver says but it is a remarkable story to take in at first hearing. Even in our line of business. If it's true and the Russians have managed to get one of theirs this close to the centre of power, it's a stunning coup. This Robinson guy must be quite something.'

'I'm not sure Harry will be able to throw much light on that,' replied Manon. 'He had no contact with the man he thought of as Igor after he walked away from the ship and didn't see him again until he was well established in Liverpool. Louise too – by the time she met him he was already a figure in local politics. But it looks as though he managed it without raising any suspicion.'

'The last thing in most people's mind is that the man planning their kitchen is a Russian spy,' said Saunders from his seat on the sofa. 'What I find surprising is that, from what this driver Harry says, Robinson seems to have survived the break-up of the Soviet Union and all the turmoil in the intelligence services without being recalled or giving himself up. Whoever masterminded this operation and sent him here in the first place is unlikely still to be around. So who took him over, or has he been flying solo? Where do his loyalties lie? Who is he working for now? Are we to suppose it's Denisov – even though he's not been in his post long according to the analysts? Or am I running too far ahead too fast?'

'Those are all good points,' Wilberforce said, 'and once we get this journal that the driver's kept, we can get the analysts to work out the chronology; that will certainly help answer some of the questions we have. But I'm still uneasy about this Harry guy, the driver. You haven't met him, Manon, have you?' Manon shook her head. 'So you can't answer why, knowing what he did about Robinson, he nonetheless went to work for him. You said earlier that he was doing quite well in the police till he left to take the job of driver to a man he knew was a spy. Why on earth would he do that?'

'I can't really answer that. I think he was being threatened with exposure by Robinson, from what Louise said. Also he has two children and a wife, though they are divorced. He might have been afraid of shaming them if the story of the bribe came out.'

'Hmm…' Wilberforce sounded unconvinced. There was silence in the room, then Saunders looked at his watch and stood up.

'We're not going to be able to resolve all the ins and outs of this now. None of us has met this Harry and only Manon knows Louise. We have two irons in the fire here. The first is our cultivation of Tatiana Denisov, who we're hoping could lead us to her father and a possible recruitment approach to him. The second is this MP Robinson, who might turn out to be a very successful Russian illegal – or might turn out to be an unremarkable British MP with a very imaginative driver.'

Manon couldn't stop herself. 'I'm sorry to interrupt but before you decide anything can I just say something? It's been bugging me ever since Louise told me Harry's story. Before I came over here, I went to a lecture in Langley from a former KGB general named Kazikov. I told you about it when you first interviewed me for this job.' She was addressing Saunders, who nodded. 'He was talking about the period before the break-up of the Soviet Union when it became very difficult for them to recruit Western sources. He described a programme he devised for planting illegals in Western countries. He said that most of them were exposed and those that were not returned during the chaos of the nineties. Then, and it was strange because it seemed almost an afterthought, he said there had been one illegal sent to the UK who didn't return. After the session ended I went up to him and asked him to tell me more about this illegal – I was interested because I knew I was coming here. He wouldn't tell me – he said he couldn't remember but I thought he just didn't want to.'

Wilberforce and Saunders glanced at each other, exchanging a slight smile. Manon caught the look, and she flushed.

'You think I'm imagining things. I'm not. I've met this man and he's very watchful. He listens; he asks questions; he doesn't say much and nothing about himself. Louise says she can't get him to talk about his childhood or his parents. Isn't that just how an illegal with a fake life story would behave?'

'OK, OK, Manon,' said Saunders. 'We don't think you're making it up but we just have to go carefully here. For better or worse this guy is an elected Member of Parliament and we have to be very cautious about getting involved with him.'

'General Kazikov,' said Wilberforce thoughtfully, from his place by the window. 'I met him briefly last year – thought he was an impressive old boy. The British agencies heard about that talk you went to, Manon, and asked if he would come do the same here. I've got an invitation from MI5 to the talk at Thames House. After what you just said, I think I'll go to his lecture but also ask if I can have a word with Kazikov afterwards. I'll see if Peter Robinson rings a bell with him.'

Manon smiled. So they were taking her seriously after all. She listened as her two bosses discussed the protocol of investigating an MP and what they should and shouldn't share with their British colleagues at this stage. She didn't really care about that. All she wanted was to make sure they were going to do something about Louise's story, and apparently they were.

27

T HE SEMINAR THAT WEEK was dreary. Annoyingly, it had been rearranged for the morning for unspecified reasons, so Manon had to get up extra early to be in Oxford on time. The speaker, a Canadian postgrad, talked in an almost inaudible whisper, and his topic – the influence of medieval Christianity on modern-day Islamic Iran – seemed pretty obscure at this point in the history of the Middle East. At the eleven o'clock coffee break, Manon found Tatiana standing alone, looking pensive. 'I was planning on coming to stay tonight,' said Manon. 'Is that still OK?'

'Of course,' said Tatiana, breaking into a smile that did not entirely disguise the worry on her face.

'I thought I could cook us supper if you like.'

'That would be lovely. I may be home a bit late – I can't stay for the rest of the seminar.'

Manon resisted the temptation to ask why, and just nodded. No more sleuthing, Saunders had ordered. 'That's no problem. I'll have supper ready when you get home.'

Later she stopped on her way to the house in Jericho to buy some food and a bottle of red wine. It had been a curious few days, she thought as she shopped; over a week since Louise had called her, sounding tense, asking if they could meet at the end of the day for a drink. It had not been particularly convenient for Manon, who had planned to go to a film with a colleague, but the urgency in Louise's voice had led her to cancel her plans and meet her old friend in a wine bar on South Audley Street.

Once they were seated in a dimly lit corner, Louise had taken a deep breath, and then plunged into her story. The details still stuck in Manon's mind: how Louise had met Harry through Peter Robinson, and how they had become friendly; their odd discovery of Russian books in Robinson's flat; the hesitancy to share their mutual suspicions after that until some psychological bubble had burst in the chauffeur and he had come to her, almost distraught, and told her everything he knew.

And what an 'everything' it had turned out to be. Manon remembered the barely suppressed excitement with which she had contacted Wilberforce and Saunders, and her disappointment at first when on meeting them they had been sceptical, showering her with questions, some of which she couldn't answer. But throughout she had retained her belief in what Louise – who was by no means gullible – had relayed, and though Manon didn't know Harry from Adam, she could think of no conceivable reason why he would have made the story up.

Right now, though, she knew her focus had to be on Tatiana. She was nervous about how best to behave with her; she sensed a slight cooling on Tatiana's part since she had run into Manon in the covered market. But Manon was also exhilarated too, just as she was at the end of her meeting with Wilberforce and Saunders, when it became clear they were planning to include her in whatever they decided to do to investigate Robinson further. She knew she was not entirely sure what she was doing – she was an analyst, after all, not a trained field agent or agent runner – but she was excited to be doing it, and it was so much more engaging than her usual desk work.

Tatiana did not return to the house all afternoon, but early that evening, when Manon was in the kitchen preparing some pork fillets with mushrooms and crème fraiche and just thinking about putting the rice on to boil, the front door banged, and a moment later Tatiana came in. She looked stressed and Manon gently said as much. 'Have a glass of wine,' she added, pointing to the bottle of Rhône she'd bought. 'Dinner will be ready in a few minutes.' She emptied a cup of rice into the saucepan full of boiling water and watched it start to bubble.

Tatiana poured herself some wine and sat down at the little kitchen table. She was usually quite talkative but seemed quiet and thoughtful now, even troubled. Manon said, 'You didn't miss much after the coffee break. Whatever you had to do must have been more interesting than our speaker.'

'You think so?' said Tatiana, then shook her head. 'I was doing another "favour" for my father. The second time. I thought when he came to England and visited me here it was because he wanted to see me, his daughter. I told you that I haven't seen him much since he left my mother. I was angry with him and let him know it.'

'I can understand that,' said Manon sympathetically.

'But enough time had passed that I was very pleased when he first made contact with me again. Now I think he just wants to put me to work for him.'

'Oh I'm sure that's not true,' said Manon as brightly as she could. 'I can't remember – is he a businessman?'

Tatiana snorted derisively. 'Hardly. He is employed by the government.' Manon stayed silent until eventually Tatiana sighed and went on, 'He's in intelligence work, if you must know.' She added bitterly, 'My father, the Russian James Bond. Only it's not like that at all. He's at the beck and call of his superiors, just like any civil servant. Better that he had been a businessman; at least then he'd be his own agent –' she smiled at the double meaning of the word '– and at least he might leave me alone.'

'I don't understand,' said Manon, keeping her eyes fixed on the pork cooking on the stove top. 'Why is he involving you in his government work?'

'Because I'm here.'

'In England?' When Tatiana nodded, Manon said with a small laugh, 'I think you're very clever, Tatiana, but if you're writing a thesis how on earth are you supposed to help the Russian government?'

'You'd be surprised,' said Tatiana bitterly, but added nothing more.

Manon decided to leave it alone for the time being. 'Let's eat,' she said, and served the food while Tatiana laid the table.

They ate quickly and mostly in silence, though occasionally they made small talk – Manon was determined not to press things, since she sensed Tatiana might be scared off if she did. After the meal she made some coffee and they were about to adjourn to the sitting room when Tatiana's phone rang.

She answered it, saying 'Hello' in English. As she listened to the caller, her face darkened and she spoke rapidly in Russian. Manon gestured for her to go into the sitting room, then closed the kitchen door and sat down again at the table, not bothering to try and eavesdrop since it wouldn't be of any use – she knew no Russian. Tatiana spoke in an inaudible murmur in any case, though at one point her voice rose sharply – in anger? Manon wasn't sure.

The call lasted only a few minutes, and then Tatiana opened the kitchen door. 'Thanks,' she said, sounding shaky. When Manon looked at her she saw she was close to tears.

Manon brought the two mugs of coffee with her into the sitting room and handed one to Tatiana as the Russian sat down on the sofa. 'Just a little milk, right?'

Tatiana nodded weakly. Manon said, 'I hope you don't mind my saying so, but you seem very upset. I hope you haven't had bad news.'

Tatiana shrugged. 'It was my father again. He wants another "favour".'

'It doesn't sound like it's something you want to do.'

'I don't,' Tatiana said angrily, her cheeks flushing. She hesitated, but only momentarily. 'I receive information from some man from London and post it on to an address in Leipzig. My father gave me a stack of pre-addressed envelopes.'

'Leipzig? Why Leipzig? It's in Germany.'

'I asked my father the same thing. He mumbled something about it being more secure. I had the impression there was another person in the loop who gets it to my father. I don't know why it's got to be me doing this for him. It's not exactly rocket science.'

'So can't you say no?'

'I tried to – believe me, I tried.'

'And?'

'He threatened me. He said that if I didn't help then the Russian government would take steps against me. Can you believe it – my own father?'

Manon's feeling was that she could believe Denisov would do exactly that. The FSB was not known for its gentleness. 'But what can the Russian government do? I mean, you're a student after all, not an employee.'

'To Putin's people, we are all employees – of the state, of their regime. And what they would do first is take away my grant to study here. They know I don't have any money of my own, and my mother doesn't either – my father was not exactly generous in the settlement of the divorce.'

'That's outrageous.'

'I couldn't stay here if I weren't a student; I would have no choice but to go back to Russia.'

'Would that be so terrible?'

'Yes,' Tatiana said without hesitation. 'You have no idea what life is like there now. Especially for anyone with a mark against their name.'

'So you want to stay here if possible?'

Tatiana wiped an eye dry, then looked at Manon. 'Actually, what I would really like is to go to America.' She added wryly, 'Like every good Russian.'

Manon laughed, and Tatiana did as well. But then her face sobered. 'If I lose my grant to study here, my government is certainly not going to underwrite my studies in the home of the arch-enemy instead. I would have to try and find support from an American university – and it's too late to apply for the autumn.'

'Yes, I suppose it is.' Manon paused, trying to look deep in thought. Then she said, 'If you can't study there next year, would you be willing to work instead? Paid work, of course.'

Tatiana's eyes briefly widened. 'I would if it got me to America. But I have no visa, no work papers, and let's be honest – no credentials other than an unfinished Master's thesis.'

'Well, let me think.' Manon allowed the silence to build between them. 'You know I work at the Embassy,' she said tentatively.

'Of course.'

'I could ask my colleagues back in the States if there was anything available over there – at the State Department, perhaps. Or some other agency...'

'That's very kind, but you should know that I really don't type very well.'

'I wasn't thinking of secretarial work. No, something more stimulating than that – analysis, research, that kind of thing.'

'You think I could do that?' Tatiana sounded nonplussed. Manon suddenly realised that, for all her apparent verve, Tatiana was lacking in self-confidence. Her bloody father no doubt, she thought.

'Yes, I do. More important, I think my colleagues will too. You are extremely knowledgeable about international relations, and you'd bring an interesting perspective. Being Russian, that is. And of course it doesn't hurt that your father works for the government. That's almost a credential in itself.' Manon gave a small laugh, and hoped it didn't sound phoney. She added lightly, 'We're always interested in people who know about Russia.'

Tatiana might be unconfident, but she was no fool. She looked at Manon, as if to check the veracity of what she was saying, and Manon gave a quick nod. Tatiana nodded back, though more slowly, and as she considered the full implications of what was being suggested, her eyes widened again. 'I would like very much to talk with these colleagues of yours. Perhaps it is just as well that I agreed to help my father after all.'

'Yes,' said Manon. 'I'd go along with that. Even if it was under duress.'

28

P ETER ROBINSON HAD HAD a good day and was feeling rather pleased with himself as he walked across Lambeth Bridge back to his flat. He had made a short speech in the defence debate during the evening for which he had been congratulated by one of the whips. Afterwards he had enjoyed a few drinks in the Strangers' Bar with some colleagues and the word seemed to be going round that he was well on his way to a step up – perhaps Parliamentary Private Secretary. As he passed the MI5 building at the end of Lambeth Bridge he smiled to himself. The lights were on but no one inside had any idea that their famed seat of democracy, of which they were so proud, had been infiltrated. Not, he had to admit to himself, that he had yet managed to do them much harm. But he was playing the long game and his time would come.

As he went into his block of flats he scooped up the mail from his letter box. There wasn't much; most of the important correspondence went to the House of Commons or to Liverpool, where it was dealt with by his constituency staff. The stuff at the flat was mostly flyers for pizza restaurants or minicab firms. He dumped the small heap on a table as he went in and headed straight into the kitchen to get another drink.

He had been drinking more than usual recently and knew he needed to watch it. It probably accounted for the mood swings he'd been having. Tonight he felt euphoric; everything was going well, he told himself. But always just below the surface lurked the question, what was it all for? He was on the crest of a wave but in his dark moods he was afraid the wave had already broken, deposited him alone on the shore, and gone.

He made himself a sandwich and took it with his drink into the living room, where he turned on the Parliament channel and watched himself speaking in the debate. As he got up to go to bed he noticed the pile of stuff he had collected from the letter box. He flicked through it, preparing to throw it all away. There was just one thing out of the ordinary, a postcard. He examined the picture on the front – an old church. It looked familiar; he read the caption printed in italic script: 'St Nicholas Church, Islip'. His stomach lurched. It was where he had met Denisov. He turned the card over quickly. No stamp; it had been hand-delivered during the day by someone who knew where he lived. Handwritten, it read: 'Thursday. 11.30.'

Denisov must be in Britain again. What did he want? And why this summons for another pointless meeting? Why risk it, and in that church of all places? It was insecure, set up by Kazikov as a place for assignations in a different era when that village must have been off the beaten track. Now everything had changed.

He thought again about the people in the MI5 building he had just passed, whose lights he could see from his living room. What if they had Denisov under surveillance? Would he know? Would those idiots in the Embassy know? Were they all working together, Denisov and the Residency? He sensed they were not.

His euphoric mood of earlier in the evening had died. Now he was angry, anxious; he felt purposeless and directionless. He toyed with the idea of ignoring the card; then he decided he needed to know what was going on – so perhaps he'd better go to the meeting. He poured himself another drink and went to bed, where he tossed and turned all night.

By Thursday morning he had changed his mind several times and he still hadn't decided whether to go to Islip. But he had avoided making appointments that day and while he was drinking his coffee he suddenly picked up the phone and asked Harry to bring the car round at ten, telling the driver he needed to go to Oxford.

They were out of London and well on their way before he told Harry to bypass Oxford and continue to Bicester instead, then head south on the A34 for the village of Islip. It was twenty minutes past eleven when they arrived, and Robinson told Harry to park the car – he would join him later. As before, the church was open but completely deserted. Denisov had not yet shown up. Robinson sat down in a pew in a dark corner of the nave to wait.

After a few minutes the silence was broken by the sound of a car. He heard a door slam and footsteps on the gravel path. The door creaked open and a man walked in. It was not Denisov. Robinson's heart pounded. Was it the police? Had Denisov been arrested? But the man called his name in Russian, and as the light from a window fell on him, Robinson saw it was the idiot who had threatened him that evening at the Embassy – Ivanov.

'What are you doing here?' said Robinson. 'Where's Denisov?'

'Denisov is no longer your controller,' said Ivanov. 'He should never have become involved and he has been reprimanded. Your case falls in my area of responsibility and from now on I will direct you.'

'Like hell you will,' snapped Robinson. 'You don't know anything about me.'

'I know more than you think,' said Ivanov. 'We have been studying you and your activities for some time and we have discussed your case at the Centre. I have brought with me a list of our requirements – for now.' And he produced a document which Robinson took unwillingly; he could see it was typed in Cyrillic.

Ivanov went on, 'You will see we want you to supply character studies of your Parliamentary colleagues, with special attention to their weaknesses. And of course copies of the papers you receive, particularly on defence policy. The arrangements for making contact which Denisov set up using his daughter are insecure and will be changed. You will be informed of the new ones.'

Robinson listened to all this with growing anger. He replied, 'These are moronic requirements for someone in my position. I am not some low-level source, and I am controlled by no one. I refuse to take direction from you. I know my objective, and as I achieve it I will report in my own way.'

Ivanov was shaking his head. 'I think you will find that this cannot be the case, my friend. If you do not do as you are directed you will be recalled; life at home would almost certainly prove less pleasant than your life here.'

At this, Robinson got up from his seat in the pew and walked out of the church, leaving the door ajar behind him.

He strode quickly past the black Range Rover that was parked alongside a low wall outside the church gate. He glanced at the two men sitting inside it; he recognised one of them from the evening at the Embassy. This only increased his fury as he went to find his car and driver.

29

Four days later, Robinson was walking across Green Park on his way to lunch at the RAF Club in Piccadilly. He and Louise had been invited by her friend Manon to celebrate Louise's birthday, not an exciting prospect as far as Robinson was concerned – Manon might work at the Embassy, but she was obviously a junior employee, and he could not conceive of her doing anything there or having access to information that would be of significant value. On the other hand, the fourth member of the party was someone he did want to meet – a senior colleague of Manon's who worked in the Defense Department of the Embassy. He was hoping this man might turn out to be useful.

He had been wondering recently whether it wasn't time to break up with Louise. She'd been acting oddly since her return from a short visit to her parents in Devon. She still stayed at his flat from time to time, but not so often as before, and her casual mentions of moving in, which he pointedly had ignored, had now ceased. Sometimes they talked as easily as ever, but more often conversation was awkward. And she had started asking questions about his family and the years before they had met. She had always been interested in his personal history, but he sensed that her recent questioning was at least in part the result of a new-found suspicion that there was a lot more to his back story than he had told her.

Up to now, he had kept hold of Louise because of the value of her many party-political connections – domestic UK politics remained Robinson's focus and priority. On that front, things were looking distinctly promising for his own prospects. He had met the Chief Whip the previous day, who had not only congratulated him on his early performance as an MP, but had also praised his speech in the defence debate. The whip had encouraged him to continue to focus on defence matters, with the carrot of a seat on the Defence Select Committee held out as a possible reward for his future loyalty. If he managed that, Robinson would have reached the sort of position he and Kazikov had dreamed of at those meetings in that office high up in the Lubyanka so many years ago.

At the thought of Kazikov a wave of sadness swept over him, followed by the angry frustration he'd been feeling since that meeting in the church and the crass approach by Ivanov. That fool of a man had actually claimed to be his controller. The thought of such a low-grade cretin trying to run him would normally have made Robinson laugh, but he was worried to learn that he had been the subject of discussion in Moscow. This made him feel very insecure, despite the solidity of his own progress.

He had also not been impressed by Boris Denisov, whom he vaguely remembered from the training school and who had turned up without warning, also claiming to be his controller. The arrangements for communicating through Denisov's daughter in Oxford too were unprofessional and dangerous. So far Robinson had used the cumbersome system just twice, and then only to keep Denisov off his back. None of the information he gave to Denisov's daughter had been earth-shattering, to put it mildly, for the simple reason that he didn't trust Denisov further than he could throw him. The man had seemed untrustworthy, autocratic and, most of all, incompetent.

It strengthened his growing concern that he was in the hands of imbeciles, fighting over him. He felt insulted – but also anxious about the risk their poor tradecraft posed for him.

At the RAF Club he found Manon standing by the stairs in the entrance hall, accompanied by a round-faced, middle-aged man with a receding hairline and a pleasant smile. As Manon introduced him to Major David Saunders, Louise arrived. He hadn't seen her for a week; he'd been in his constituency and when he had got back, she had been busy with some crisis at work. He thought she looked unusually pale with dark circles under her eyes, as though she hadn't been sleeping. Even her copper-coloured hair looked somehow faded.

Introductions made, they moved into the dining room where a circular table in a corner by the window had been reserved. Saunders had ordered a bottle of champagne and they all drank to Louise's birthday. She thanked them, then announced apologetically that she had to leave at two fifteen as the party leader was going to address a meeting of staff at three o'clock, and she had to be there, birthday or not. She responded to the interested looks she got from them all with a shake of the head. No, Louise said with a laugh, she couldn't tell them what it was about, but it would most likely hit the headlines in due course.

The dining room was rather elegant; nothing like as grand as those in the Pall Mall clubs Robinson had visited, but with the advantage of being more friendly, even intimate. Saunders greeted one or two people as they passed their table but no one stopped to be introduced. After general chat about holidays and the weather and a further fruitless effort on Saunders's part to find out what had caused the crisis at Louise's party HQ, conversation broke into two. Robinson was interested when Saunders mentioned a visit he was making to view a new weapons system at an airbase in Suffolk, and Manon and Louise were talking about a film they were planning to go and see.

After they had finished their main courses and everyone had declined a dessert, Saunders suggested they move upstairs to the drawing room for coffee. He wanted to show Robinson the pictures of aircraft which lined the corridors on the first floor. Louise said she must go as she didn't dare risk being late, and as it was pouring with rain now she might have trouble hailing a taxi. Manon said she would go as well as she had masses to do.

Fifteen minutes later, Robinson and Saunders were installed at the far end of the drawing room with a tray of coffee on a low table in front of them. Robinson was sitting on a sofa facing the window, while Saunders sat opposite him in a chintz-covered armchair. The MP accepted a brandy and was settling in, comfortably enjoying the surroundings and the conversation and hoping to pick up something he could use. He didn't notice the tall man in the blue blazer with military-crested gold buttons until he suddenly appeared beside his shoulder.

Saunders stood up to greet him and introduced him as his colleague, Jeff Wilberforce. The new arrival, who to Robinson's surprise seemed to know who he was, sat down and said, 'Very pleased to meet you, Mr Robinson. I noticed you lunching downstairs and it seemed an ideal opportunity to ask you about something.'

Robinson was taken off guard and his mind began racing to try and catch up with what was going on. 'Yes?' he asked cautiously.

'We've noticed that you are in touch with someone closely involved with the Russian intelligence service. That's very interesting to us as we keep a pretty sharp eye on those guys, as you can imagine. I wonder if you'd tell me a bit about how that transpired?'

A wave of relief swept over Robinson. He knew what this was about. This man must be from one of the intelligence agencies. He thought it a very crude approach but he decided to play it cool. Someone must have seen the kerfuffle at the Russian Embassy and reported it. But no one could possibly have heard what was being said as only the Russians were in earshot.

He replied with a nonchalant smile, though he was now very much on the alert. 'Oh yes. You're talking about that evening at the Russian Embassy. I was there with half a dozen other MPs. It's a regular event, I understand. Some of your chaps were there as well; I expect that's how you got to hear about it. I got myself stuck in a group of Russians – couldn't understand what they were talking about and I swung round too quickly to move away and unfortunately I knocked a tray of drinks out of a waiter's hands. It made a frightful mess. I was embarrassed – got out of there as soon as I could after that.'

The man named Wilberforce waved a hand dismissively. 'That's not what I'm talking about. I was thinking of the Russian woman you know in Oxford.'

'In Oxford?' Robinson repeated, buying time. His mind froze; he was totally unprepared for this. He had only seconds to decide how to play it and he had no idea what they knew.

Wilberforce nodded. 'Yes, Oxford.' There was silence. Robinson frowned as though he was trying to remember, then his face cleared and he said, 'Oh, I remember. That girl. Of course, she's Russian – she's the niece of one of my constituents. He's had an accident and can't travel so he asked me if I would check up on her, make sure she was all right. He knew I had business in Oxford occasionally.'

'That's very interesting,' said Wilberforce. 'She is in fact the daughter of a senior Russian intelligence official. What you have just said makes me wonder about this constituent of yours. I think it's possible you may have got involved in something you don't understand and I'd like to invite you to meet us to talk it through so we can advise you how to deal with it.'

Listening to this with growing alarm, Robinson decided it was time to assert himself. 'I assure you, gentlemen, that I have not got involved in anything,' he said, blustering now, playing the role of the northern MP on his high horse. He was gambling on their not having any proof to use against him. 'I know the Russians still get up to some dirty tricks but a lot of them are perfectly friendly and well intentioned and I am happy to talk to them.'

'That's all very good,' said Wilberforce, 'but I am afraid that when it comes to the daughter of a senior intelligence official, who we know to be involved in her father's business, then it's another matter. We will have to bring this to the attention of our transatlantic colleagues here in MI5, but if you would like to talk to us again, we may be able to help you out of a tight spot.'

'Think about it,' said Saunders. 'If you change your mind,' he added as he pushed a business card across the table, 'please give me a call.'

With that, both men stood up. With a curt 'Good day', Wilberforce walked away, while Saunders stayed behind. Robinson also got to his feet, shaken but also seething at the patronising tone of the two Americans. He felt his legs trembling and stood still for a moment, taking his time to put Saunders's card into his wallet while he took control of himself. Saunders waited until he was ready, then the pair of them walked together in silence down to the door of the club, where with no farewell or handshake Robinson turned left and strode off along Piccadilly, while Saunders stood on the steps and watched him go.

30

T HAT EVENING, ROBINSON – NOW feeling very much Pyotr Romanov – was pacing up and down his living room in front of the big windows that looked over the Thames towards Parliament. For the first time since his arrival in England so many years ago, he felt threatened.

He was proud of what he had achieved; working for years on his own without support, advice or praise, he had manipulated, lied and deceived his way into the centre of the British state. He had so completely adopted the persona and habits of his assumed character – Peter Robinson – that no one suspected he was anything other than the self-made British businessman he appeared to be.

He had brilliantly carried out the task that Kazikov had set him all those years ago in his office in the Lubyanka. But now he had done it, there was no one there who would understand the extent of his success. The great days of the Soviet intelligence services, when men like Kazikov dreamed up magnificent daring operations, were gone. Now in Kazikov's place there were pygmies like Ivanov, with small minds and no imagination, trying to tell him what to do and completely failing to understand the huge possibilities of the position he had achieved. Denisov was no better, using his daughter for communication, a girl with no training who seemed reluctant to do what was required, and who had somehow exposed him to the scrutiny of the CIA.

As if things could only get worse, there seemed to be an internal argument about which of these buffoons was running him. Robinson's own view was that it was neither of them; he would refuse to take direction from either man.

But in taking that decision, his mood changed as he sat down in a chair in front of the panoramic view. Here at the centre of public affairs he was playing in a different league – one in which the challenges were greater, more difficult and more dangerous. The people he met now were less inclined to take him at face value – more inclined to question what they were told. Now for the very first time he found his profound aloneness alarming.

He thought back to Louise's birthday lunch earlier in the day with the Americans. They were obviously CIA. He had suspected Manon ever since Louise had introduced her, but he had been off his guard at the RAF Club when she introduced her colleague Saunders. He had let himself be lulled by the man's friendliness and talk of visiting airbases. He had drunk too much wine at lunch and then accepted a brandy. He was far too relaxed when the tall man moved in with his probing questions about Denisov's daughter. As a result he had made a stupid mistake, saying she was the daughter of a constituent. It would be easy to prove that she wasn't. It was the first time he had directly encountered Western intelligence and still he had managed to make that elementary error.

As he watched a tug chugging up the Thames he felt the room start to shrink. It was as if its walls were moving inwards, giving him a claustrophobic premonition that one day there would be no space to breathe, and that he would be crushed as the sides of the room converged. It was a mad idea, he knew that, but it came out of the real fear he was starting to feel – that outside forces were moving in on him, in a series of pincer-like strikes. And he had only himself to rely on.

Perhaps, he thought, the CIA would take it no further. After all, he was a British MP. But what if they were interested in Tatiana Denisov rather than in him? Louise had mentioned that Manon was attending a course in Oxford – would that have brought her into Tatiana's orbit? How loyal was Tatiana to her father and thus to him? She had seemed surly and unfriendly. Would she betray them both? It was a risk.

But there was someone much closer to him than Tatiana. If they were suspicious, then Louise would be their best source of information about him, and she was already close to Manon. But he could not see how she was any threat; even if she suspected there was something fishy about his background story – and she was always asking questions – she couldn't prove a thing. In any case, when he'd asked about the tall American who turned up after lunch, she didn't seem to know anything about him. It could be that even though she was a friend of Manon, she didn't know Manon's colleagues or anything about her friend's actual work. But he couldn't get out of his head the tall American called Wilberforce. His showing up when he did was no coincidence; that was obvious, and Manon must have steered him towards Robinson. As for Louise, whatever she knew – or thought she knew – he was right not to break up with her, for she could be a way of monitoring what the Americans were up to.

Feeling slightly better after his review of the situation, he went into the kitchen and poured himself a whisky, bringing the bottle back with him to his chair. As he did so a new wave of panicky thoughts suddenly washed over him. There was someone he'd forgotten; someone he took for granted and rarely thought about. Harry Bristow, his driver.

He'd noticed Harry had struck up a friendship with Louise, but he had thought nothing of it. But now he realised that Harry was the real threat; the most dangerous threat of all. It was Harry after all who could trace his arrival back to the *Bogdana*; it was Harry who could get the British security services to dig deep into Robinson's background – deep enough to reveal that his Canadian upbringing was a myth, that Peter Robinson was about as real as Santa Claus.

He remembered the words of an instructor, a wizened veteran of the KGB who as a young man had fought at the Battle of Stalingrad. Romanov had seen him soon after being told he would be sent to Great Britain as an illegal. The man had said that if he ever found he was under suspicion in his new identity, he should proceed cautiously, and only act to protect himself if absolutely necessary. 'Think of yourself as a submarine. Once you fire a torpedo you risk giving away your position.'

Now, assailed on both sides by supposed friends and outright enemies alike, he remembered what else the instructor had said. 'But if you must act, do so swiftly. And choose the one who knows the most about you, and has the most reason to reveal it.'

31

I T WAS RAINING AS Wilberforce got out of the taxi at
the Millbank Studios opposite the Houses of Parliament,
a few hundred yards from the MI5 building. Out of long-
standing habit (he had worked in the field for many years) he
never took a taxi to his precise destination. He looked around
as he paid the driver, but saw nothing untoward so he walked
straight along Millbank to the entrance of Thames House.

There he proceeded through the security checks, depositing
his phone with the guards, and emerged into a waiting room
where he found Stanston, one of the deputy DGs of MI5.

They had last seen each other three days before, after
Wilberforce's urgent request for a meeting with the DG
himself. He was away on business in Australia, but Stanston
was standing in during his absence and had more than enough
clout to act on what Wilberforce had to tell him. They had
met here, high up in the building, where Stanston's corner
office overlooked the streets at the back, away from Millbank
and the river. Stanston looked about fifty, and seemed to
Wilberforce almost classically English – average build and
height, a calm expression on his face, wearing a nice but
nondescript suit, cordial enough but initially reserved.

For all his own easy manner, Wilberforce could be profes-
sionally succinct, and he outlined what they had learned from
Harry Bristow (via Louise Donovan) about Peter Robinson

in a short series of bullet-like points. He mentioned the recent lunch when he and a couple of colleagues had met the MP for themselves and that when he had asked Robinson what his connection was with Tatiana Denisov, he had not denied he knew her but had said she was the daughter of a constituent, which was plainly untrue.

He and Saunders had discussed omitting this last incident from his account, since the British might regard their approaching Robinson without informing them first as a breach of protocol. But eventually the two of them decided it was better to come clean about everything they knew. That way, if it all blew up there could be no recriminations, especially if they were somehow wrong about the MP. They had hesitated even longer over revealing that they had manoeuvred one of their colleagues into close contact with Tatiana Denisov in Oxford and that they believed she was working for her father, the senior FSB officer who had recently been in the country for counter-terrorism talks. But again they decided that the information was vital to an understanding of the story.

Stanston had taken a few notes during Wilberforce's recital, and once it was finished he was silent for a moment or two, glancing down at what he had written. Then he started asking questions – about Harry's credibility, about how much Manon had learned about Tatiana's connection with her father; what was Robinson's connection to Tatiana and was Manon sure about the exchange of envelopes in Oxford? Wilberforce admitted that there was a great deal unknown about the story but he was confident enough that something untoward was going on involving the MP, to feel obliged to tell his British counterparts about the CIA's suspicions.

'And thank you for doing so,' said Stanston. He looked thoughtful. 'It does sound as though we have a serious problem here. But we'll have to tread carefully – he is an MP after all.'

'I understand. It would be the same if we learned this about a senator or Congressman. Louise Donovan is going to get the journal that Harry Bristow, the driver, has promised to give her; apparently he's done his best to document his relationship with Robinson from the beginning. As soon as we see it, I'll let you know – and bring it over here for you to inspect.'

'Yes, please.' Stanston looked out of the window, and Wilberforce knew he must be shocked by what he'd just heard and reviewing who he needed to inform. Turning his gaze on Wilberforce, he said, 'In the meantime, I think we will put Mr Robinson under surveillance.'

'Good idea,' said Wilberforce. Both men knew that a warning had been given and understood. From now on any involvement the Americans had with the MP would become known to the British.

'Also, we'll start to dig into his past, and see if any of his back story – you said he claimed to come from Canada – holds up. Though after what you've told me, I don't think it will. As he must have a British passport we should be able to trace when and where it was first issued.'

'It's been years – will the records go back that far?'

'They're meant to be kept for eighty years, so in theory they do,' said Stanston. 'Fingers crossed for Mr Robinson's passport history.'

Now, three days later, Wilberforce again shook hands with Stanston in the waiting room and followed him through into a large atrium with a high glass roof. Rows of folding chairs had been set up for the occasion. 'I've had two seats saved for us. A good thing too,' Stanston added, since most of the seats were occupied and more people were coming in.

They sat down at the back, Wilberforce on the aisle, which he was grateful for since he was long-legged. Stanston said, 'I've spoken to Kazikov and explained we'd like a chat after his talk. We've got a meeting room reserved, and I told him you'd be present. I imagine he thinks it's just a courtesy call,' he added wryly.

After a few minutes, two men walked on to the small stage at the front, where a couple of armchairs, a table and a microphone and lectern had been placed. The younger man stepped up to the microphone while his much older companion sat down slightly slumped in one of the chairs.

The murmur of conversation gradually stilled. Stanston whispered, 'That's Hugo Wilson, our Director of Counter Espionage.'

Wilberforce nodded; he knew Wilson quite well already. Wilson introduced the former KGB general as the leader of Soviet espionage against the West during the dying days of the Cold War. 'Now resident in America,' he went on, 'General Kazikov is a valued speaker, author and authority on all aspects of Soviet intelligence. There will be an opportunity to ask questions after the talk and I encourage you to take this rare chance to learn from a man who worked through the Cold War and its ending and knows many of those in power in Russia today.'

When Wilson finished there was a brief, expectant round of applause, and then the Russian stood up and walked slowly to the microphone. He was wearing a brown tweed jacket with a bright blue tie and a white shirt. Wilberforce thought he looked like an ageing professor of philosophy who had once done military service.

Kazikov spoke for about forty minutes, which left plenty of time for questions, of which there were many – both about the KGB and its new manifestation and about Russian politics. Much of what he said was a repeat of his talk in Washington, which Wilberforce had listened to the day before in his office – the talk had been video-recorded and circulated to all stations abroad. But he noticed that, whether by design or chance, Kazikov did not discuss the illegals programme, as he had done in Washington.

At the end of an hour Hugo Wilson brought the proceedings to a close, even though there were still plenty of eager hands waving with questions to be asked. Kazikov looked relieved and slumped down in his chair again while a woman in the audience gave a vote of thanks.

The atrium emptied quickly, and Stanston said, 'If you come with me, we can have our talk with Kazikov.' The Russian was speaking behind the podium with a couple of young-looking MI5 staff while Wilson stood by patiently. Stanston and Wilberforce passed them and went into a small meeting room. It held four comfortable chairs and a table on which glasses and drinks were set out.

'Have a seat,' said Stanston, pointing to a chair. 'They should be with us in a minute.' Sitting down himself, he asked, 'Had you heard it all before?'

'Pretty much,' Wilberforce acknowledged. 'Though, interestingly, this time he didn't mention operations in the UK. Or any country other than mine, for that matter.'

'I noticed that too. I hope that doesn't mean he'll go mute with us as well.' Stanston looked up and quickly stood as Kazikov and Wilson came into the room. 'Ah, General Kazikov. Thank you so much. The audience was enthralled. They could have gone on asking questions all evening. May I introduce my colleague from the CIA London Station, Jeffry Wilberforce.'

They all shook hands.

Wilson was hovering by the table. He said, 'General Kazikov, can I get you a drink? A glass of wine, a Scotch or there's vodka if you prefer.'

Kazikov smiled. 'A Scotch with a little water would be most welcome.'

Soon Wilson had supplied them all with drinks and he sat down in the fourth chair. Kazikov took a long pull on the hefty glass of Scotch he'd been handed. 'Ah,' he said, 'that's most invigorating. However often I give a talk, I still find it exhausting. Especially in front of such a well-informed audience.'

Stanston said, 'They enjoyed your talk very much, as you could tell by the questions.'

'I thought it was excellent,' said Wilberforce. 'Very well pitched.'

'That is very kind of you. It was good of so many to come to hear me.' Kazikov looked at Wilberforce. 'I spoke on a similar topic at Langley. Did you know that?'

'Yes. I did. It was also very well received.' Wilberforce wondered how long these banal pleasantries had to go on, but told himself to be patient. He must let the Brits move things along at their own speed.

'I am afraid much of this repeats what I said there.'

'Different audience,' said Wilberforce. 'Doesn't matter at all.'

'And very useful for our intelligence community here to get your views,' added Stanston.

Wilberforce could stand it no longer and, putting down his glass, said, 'I am very glad I came this evening. You see, there are a couple of things I'd like to ask you about – you touched on them in your talk at Langley but not today.'

'Oh?' Kazikov suddenly sat up, as if realising this meeting was not just a post-talk piece of etiquette. He looked enquiringly at Wilberforce. 'Did I leave something important out? It's difficult to say precisely the same thing when you speak without notes.'

'Illegals. When you spoke at Langley you mentioned that during the eighties you began to realise that recruitment of foreign sources was proving much more difficult with the increasing chaos in the Soviet Union. So you created an illegals programme mainly targeted at the United States, but I seem to remember that you also said a few were sent to Europe.'

'Yes,' said Kazikov nonchalantly, 'the United States was almost the exclusive focus of our attention.' He took another sip of his whisky, and continued, 'Which is why I didn't mention it today. One cannot cover everything in forty minutes.'

'I understand,' said Stanston smoothly, taking over the questioning, 'but you'll appreciate that our focus is on what may have happened in the UK.'

There was silence for a moment. Kazikov took another sip from his glass. 'Were you thinking of anything in particular? The details are rather hazy now and I had a team of people working on the illegals programme so I wasn't aware of everything that was done.'

Stanston said, 'We have reason to think an illegal was sent to the UK. A long time ago, in the hope he could infiltrate British society, establish himself, possibly even attain a position of influence and power.'

There was another silence. Kazikov said at last, 'What sort of power?'

'Political, mainly. Something that would allow him access to information, which could be political – or better still, military or even intelligence. Information of huge value to an enemy.'

Kazikov was looking thoughtful. 'When do you think this person came to your country?'

'In 1988. We assume it must have been planned and authorised by your Directorate.'

A faint hint of pinkness was surfacing in Kazikov's cheeks. 'You mean during my time as its head?'

'Yes.' The word hung in the air.

Stanston gave a gentle cough, then said, 'We think this operation was not widely known – or it would have come out before now, along with all the other information we've had from disaffected former Russian intelligence officers. They've been very forthcoming,' he added pointedly.

'So you think I knew about this operation?'

'Yes. We think it very probable,' Stanston replied.

Kazikov leaned back in his chair, he closed his eyes and his face suddenly looked very old. 'So,' he said, 'you have found a man and you think he was sent by us. Has this man achieved a position of power, as you put it?'

'Yes,' said Stanston. 'If you sent this man you can be proud of him. He has done what you asked him to do.'

'But I do not think he can have helped his country,' said Kazikov. 'His country fell apart and if he is still here he must have worked alone.'

The Russian sat very still. Then he said, 'Very few people knew about him. I selected him and we worked together on his cover story. When I left the service I sealed his file because I did not trust the incomers.'

No one interrupted as the old man reminisced. 'Pyotr Romanov,' he went on. 'He was the most brilliant student for years. He was the son of a former ambassador in London, a friend of mine, and he spoke beautiful English. You say he has achieved a position of power. What position?'

'He is a Member of Parliament,' said Stanston.

Kazikov smiled. 'He has done well. But now that you have found him, what will you do?'

'That will to some extent depend on him,' replied Stanston. 'Whether or not he helps us.'

Kazikov sighed. 'When you talk to him give him a message from me. Tell him I said he has done more than I could have hoped for. Say that our country is now not worthy of him and he should help you. Then I hope that one of your countries will welcome him as the United States has welcomed me.'

The old man pulled out a handkerchief and wiped his eyes while Hugo Wilson reached for the now empty glass and poured him another drink.

Fifteen minutes later Hugo Wilson returned from taking General Kazikov out to his car and the three men sat down to finish the bottle of wine.

'Well,' said Stanston, 'what do we make of that?'

'He's an old pro,' said Wilberforce. 'He's hamming it up and telling us just a part of the story to protect his protégé.'

'I don't agree,' said Wilson. 'I thought his story rang true. He left Russia while things at the KGB were chaotic. I can believe he didn't hand the case on to anyone else. He probably didn't trust any of the new guard and thought it best to let his golden boy look after himself – which he seems to have done very well.'

'Whatever the truth of that,' said Stanston, 'it doesn't help us with what's going on now. Even if it's true – what the old boy said about sealing up the file and cutting Robinson/ Romanov free – it looks as though someone has found the file and reopened the case. Presumably Denisov or one of his people. What I'm wondering is why Denisov's daughter has got involved. Why isn't the Residency here running him – Ivanov and his mob?'

'We can only speculate about that,' said Wilberforce. 'But one thing we have learned tonight is that the story we got from the driver is pretty much true. Maybe when we get hold of his journal it will give us a bit of a clue about what's happening. Apparently he's kept it up to date.'

'Right.' Stanston was winding up now. 'What do you think, Hugo?'

'Surveillance has already started on Robinson and we'll step up observations on the Residency to try to capture any contacts with him. We'll leave Denisov's daughter in the capable hands of your colleague for the time being. But please keep us closely informed.'

Wilberforce went down the steps of Thames House and along Millbank. The rain had stopped and it was a pleasant, mild summer evening; he decided to walk home. As he set off he began to go over what had happened. He was pleased with himself and his team. They had uncovered something really big, which the Brits had no idea was going on under their noses. The only downside was that now the Brits were in the driving seat – but he consoled himself he still had a horse in this race.

LOUISE HAD PROMISED MANON she would be in touch just as soon as Harry handed over his journal. But it had been more than two weeks since Harry had visited her in her flat, and there was still no sign of it – or of him. She had thought of ringing his mobile, but there had been her birthday and that odd lunch Manon had arranged so her colleagues could meet Peter. She had seen Harry once, when he had driven her and Peter Robinson to a drinks party in Chelsea, but with Robinson present there had been no chance to talk to him, though she had noticed he looked very strained. That was also the only time she had seen Robinson since the lunch. He seemed to have been very busy and preoccupied, which was a relief as it meant she hadn't had to make excuses not to see him. After hearing Harry's story she would find it very difficult to behave normally.

She wasn't anxious about Harry, she told herself, just impatient to see the journal he'd promised to give her. But her vague concern crystallised when Peter Robinson arranged for the car to collect her one evening so they could go to a charity concert together. When she came out of her flat, the driver waiting for her wasn't Harry, but a man with a chauffeur's cap and oversized ears who said he was the replacement driver for the MP. It was clear he didn't know anything about Harry, and when they collected Robinson from the House of Commons and she asked what had happened, he replied that Harry had requested a few weeks off from work – he was needed up north by his family for some reason. Then he changed the subject.

This seemed odd to Louise. Harry had told her about his son, but she thought he was still in London. And Harry had never talked about his ex-wife; there was no sign that they were often in touch. The following day she tried several times to reach him on the mobile number he had given her, but it just rang and rang and rang. No answer and no way of leaving a message. That seemed odder still – or rum, as her father used to say.

She rang Manon and explained that she hadn't heard from Harry, and that he didn't seem to be working any longer for Robinson.

'I don't like the sound of that,' her friend said. 'Do you think he's done a runner or something?'

'I don't think so. And Peter's explanation just doesn't ring true. I think I'll go round to his flat. He may be ill or something. I've got a set of keys, so if needs be I can let myself in.'

'Do you want me to go with you?'

'No. I'll be OK on my own.'

'You sure?' Manon sounded concerned.

'I don't know if he's even there. But I want to check – and also find out if the journal has gone AWOL as well.'

'All right. Please keep me posted, and don't hesitate if you change your mind and want company.'

So after work the next day, Louise hailed a cab and gave the driver the Marsham Street address where Harry lived. It was not a pretty part of London, more functional, and popular mainly with MPs – it was within walking distance of Parliament – and people who worked in the many government offices nearby.

Louise got out of the taxi and stared at Harry's building. It was one of the older, less attractive blocks – red-brick, flat-fronted, with rows of small sash windows. It looked as though it had not had much refurbishment since the end of the war. She took the key ring that Harry had given her out of her bag and pressed the fob against the electronic entry device, until the double doors opened and she walked through into a vestibule, which had a little side room that years ago must have been occupied by a porter. She started up the mahogany staircase and climbed three flights, then walked down a dark brown corridor until she came to the door of number 35 – Harry's flat.

Ringing the buzzer, she waited, an ear cocked for noises from inside. There were none, and no one answered the door. She told herself to be patient – maybe Harry was sleeping – and she rang the buzzer again, but there was no response.

She was still holding the key ring so she turned the top lock, and was surprised when the door swung open straightaway – the second deadlock at the bottom had not been set. If Harry had gone away wouldn't he have double-locked his door?

Pushing the door wider open, she ventured inside cautiously, loudly calling out 'Hello'. But again nothing stirred.

The front door opened directly on to the sitting room, which had a view through its windows of the dark brick side of the adjacent mansion block. This was a bachelor's flat, and a rather grim one, dimly lit, with none of the warmth a couple would bring to it, or a single woman. There was exactly one picture on the sitting-room wall – a map of the West Country – which Louise guessed had been there before Harry moved in. The furniture was equally basic: a sofa, two chairs, one rug, a large television set in the corner. The carpet had not been vacuumed recently, and there was a curious sour smell in the room – but not from dust. Instead it reminded her of bacon – uncooked bacon that might have gone off slightly. The smell was mildly nauseating, and as she crossed the room it grew stronger; Louise only just managed to prevent herself from retching. There was a distant buzzing noise as though a fan was running, but it was so faint she couldn't be sure where it was coming from – it might have been from outside.

In the corner of the room sat a squat two-drawer filing cabinet. Under it must be the loose floorboard which concealed the box holding Harry's journal and notes. She considered retrieving it, then decided she should first make sure no one was in the flat.

The mere thought of that made her scared. She was starting to wish she had accepted Manon's offer to come with her. Steeling herself, she walked slowly down a short corridor past a small kitchen. She glanced in and saw that it was tidy with no unwashed dishes lying about. It didn't seem to be the source of the smell. The corridor ended with two doors side by side. The smell had grown more intense; so had the buzzing.

She chose the left door first, and rapped on it. No answer; she slowly turned the doorknob, unsure what to expect.

It was the bathroom. A white enamel bath that looked as old as the flat doubled as a shower; the curtain was pulled to one side. There was a towel strewn on the floor, but she ignored the instinct to pick it up and backed out of the room.

One room to go. She was holding a hand over her nose, so bad was the smell, and the buzzing now was louder, though erratic. She was tempted to go back to the sitting room, retrieve the journal, and get out, but she knew she had to be sure that Harry had gone. This time she didn't knock, but took a deep breath and flung open the door.

Immediately a swirl of tiny black things rushed towards her, twisting and circling all over her eyes and face and head. Lifting both hands she swatted at them and only then realised it was an enormous pulsing cloud of flies. She took a quick step forward, swatting all the while with her hands, and saw that the entire room was fly-ridden – there must have been thousands of them. The window was open, its cheap curtains not quite meeting and flapping gently in the draught. That was how the flies had got in. But what for?

The stench was almost overwhelming – of putrid, rotting flesh. She took a step towards the bed, which was neatly made, a contrast to the hovering black cloud that seemed to form a grotesque column beside it. And then she saw why the cloud was there.

A decorative mock-Tudor beam, once so fashionable in pre-war buildings, ran across the middle of the room, with a small gap between it and the ceiling. A rope had been looped through this gap, and made into a noose which dropped down. It encircled a mannequin-like figure dressed all in black. No, not dressed in black; instead, almost every inch of the figure was covered in flies.

As she looked she gradually realised it was not a mannequin, but a man, hanging by the neck, his feet dangling a few inches above the floor. He was dressed for work – a white shirt that was just visible through the nests of flies, black lace-up shoes smartly polished, dark trousers neatly pressed.

She forced herself to look at the man's face – the bulging eyes, the swollen cheeks, the extended tip of the tongue on which yellow maggots were crawling.

'Oh Harry,' she cried out as the flies continued to swarm over the corpse and buzz round her head. Why had he done this to himself? She – and Manon and the other Americans at the Embassy and probably the UK authorities too – would have never punished him for what he'd done so many years before. Not when he was helping them get to the truth about Peter Robinson. Had the guilt he said he'd lived with for years proved too much at last?

Suddenly her stomach started to churn. She had to get out. She turned, slammed the bedroom door and ran down the corridor. Her impulse was to run out of the flat altogether – she wanted to be anywhere else in the world other than this squalid den of death. But then she remembered what Harry had said: 'If anything happens to me, get the notebook.' She couldn't do anything for poor Harry now except carry out that request. So, forcing herself not to think about the thing in the bedroom, she set about the task.

The filing cabinet was heavy, and it took all her strength to budge it, but, once moving, it slid along the old-fashioned parquet. She got down on her knees and pressed on the floor-boards one by one, until the thinnest board suddenly flipped up, almost vertically, and she lifted it out and put it aside. Reaching down into the hollow space underneath the floor, she felt round until her hand connected with something smooth and metallic. She drew it out carefully – it was a flat steel box just as Harry had described.

She used the little key on the ring Harry had given her and opened the box. Inside there was a thick A5-sized notebook with a black shiny cover and some loose sheets of paper. Even though every instinct was telling her to grab the stuff and go, she needed to make sure she had found the right notebook.

So she opened it and flicked through the pages. She saw at once that Harry had written a lot. The last few pages were about recent events, with dates and times marked down in a neat precise hand, but the rest was a narrative that began with how he had first met Robinson, followed by a section headed 'Liverpool' and another headed 'London'. The loose papers seemed to be notes – observations that perhaps he had intended to write up more fully later on.

That was enough for her – she had the right book and now she needed to get things back as they were. So she knelt down again and, grabbing the empty box, relocked it and reached into the hole under the floor to put it back.

Then she felt a light touch on the nape of her neck. She froze, paralysed with fear. Had someone come in without her hearing and been watching her? Who was it? What did he want? Was he going to hurt her? Would anyone hear her if she screamed? The touch turned into a tickle and moved along her neck. She heard a low buzz. One of the flies had followed her from the bedroom, and was now turning its morbid attention to her.

Swiping wildly behind her head, she got up quickly, replaced the board and finally managed to push the filing cabinet back in place. Then, grabbing the notebook and papers and shoving the key ring into her bag, she ran out of the flat, along the dark corridor, down the stairs and into the street where she hailed a passing taxi and headed home.

33

M ANON HAD JUST GOT back to her flat when her phone rang.

It was Louise. She was gasping as she spoke, as if she had been running. 'Manon. Something awful's happened.'

'What's wrong? Where are you? Are you OK?'

'I'm at home. I'm OK. But Manon, I went to Harry's ... ' and she stifled a sob.

'What's the matter? Was he there?'

'Oh Manon, it was awful. In the bedroom ... flies ... there were flies everywhere and a terrible smell. Harry was hanging there. He's dead. Been dead for days, I think.'

'Oh God, that's dreadful. What a shock. Tell me exactly what happened.'

'I went round there, like I told you I was going to.' Louise was speaking in staccato sentences, gasping for breath. 'I let myself into the building – with the fob thing he'd given me – and went up to his flat and rang the bell several times. There was no answer so I let myself in. It's not very nice – sort of dark and gloomy. There was a funny smell, but I thought it might be coming from outside. I looked in all the rooms then I opened the bedroom door ... oh ... it was ghastly,' and she started to cry. Manon waited. Then, as Louise sobbed, Manon said, 'I'm so sorry.'

'It was the last thing I expected to find. He didn't seem depressed at all. He just seemed determined.'

'Louise, listen. Stay right where you are. I'm coming over. Pour yourself a drink. Sit down. Wrap yourself up in something warm. Then you can tell me everything that happened. OK?'

Louise sniffed. 'OK. Thank you. But Manon, I'm worried. I haven't rung the police yet, but I'm sure I ought to – so they can go and get poor Harry. It's horrid to think of him still hanging there. Oh Manon, it was frightful. He was all covered with flies.' She started sobbing again.

'Don't ring the police,' said Manon. 'Don't talk to anyone. Not yet. I'm going to call my boss. I think we may need some advice. Don't do anything till I get there.' Manon's mind was racing. There was something else she must know before she rang Saunders.

'One thing,' she said, trying not to sound overly tense. 'I don't suppose the journal was lying around anywhere?'

'Oh yes. I got it. It was in the place he said. Under the floorboards. I was really scared looking for it. I kept thinking someone was going to come in. But I knew he would have wanted me to take it. So I did.'

'Louise. You are a hero,' said Manon. 'Sit tight till I get to you.'

Manon rang off and sat down suddenly. She felt shaky now. Pull yourself together, she said to herself. After all, she hadn't even met Harry.

But questions were swirling round in her head. Why would Harry kill himself? It seemed utterly bizarre – and unexpected, coming just when he had decided to tell his story and help to nail Peter Robinson. Why would he do it just when he had promised to hand over his journal, full of detail about Robinson's true identity? What had happened seemed, at least on the surface, inexplicable. But she realised she was now in the business of finding answers.

She picked up the phone and rang Saunders.

Saunders was at home, watching TV with his children. He listened to Manon's story with hardly any questions except to ask, 'Did she get the journal?'

'Yes. I'm going over to her place now,' concluded Manon. 'She's very shaken up.'

'Not surprised,' he said. 'Anyone would be. Stay there till I ring you. I'm going to talk to Wilberforce. I think he'll want to tell the Brits straightaway. Don't let her talk to anyone and I'll get back to you soon.'

It was after ten o'clock when Manon and Louise, sitting in a black car with smoked-glass windows, drew up outside a terraced house in a quiet street near the Tate Gallery in Pimlico. The man sitting beside the driver leapt out and rang the doorbell, then returned to lead the two women to the house's front door.

There a young man in a bomber jacket greeted them with a smile. 'Good evening, ladies,' he said cheerfully. 'The gents are ready for you; please follow me.' He ushered them along a short corridor and opened a door.

The first impression was of a crowded space, but in fact there were just four men standing round the fireplace. Two of them were very tall, and as the room was quite small, with fairly low ceilings, they seemed to fill it up. The two women hesitated in the doorway.

One of the men stepped forward and held out his hand. 'I'm James Stanston,' he said. 'From MI5. We're most grateful to you for coming out so late.' He turned to Louise.

'Especially as I understand you have had a very distressing evening.' Louise smiled weakly.

The other men then introduced themselves, Wilberforce and Saunders from the American Embassy and – the other tall man – Hugo Wilson from MI5.

A tray of coffee and bottles of water was brought in by the young man in the bomber jacket, and everyone sat down, the women on a sofa and the men facing them in a semicircle mix of armchairs and dining-room chairs brought in from the adjacent room.

While Louise went over her story of finding the body, Manon thought how far everything had progressed since her friend first rang her earlier in the evening. It hadn't taken more than a few minutes' examination of Harry's notebook for Manon to realise it was a time bomb that desperately needed a controlled detonation. She was glad now that everyone seemed to be taking the situation seriously.

While she and Louise had waited for Saunders to ring back, Louise had tried to rest and Manon had read Harry's journal. There was a first-person account of how he had first met the 'sailor' who came ashore from the *Bogdana*, with lots of detail, including description of the gifts Harry had received – and the large cash bribe. He went on to recount how purely by chance he had run into Robinson several years later in Liverpool – and gave the specifics of their encounters, including the mayoral dinner at St George's Hall in Liverpool that both had attended, as well as the exact wording of the letter Robinson had sent him, demanding a meeting. Then followed a description of the Robinson 'offer' of a job as his chauffeur, and a heartfelt account of how Harry had struggled with his conscience before accepting.

The recent history of Harry's work in London took the form of diary entries rather than a narrative, including the day when Harry and Louise had discovered the Russian books in one of the boxes he had brought down from Liverpool, and the date and time (4.21 p.m. on 24th May) when Harry first heard Robinson speak Russian on his mobile phone. And most important, since it suggested actual contact with his controllers, a note about the day (26th May) he drove Robinson to Islip and saw him meeting a man in the church there.

She had read fast, flicking through the pages, and had not had a chance to look at the loose papers when Wilberforce had rung. He said he had spoken to the British and they were taking the incident very seriously, and could she please come to a meeting right away? He didn't apologise for the hour, but he didn't need to. When Manon asked if she should bring Louise with her, again he didn't hesitate. 'Absolutely. I want Stanston to hear it from the horse's mouth, so there won't be any doubt – both about this poor chauffeur and about the notebook. They may well want to question her about Robinson and her relationship with him. Do you think she's up to that?'

'I think so. She's been having a bit of a rest.'

Now Louise was coming to the end of her recital of the evening's events. It was a calmer version of the story Manon had already heard. When Louise had finished, Stanston, who was leading the questioning, asked, 'Have you brought the notebook with you?'

'I have,' interjected Manon, and pointed to her bag. Louise had seemed relieved to let Manon take charge of it. Manon fished inside the bag and brought out the black notebook and the loose papers. She handed them to Stanston, who passed them across to Wilson saying, 'Hugo. Could you ask Rob to copy these?' Wilson went out with the documents and returned without them; soon there was the soft whir of a photocopier at work.

Stanston said to Louise, 'Thank you so much, Ms Donovan. You could not have been clearer. And I think you've been very brave.'

Louise seemed relieved by the compliment.

Stanston went on, 'I won't ask you to do this now, as you must be extremely tired, but we would like to talk to you about Peter Robinson. You must know him very well and we would like to hear everything you can tell us about him. As you now know, it seems he isn't the person he claims to be, and I wonder whether you had any suspicion of that before Harry Bristow told you his story.'

Louise started to speak but Stanston waved a hand. 'No, don't tell me now. It's far too late to ask you to do any more. But would you come in tomorrow and talk to Hugo?'

Hugo Wilson smiled at her and said, 'I'll ring you in the morning and we can fix a time.'

Turning back to Louise, Stanston said, 'I think you should avoid Robinson as much as you can. I would advise you not to be alone with him and don't talk to anyone about today's events. Can you take a few days off work and say you are ill?'

'Yes, I think so,' replied Louise. She hesitated. 'Can I just ask you one thing?' and she looked round the room. 'Do you think someone killed Harry?'

'Well,' replied Stanston slowly. 'We won't know how he died till the autopsy.'

'But it's possible?' There was a silence.

'Yes. I suppose it is possible,' Stanston said at last. 'But it looks more likely at present that he killed himself.'

'Why would he do that now? Just when he had decided to talk about Peter?'

'Who can ever know why people decide to kill themselves?' said Saunders. But Louise wasn't listening.

'Do you think Peter killed him?' No one spoke. She had just asked the question everyone was asking themself.

'I think,' said Stanston, 'Peter Robinson is very probably a Russian spy. But at present I have no reason to think he's a murderer.'

Manon could see that Louise was running out of internal resources, so she said, 'Do you mind if I take Louise home now? I think she has done all she can for this evening.'

'That's an excellent idea. The car is still here and will take you. We are really grateful to you both for coming out so late.'

'Manon,' said Saunders quietly, taking her to one side after the young man in the bomber jacket had been summoned to escort them to the car, 'I think Louise should stay with you tonight. Don't answer the door to anyone and call me if you need anything.'

Manon nodded and, with handshakes and thanks all round, followed Louise out of the room.

'Where to, ladies?' asked the driver as they got in the car. 'Same place?'

'Would you like to come to my flat tonight?' asked Manon.

'Yes,' said Louise immediately. 'I think I would. I'm so glad you suggested it. I have to admit I think I would be scared at home.'

When Louise and Manon had gone, Stanston said, 'Well, Jeff, any doubts I may have expressed to you before have pretty much gone away. The problem remains that we need hard evidence before we move on Robinson, though this notebook of the chauffeur's certainly gets us part way there, I think.'

Wilberforce nodded. This was Stanston's territory and he must decide the next moves.

'Meanwhile,' continued Stanston, looking at Hugo Wilson, 'we need to put the Met in the picture. Would you handle that? And they'll need to get the body out. Judging by what Louise said about its condition, that needs to be done straight away before someone reports the smell. Top secret. MP involved. No leaks.' Wilson nodded and went out again.

'As you know,' said Saunders, 'before all this business with Robinson blew up, Manon had been cultivating Tatiana Denisov, who we hoped might lead us to Denisov himself. That was before we knew that Tatiana's father had got her involved as Robinson's contact. According to Manon, the girl has been getting more and more fed up with her father and she seems to regard Manon as a sympathetic ear.

'Manon goes up to Oxford every week to attend a seminar that Tatiana also attends. She'll be going there again in a couple of days and she'll stay at Tatiana's place. It's possible she may get some more information about Robinson – especially if he wants another meet with Tatiana. Obviously, we'll let you know right away if anything emerges.'

Hugo Wilson had come back into the room during these remarks and he nodded. 'If we can catch Robinson in flagrante handing over something incriminating to Tatiana that would be the best outcome. He could be arrested for that and the rest could be investigated.'

There was silence for a moment, then Saunders said, 'I have to admit that I'm nervous about Manon getting any further involved in this business. I don't think it's at all likely that Harry Bristow killed himself. Why would he do that? From what Louise said, he had made his decision – and was determined to expose Robinson. He was the only one who knew the whole story and so he was the biggest threat. I think Robinson got an inkling that Harry had come to the end of his endurance and was a risk, and so he killed him. If that's true, he's very dangerous.'

No one spoke. Finally Wilson said, 'It looks as though we'll have an answer on Harry Bristow's death quite soon – the autopsy will be done first thing. With luck we should have the results some time later tomorrow.'

'Meanwhile,' said Stanston, 'between ourselves and the Met we'll keep a sharp eye on Mr Robinson, and if there's reason to believe anyone else is at risk, we will take action. So it's crucial that word doesn't leak that Bristow's death is thought to be suspicious, or else Robinson will run for the hills.'

'Or kill somebody else,' said Saunders grimly.

34

'AH, JUST THE MAN I'm looking for,' said Jerry Dukes, the assignment editor, with a cheerfulness which George Bennett knew did not bode well. 'Anything special you're working on right now?'

Such was his headache that the young reporter found himself incapable of concocting even a mildly plausible project, one that would force Dukes to look elsewhere for whatever he had in mind. Instead, George told the truth. 'No, nothing urgent,' he said, massaging his throbbing forehead.

George knew he was suffering the punishment for straying from his usual strict regimen, not because he was late for work (he wasn't) but because he was hungover. Working on a midday paper usually put a serious damper on George Bennett's night-time social life, since the job required a five a.m. start from home – he was supposed to get to the newspaper's offices in Kensington by six.

But it had been a stag night for an old school chum, and he couldn't really miss it. It started with drinks in a hotel on Piccadilly, followed by dinner in a private room at the Ivy, and ending – this was the fatal misstep, and made only after yet more to drink – in one of the few establishments in Soho that remained distinctly seedy. By the time they had piled the inebriated groom-to-be into a taxi, it was after three o'clock in the morning; when George got home – a studio flat in North

Kensington – it was four. It wasn't worth going to bed so he'd tried to sober up with a shower and coffee but he was still very fragile when he set off for work.

'Good,' Dukes said now. 'Here's the address,' he added, putting a yellow sticky on George's desk. 'I had a phone call just now with a tip-off – it sounded like an old codger, but he's quite insistent in his story. Said a neighbour of his died, and the police showed up late last night with an ambulance and carted him away. Wouldn't tell him what happened but then – get this – they sealed the dead man's flat and kept a cop outside the door. God knows what it's about, but the old geezer who called it in swore it's something to do with an MP. Since it's on Marsham Street that rings true – half the flats down there are rented out to MPs, and they all have division bells.'

'Who is this source?' asked George sceptically.

'A neighbour, as I said. His name's on the slip,' Dukes added, pointing to the sticky. 'So be a good boy and run down there and see if there's anything to it. Don't look so doubtful; I know it's a long shot, but we'd better check it out. I don't want it in *The Times* tomorrow morning if it could make our page this afternoon. The old boy's up and about so you needn't be scared of waking him.'

An hour later, George was knocking on the door of flat 34. There was no sign of a policeman guarding flat 35, but yellow tape ran in a series of criss-crosses across the doorframe. When the door opened at last, George faced a middle-aged man wearing a not-so-clean vest and baggy khaki trousers. He was bald on top and in compensation had let the uncombed hair on the side of his head grow wild. 'Mr Loudon?' asked George.

'That's right. To whom do I owe the honour of this visit?'

George explained why he was there and the paper he worked for. Mr Loudon nodded, as if the reporter had passed a test. He showed no sign of inviting him in, so George continued to speak where he stood. 'Who was the gentleman who died next door?'

'What's this worth, sonny?' said Loudon.

'Dunno till I've heard it. Could be worth a tenner if it works out.' George knew the ropes.

Loudon contemplated this for a moment, then seemed to make up his mind. 'A Mr Bristow. He was friendly enough, but kept himself to himself.'

'Was he an MP?'

'No, but he worked for one. He was a chauffeur.'

'Do you know which MP?'

'I don't know the name,' and George's heart sank. What was Dukes expecting him to find? This man didn't seem to know much. But then Loudon said, 'I know the MP was new. Got in at a by-election. For Liverpool – his constituency is in Liverpool. Sometimes Mr Bristow drove him up there; but sometimes the MP took the train and Mr Bristow was here at the weekends.'

'Do you know why the police were here? Were there many of them?'

Mr Loudon grew slightly more animated. 'There were four cars in front, and an ambulance.'

This seemed to George a bit de trop for the chauffeur of some obscure MP. 'Did you speak to them?'

'Oh yes, but they wouldn't tell me much. I asked why they were sealing off his flat and they as good as told me to piss off. There was a copper standing right there –' he pointed next door '– all through the night. He only left an hour ago.'

'Is there anything else you can tell me about Mr Bristow? Do you know what he died of?'

'Not a clue, and the police wouldn't say.' Loudon seemed to sense George's disappointment, for he said, 'He had a son; I know that. He just graduated from the police academy and Bristow was very proud of him. He showed me a photo of the graduation ceremony and said his boy had won some award. The sword of something.'

Damocles, George was tempted to say, but thought this would be lost on Mr Loudon. His hangover was only now beginning to recede. He'd go back, check with the Met press office (he was not optimistic about what he'd learn); he'd find out who the new Liverpool MP was and file before lunch. Lunch – he imagined a large glass of white wine. The hair of the dog had done the job before; pray God it worked again this time. And unless the Met press office had anything of interest to say, it was unlikely this story was going to go anywhere.

35

ONE THING MANON HATED above all else was hanging about doing nothing. Wilberforce had rung her that morning and asked her to come to his office after lunch. He'd expected to receive a copy of the autopsy results for Harry Bristow from the Met's special pathology lab by then. It was now two thirty and it hadn't arrived.

When she'd suggested going back to her desk and returning later, Wilberforce dismissed the offer with a wave of his hand. He gestured at the two chairs facing his desk, and she sat down in the nearest one. 'They'll be along shortly; they would have called to say if they were delayed. While we wait, tell me – any news from Oxford?'

Manon shook her head. 'No, but I'm spending the night there tomorrow, and on Wednesday too. I should find out if she's heard from her father – or from Robinson.'

'And you think she's definitely on the level, yes?'

He'd asked this several times before, but she couldn't blame him; in his position, she'd also be worried that Tatiana might be leading them up the garden path. She gave much the same answer as she had previously. 'I'm confident she's on our side now. She seems completely disillusioned with Russia, and with her father as well. And really eager to move to the States. Speaking of which, is there any news on that front?'

'It looks very promising though of course they won't let her work at Langley – too risky.' He added after a moment, 'I don't think I'd tell her that yet.'

'OK, I won't.'

'In fact, for the time being let's not give her too much good news. Why don't you just say there *might* be a job for her in DC?'

She understood at once; if the carrot being offered was firm rather than contingent, there would be little incentive for Tatiana to help them.

There was a knock on the door, and Wilberforce's assistant came in, a young man who Saunders had told her had been a graduate of West Point and then a Rhodes Scholar at Oxford before joining the agency.

'Hot off the press, sir,' he said, putting an envelope on Wilberforce's desk.

'Could you get a hold of Dr Peterson for me please? He's expecting the call.'

'Actually, he's already here, sir. He's waiting in my office.'

The assistant left to get the doctor, and Wilberforce smiled at Manon. 'If I've asked him once, I've asked him a hundred times – don't call me "sir". It makes me feel I'm back in the army.'

'Who is Dr Peterson?'

'He's a consultant we use occasionally if there's some medical or forensic issue. I'm hoping he can explain the autopsy report to us – they're always written in medical jargon I can't even pretend to understand.'

Dr Peterson was a short trim man with a Van Dyck beard, which like his hair was the colour of burnt oranges. He was also obviously American – he wore a grey Brooks Brothers herringbone jacket, a button-down shirt and blood-coloured penny loafers. He shook hands with Manon and nodded at Wilberforce, who stood up and handed him the file. He sat down in the chair next to Manon, facing Wilberforce, and, putting the report on the side of the desk, started to read.

Wilberforce glanced at Manon and rolled his eyes while the brought-in boffin went silently through the report with painstaking care; he looked utterly rapt. Finished at last, he said, 'Well, what would you like to know?'

'Everything,' Wilberforce declared. He added with a grin, 'Provided it's in English.'

'I'll do my best,' said Dr Peterson. 'Let's start with the state of the corpse. The best estimate of the pathologist is that the man in question –' he looked down at the report '– a Mr Bristow, had been dead five or six days when he was discovered. There was some natural decomposition, made worse by insect infestation – mainly flies of various kinds and their maggots.'

'Did that affect the autopsy?'

'Not really,' Peterson said with a shrug. 'Just slowed them down a bit, I would think.'

'OK. Let's go on – how did he die?'

'I thought that's what you'd want to know,' said Peterson. 'It looks like a pretty straightforward suicide. Death by hanging. There was a chair he would have stood on and then kicked away. The rope he used was more than long enough and very strong – you could tow a sailboat with it. It was looped around the beam and carefully secured; and the noose around his neck was simple but effective and tied tight as the proverbial drum. Death by asphyxiation, seemingly by his own hand. Open and shut, you could say.'

Wilberforce scratched his cheek, looking a little worried. 'I hope I'm right to think a big "but" is coming…'

'You are, and I have to say, whoever did this autopsy is a clever boy. Or girl,' he said, glancing at Manon.

'Why's that?' asked Wilberforce, trying to hurry him up.

'Most of the damage done by the hanging fits the suicide model. The toxicology report is pretty thin – but it would be after so long a time between death and discovery.'

'What would that have shown?'

'Nothing definitive, but it might suggest a state of mind – if he were drunk or doped up with Valium, for example. It takes a certain gumption to hang yourself, and booze or drugs can make it more palatable, I guess. In any case, drugs or alcohol are often present in this kind of suicide.

'Also, the ligature was tight, certainly tight enough to choke him to death. One vertebra was snapped – no surprise in a hanging. The hyoid bone was broken too – it supports the tongue and larynx, and lies in front of the third vertebra. Right here,' he said, tilting back his head while he put his thumb and first finger on either side of his throat where it met his lower jaw. He withdrew his hand and lowered his head. 'A common misperception is that this bone doesn't get broken when death occurs by homicide rather than suicide. But it's not true – it's perfectly common.'

'OK,' said Wilberforce patiently, and Manon wondered what was coming next.

Peterson said, 'So far, so normal – if you consider suicide normal, I guess. But this is where the pathologist got smart – the Met might want to give him a raise.' He paused momentarily, then said, 'Before I go on, I wanted to ask something. Was Mr Bristow a violent man?'

Wilberforce gestured for Manon to answer. She thought quickly, then said, 'I don't think so, but I'd have to ask people who knew him; I didn't. He was a policeman, so he must have seen his share of trouble, but as far as I know in his private life he was a peaceful kind of guy. Gentle, in fact, from the sound of it.' She was thinking of how Louise had described him. 'Why do you ask?'

'Because it looks like he'd been in a fight recently.' Waving the file, Peterson said, 'He had a broken bone in his left cheek and really bad bruising as well – with a considerable contusion. I don't think he walked into a door; you'd have to be running at full speed before a door would do that kind of damage. Somebody hit him.'

He paused, then went on, 'Here's the thing: if you're hung by a rope, then the ligature creates what we call a furrow – a trench in other words, the marks around the neck left by the rope. If someone has committed suicide by hanging then the furrow is inevitably at an angle – a downward angle created when the body falls from the height you need to hang yourself. Does that make sense?'

'Yes,' said Manon and Wilberforce, almost in unison.

'But if someone is strangled, then the furrow is going to be horizontal – because the victim hasn't jumped from a height, which is usually the seat of a chair. Instead they are being strangled, almost always from behind. There's no downward pressure on the ligature so the furrow isn't at any angle at all – it goes straight around the neck.'

Suddenly a different possibility had emerged. Peterson said, 'You can probably see where this is headed.'

Wilberforce gave up any pretence of patience. 'Tell us about Bristow's furrow.'

'Completely horizontal and deeply etched into the skin. It would take a very powerful pair of hands to get the ligature to leave such a deep mark. But hard to do to yourself, especially when the ligature is tied *behind* the neck.'

Peterson pursed his lips and said nothing further. The three of them sat in silence for what seemed to Manon an eternity. Finally, Wilberforce emitted a deep sigh. 'And therefore the conclusion is … ?'

Peterson didn't hesitate. 'The report is unambiguous. Our Mr Bristow was no suicide.'

36

Robinson was in the Members' Tea Room. As usual the place was crowded, but he was sitting by himself in one of the deep shell-pink armchairs. He had been in the Chamber for Prime Minister's Questions, where MPs were expected to show support for their leader. He found the loud barracking and jeering of the weekly televised ritual remarkably immature for such an august setting, but he joined in nonetheless, cheering with his colleagues when the leader of his party scored points against his counterpart across the despatch box. After PMQs, he had stayed in the Chamber, while most of the MPs left, and listened to a debate on defence priorities.

The day before he had met the Secretary of State himself, ostensibly for a chat – the minister had said, 'I gather you're particularly interested in defence matters, so I thought it would be a good idea to get to know each other.' But when he'd seen the whips afterwards, it was clear that it had been an audition for a role as the minister's PPS – Parliamentary Private Secretary – and it seemed that he had passed. At least the Chief Whip had indicated as much, and suggested there could be an announcement of the appointment at the next reshuffle later in the month.

Alternatively, if that didn't work out, a member of the Defence Select Committee from his party was in the terminal stages of liver disease, and there would be a vacancy in a matter of weeks, if not days. Would Robinson be interested in being considered for a seat on the committee? Yes, he had replied calmly, though inwardly he felt a surge of excitement. He was in – inside the inner circle. All the years of subterfuge and diligence were paying off.

Not for the first time, someone's death was paving the way for his advancement – it was, after all, through a death that he had become an MP. There was nothing ghoulish about this fact for Robinson; it had provided the opening he had been constantly on the lookout for and, trained as he was, he had taken it immediately. What to do with the documents and information he'd have access to, if he got either of these jobs, was something he could decide when it happened. He wouldn't turn any more of them over to Denisov – that was certain – or to that Embassy goon, Ivanov. But Robinson felt confident there would be senior intelligence officers in Moscow who would understand what he had managed to do, and who would contact him and take delivery of the material which he would soon be able to supply.

He felt no emotion about what he'd done to Harry Bristow. His was just another death necessary to the plan. He was relieved to have removed the threat his driver had posed and surprised he hadn't recognised it sooner. He knew now that had been a mistake. He had taken the man for granted, ignored him, almost forgotten he was there. But when he'd come to think about his security, after that encounter with the CIA, he'd realised that of course Bristow was *the* threat. He had had no choice about it. If the man had been more sensible, and frankly more *loyal*, he might still be driving Robinson. Instead, he was, as far as Robinson knew, still hanging from a beam in his bedroom. At some point, the stench from the decomposing body would alert the neighbours to the presence of a corpse next door; or perhaps a friend or family member would start looking for him. But this might not be for weeks, which provided added cover for what anyone would have to conclude was a suicide.

It had turned out to be very easy to do. Bristow might have been a senior policeman, but he was ageing a bit, out of shape, slow on his feet. He had peered through the spyhole and opened the door right away, clearly surprised to find Robinson visiting his flat.

Robinson had walked in while Bristow closed the door; when the driver turned around, starting to offer him a cup of something, Robinson had struck. He hit Bristow so hard it lifted the man off his feet, and as he fell back, he banged the door with his head. When he landed on the floor, moaning and only half-conscious, he made the fatal error of turning over on to his stomach in an effort to get up. Robinson had sat on him then, his knees pinning Bristow's arms down while he put on a pair of latex gloves and drew out a reinforced cord he had bought that afternoon in a small hardware shop in Peckham.

It had taken less than a minute to strangle Bristow, but much longer to hoist his heavy lifeless corpse into the bedroom and on to a chair, while Robinson used another chair to stand and tie the garrotte encircling Bristow's throat around the central beam.

Now Robinson's tea was getting cold, but he left it, his thoughts roaming, considering his position. He was feeling pretty good – certainly compared to the gloomy anxiety he had felt after the encounter with the two Americans at

Louise's birthday lunch. He had made a stupid mistake, claiming Tatiana was the daughter of one of his constituents, but he was confident there wasn't much the Yanks could do about it. He guessed it was Tatiana Denisov they were interested in, not him. If so they were not going to go talking about it to the British. After all, they weren't operating on their own turf, and were probably out of order if they were cultivating Tatiana.

'Hello, Peter.' Robinson looked up. The face was familiar – another backbencher in his party – but he couldn't for the life of him remember the man's name. That was the problem being a new MP – there were six hundred and thirty-four colleagues to learn about. Then he remembered: Davison, whose constituency was somewhere down here – Beckenham? That he couldn't remember. Still, it was important to act friendly, so he smiled at Davison and motioned the man to sit down.

But Davison shook his head. 'I'd love to join you, but I've got a constituent to see in the lobby. I just wanted to say I was sorry to hear about your driver.'

At first Robinson thought Davison meant his new driver, who had an unfortunate (and expensive) habit of parking on double yellow lines. Had he been towed? Then he realised it must be more serious than that to be mentioned; it had to be Bristow the MP was referring to. 'Yes,' he said, deliberately non-committal.

'Had he been your driver for long?'

'Not long. And he left the job a few weeks ago. I didn't know him well.'

'Well, sorry anyway. I gather the police think it may not have been a suicide after all. Poor bugger either way. See you.'

Robinson got up as soon as Davison had gone out of the door and headed straight for the Commons Library. He was badly shaken by his fellow MP's remarks.

It didn't take him long to find what he was looking for. In the early-afternoon edition of the *Evening Standard*, he discovered a brief item about a dead man found in a flat on Marsham Street. He was identified as 'Harry Bristow, a chauffeur by occupation, most recently employed by the newly elected MP for Liverpool North, Peter Robinson'. Instead of the usual comforting phrase – 'police reported there were no suspicious circumstances' – Robinson read to his astonished dismay that 'police would not comment but neighbours believe there may be suspicious circumstances. An autopsy has been ordered...'

All of his subdued anxiety returned. Why on earth were there suspicions? He had been scrupulous about not leaving any evidence of his presence in the flat, and he was quite sure no one saw him going in or leaving.

No, it must be something else. Yet actually, if the police suspected him of anything, they would have been to see him. In fact it seemed curious that they hadn't had the courtesy to inform Bristow's most recent employer – Robinson – of his death.

Don't get paranoid, he told himself. There was nothing to tie him to Bristow's death, so let the police think dark thoughts as much as they liked – he was safe, from Bristow at least.

But Tatiana might be something else, and at the thought of her he realised with a sudden cramping of his stomach that actually, just like Bristow, she could do him real damage – especially if she had looked at the document he had passed her in Oxford market. That could not be explained away.

What if the Americans were cultivating her and she changed sides? Certainly she hadn't seemed very enthusiastic about working for her father. Like Harry Bristow, Tatiana was now someone – and with Bristow dead, the *only* one – who could ruin his great achievement. She would be able to expose him for what he really was: a Russian agent acting under the most brilliantly constructed cover.

What a pity that it had come to this, he thought, since she was an attractive woman, and presumably clever, with a bright future ahead of her – studying at Oxford for a higher degree. But this brief feeling of sympathy didn't last; he knew now what he had to do.

He tried to still the sense of mounting panic he felt, telling himself he had been trained to kill when it was necessary. It should make no difference whether he terminated one person … or two. What mattered was removing any threat to what he had been working towards for so many years. He sensed that if he didn't act fast – even if that made things more risky – he would find himself surrounded, and then exposed.

37

T HE *EVENING STANDARD* WAS delivered every afternoon to the SVR Residency in Kensington Palace
Gardens and examined carefully for items of useful local
news. On the day George Bennett's short article appeared,
the SVR Resident Ivanov was the first to notice the reference
to the death of the driver of the MP for Liverpool North. He
picked up the phone straightaway and summoned Yuri, who
had been supervising the monitoring of the microphone in
Robinson's car.

'Have you seen this piece in the *Standard* about Paris's
driver?' he demanded, waving the paper at Yuri. 'Paris' was
the codename SVR HQ in Moscow had given to Romanov–
Robinson. 'Did you know his driver was dead?'

'No,' replied Yuri, hesitantly, waiting for the next onslaught
from his boss. 'We'd noticed he had a different one in the last
few weeks. We heard Paris telling his girlfriend that the usual
one – Harry, they call him – had asked for time off to visit his
family.'

'You should have told me. You should have known that
might be important. I need to know everything out of the
ordinary that happens. It says here the driver was found
dead in his flat and the police think there may be suspicious
circumstances. That means they think someone killed him.
Who do you think might have done it?'

'I don't know,' said Yuri, looking confused.

'Think, man.' Ivanov was going red in the face. 'There must be a chance it was Paris. And if it was he's in big trouble.'

'Why would he do that?' asked Yuri.

'I don't know. You're the ones who are supposed to be monitoring him. You tell me. All I know is that if something's been going on there, we should have known and told the Centre. They have been considering sending one of the top field men to take him over, but if Paris has got himself into some sort of trouble and the police are involved, they need to know. They won't want to touch him with a bargepole.'

'Why should it be Paris who killed him? The driver was an ex-cop. Maybe he had enemies.'

'Well, I don't know. What do you think? Have you ever heard them arguing?'

'No. They hardly spoke except to make arrangements. Harry talked a lot more to the girlfriend when they were alone in the car.'

'Hmm. I wonder,' mused Ivanov. 'You say this Harry was some sort of a policeman?'

'Yes. That's what he told Louise. Special Branch, he said. What are you thinking?'

Ivanov said, 'I'm thinking, what if this ex-policeman Harry got suspicious? What if he noticed something about our friend that didn't seem right? After all, Paris has not been very careful. When I met him in that church he came by car – we saw it parked there when we arrived. The driver may have seen us turn up, for all I know.'

'Yes,' said Yuri, warming to the subject. His imagination was now in full flow. 'And if he saw you he may have seen Denisov. And Harry drove him up to Oxford one time. We thought he'd probably gone to meet Tatiana Denisov. We didn't follow him that time – you decided it was too risky – but maybe Harry did, and when he saw Robinson meeting the woman he dug around and found out who she was.'

'You don't know that,' said Ivanov. 'Just stick to what you've heard in the car. Don't start making things up.'

'Tatiana!' said Yuri suddenly. 'That's it.'

'What are you talking about now?'

'What first put us on to thinking Mr Paris wasn't British? It was when we heard him speaking Russian to Tatiana.'

'Yes. And the driver must have heard that too.'

Yuri hesitated. 'But the driver wouldn't understand Russian.'

'No. But he could probably guess what language it was.' Ivanov had got hold of a theory now and was feeling more comfortable. 'And even if he didn't guess the language he must have thought there was a lot of odd stuff going on. Our friend Paris has been far too cocky and unprofessional. He spoke to me as though he thought he was the greatest agent of all time. What if Harry was reporting all this to the British? What if they know all about Paris, and are just watching what we do? Ready to pounce.'

'So what about Harry, then? Are you saying you think Paris has killed him?'

'It would make sense, wouldn't it? If somebody has killed him, chances are it's Paris. He must have suddenly realised this Harry was a threat. And if Harry has been reporting on him to the police or MI5, we need to keep well clear or we'll be back in Moscow on the next plane – and it won't be to collect a medal either. I've got to tell the Centre that Paris may be damaged goods, and not the boy wonder they seem to think he is.'

So, armed with his copy of the *Evening Standard* and with a satisfied smile on his face, Ivanov went off to the Communications Room to do his best to bring Pyotr Romanov's glittering career to an end.

An hour and a half later, Ivanov summoned Yuri again, and told him he wanted to talk to the team working on the Paris case. Shortly afterwards they all trooped into Ivanov's office, looking apprehensive. Yuri had told them that the boss was in a state because they hadn't realised that Harry the driver was dead, so they were expecting to receive the usual bawling out. But instead Ivanov was stationed quietly behind his desk with a solemn expression on his face.

'Sit down, boys,' he said, waving them to chairs. They sat, perched uncomfortably on the edge of their seats, ready for Ivanov to start shouting.

He spoke calmly, his voice level and serious. 'I have just been speaking to the Centre, giving them the news of the death of Paris's driver. They asked for my interpretation of what has happened and an assessment of how this affects the security of the case. I told them my view, which, as I have already told Yuri, is that it blows the case wide open. In my opinion it indicates that the driver, who as you all know was an ex-policeman, was acting as a spy for the police. Discovering this, Paris killed him.'

The assembled group, including Yuri, tried to hide their astonishment. They had never heard Ivanov speak like this, and his suspicions seemed extreme – based as they were on one small article in an afternoon newspaper. No one spoke.

Ivanov went on sombrely, 'Although the case had seemed to be most promising, in the light of my information the

Centre has decided that the agent Paris has been acting without direction for so long that any attempt to reassert control would present a disproportionate risk. It was decided that with the apparent killing of his driver – and in such a manner that it has attracted police attention – Paris is now effectively a rogue agent and a threat to national security. Accordingly, it was agreed unanimously that he must be terminated.'

There was a gasp; this was not what they expected.

Yuri recovered first. 'So are they sending over a team to do it?'

'No,' replied Ivanov. 'We have to do it.' And, looking at Yuri, he added, 'Draw up a plan. I don't want any dramatics. Keep well clear of Parliament. This is to be done quietly and discreetly, somewhere out of sight if possible. But it needs to be done soon. They don't want him taking it into his head to kill anyone else.'

'They don't know if he's killed anyone yet,' muttered Yuri to Alexei as they left the room.

'It's called diplomacy,' replied Alexei. 'They've got bigger fish to fry and poor old Paris risks fouling their lines.'

38

Robinson RANG TATIANA THAT evening as he was being driven back to his flat by the new chauffeur. 'I need to see you at once,' he said right away, speaking Russian so she would know it was him. 'It is most urgent. I want to meet up tomorrow.' If he went there tonight, he would get there late, when the streets were quiet and the trains half-empty; someone might notice him.

'I'm afraid tomorrow's not convenient.'

'Then the day after tomorrow.' That would do.

'That's not convenient either.'

'It will have to become convenient. This is an emergency.'

'It's always an emergency,' she complained.

'I am not prepared to argue with you.' She did not reply, so he tried a different tack. 'I promise this will be the last time. I know your father is making a different arrangement.'

She sighed. 'He hasn't told me that, so I hope you're right.'

'I am. But I have something for him now and it's urgent.'

Again there was a sigh, but this time one of capitulation. She said with resignation in her voice, 'All right, but I won't do this again. I can meet on Wednesday – in the morning. And it has to be here in Oxford. I have a class in the afternoon. And I'm not going back to that market. It's too crowded and I might run into someone I know.'

'OK. Suggest somewhere else. Somewhere outside, where there's plenty of space and not too many people around.'

She thought for a moment then said, 'There's a big open space called the University Parks. It's only ten minutes' walk from the centre of town. There's a cricket ground right in the middle, with a pavilion. It's a big old building with seats in front. People go there and watch the cricket matches, and even when there isn't a match on people like to sit on the benches. I'll be there and you can join me and pass over your thing. No one will notice.'

Robinson thought about this for a minute, wondering if it would provide him with the opportunity he wanted. 'OK,' he said at last. 'I'll meet you at the pavilion at eleven o'clock on Wednesday. If there are too many people, we can go for a walk.'

'All right. Eleven o'clock at the cricket pavilion. And remember, this is the last time I will cooperate.'

'Don't worry. After Wednesday, you'll never see me again.' Or anyone else, he thought, as he ended the call.

Manon was intending to have an early night and was just getting into bed when her mobile phone rang. She resisted the temptation to ignore it and looked at the screen – she was glad she did, because it showed Tatania's number.

'Hello Manon, it's me – Tatiana.' She sounded slightly breathless.

'Hi. I was going to ring you in the morning. I was hoping to stay tomorrow night as well as after the seminar on Wednesday. Is that all right?'

'That's fine,' the Russian woman said, but she sounded as though her thoughts were elsewhere. 'I need to see you anyway – something's happened.'

'What's that?'

'He's been in touch – the English-Russian as I think of him.'

'He rang you?'

'Yes. He wants to meet. No, correct that – he *insists* on meeting. He says it's urgent, and that he has some information to be sent to my father. I resisted, but he said it would be the last time. I thought I had better go along with it.'

'You did the right thing,' said Manon. It would have been no help if she'd refused to see Robinson. This way, they might be able to catch him dead to rights – especially since he had something to give her. 'When are you seeing him?'

'Wednesday at eleven o'clock. I wanted it to be in the open air, so we are meeting in the University Parks – it's only about fifteen minutes' walk from here. There's a cricket pavilion in the middle of it – I said I'd sit there and he could give me whatever he wants me to send to my father. Or if there are too many people around, we could walk down to the river where it will be quieter.'

'OK. We can discuss it tomorrow evening.' Manon was thinking fast. God knows what Robinson was up to, but it seemed wise to assume the worst. 'But until then, can you not answer the door to anyone you don't know? Just to be on the safe side.'

'All right,' said Tatiana hesitantly.

Manon had decided not to say anything about Harry's murder. She didn't want to spook her any more than she just had. She said only, 'Good – I'll see you tomorrow.'

She rang off, then left the bedroom and put the kettle on. Bed would have to wait; she needed to ring Saunders right away, and this time she knew she didn't have to apologise for the late hour.

In the SVR Residency in Kensington Peter Robinson's call to Tatiana Denisov had been overheard by the team monitoring the microphone in the MP's car.

Ivanov agreed that the meeting in a quiet place, which Tatiana had insisted on, might provide the opportunity for them to carry out their instructions from the Centre. So at about the same time as the first high-level meeting was under way in Thames House, Yuri and his small team with their equipment were in Oxford, reconnoitring the University Parks. This was unknown territory to them; their only previous visit to the city had been when two of the team had followed Denisov from the railway station to Nuffield College when he went to meet his daughter.

They had spent the previous night on the outskirts of town, arriving just before midnight and sleeping in the back of a large white van they now parked on a side street off the Banbury Road. The Parks were almost deserted when they entered on foot – just the occasional runner and a couple of dog walkers. They found the cricket ground and the pavilion without difficulty and they stood gazing at it, like a group of sightseers.

'This is no good,' said Yuri. 'Too exposed, no cover. We're supposed to be discreet. The Centre doesn't want a diplomatic incident. Can't be done.' The others nodded.

'Poison would be best,' suggested Alexei.

'Take too long to set up,' objected Mikhail. 'They want a quick job. We need to shoot him.'

Then Yuri remembered that Tatiana had suggested that if there were too many people around they might take a walk down to the river. And that is why, the following day, sunrise saw the team concealed in bushes and undergrowth on the far bank of the Cherwell.

Saunders managed to suppress a yawn, and glanced at his watch. It was six thirty in the morning, a time usually spent letting the dog out in the Saunders family's back garden and putting on the coffee machine. Instead he was sitting in the now-familiar room on the ground floor of Thames House.

Manon's call the night before had set the proverbial cat among the pigeons. Saunders had decided it was sufficiently urgent to alert Wilberforce and as a result both men had been up until two in the morning – making their own calls. The recipients had included Hugo Wilson, the MI5 Director of Counter Espionage, and Stanston, the deputy director general, both of whom now sat across the table. Stanston had in turn contacted the woman sitting next to him – Frances Fielding, Assistant Commissioner at the Metropolitan Police, the most senior woman in the Met. She had brought along Jeremy Coates, the operational commander.

The reason for the particularly high-powered attendance at this early meeting was that later in the morning Assistant Commissioner Fielding and Deputy Director General Stanston would have to inform the Prime Minister and the Home Secretary that one of their Members of Parliament was not only a foreign citizen but also a spy and probably a murderer.

They had all read a briefing document prepared over-night by Hugo Wilson's staff so they knew the background, and now Commander Coates took them through the plan for the meeting between Robinson and Tatiana Denisov in Oxford the following day. For the purposes of the operation,

Robinson had been given the codename 'Rotation', which Wilberforce thought apt, considering the career gyrations of the man. Tatiana was 'Ariadne'.

Coates began, 'The brief I have received is that our objective is to monitor a meeting between Rotation and Ariadne. Rotation is an MP but strongly suspected of being a Russian illegal. It is also believed he may have committed a murder and may be armed, as well as violent, if we arrest him as planned. It's thought that Rotation intends to hand documents over to Ariadne. If he does so, we will arrest him on suspicion of espionage. Ariadne should not be arrested.'

Heads nodded but no one spoke. Coates went on, 'Surveillance will pick him up tonight and stick with him until we see he's settled. Assuming he sleeps at his flat on the South Bank, that's where we'll start tomorrow. We'll go with Rotation to Oxford, whether he goes by car or train, and we'll have teams there ready to take him on when he arrives. We have the advantage of knowing where the meeting is going to take place and we'll be scoping that out today. Our information is that they'll initially join up at the pavilion, but they may walk down to the river to do the handover.'

'It's more a stream, actually,' interjected Stanston – Wilberforce guessed he'd been at the university. 'But the far bank is rather overgrown, so I hope she can persuade him to stay on the pavilion side. That way they'll be visible.'

'Thank you,' responded Coates.

Hugo Wilson spoke for the first time. He asked Wilberforce, 'Do we think Ariadne is potentially in any kind of danger? Or is this just a handover meeting?'

Wilberforce shrugged. 'I can't give you a very satisfactory answer to that because we just don't know. A month ago,

I'd have said it would be another handover – the first took place near the covered market in the middle of town. But given what we think he did to Harry Bristow, it's safest to be prepared for anything.'

'Then should we let her actually meet him?'

Wilson was now looking to Stanston for the answer, which came as a relief to Wilberforce, since he had asked himself the same question. Fortunately for him, it was Stanston's call, and after a moment the deputy director general replied, 'I think we have to, though don't imagine I haven't thought long and hard about it. We must take every possible precaution to protect Ariadne, but it's critical that we get sufficient evidence to charge Rotation.'

There was silence in the room, which Wilberforce only reluctantly broke. 'I take it a few of these officers will be carrying weapons?'

At this Assistant Commissioner Fielding looked coldly at Wilberforce and said, 'The appropriate number of armed Metropolitan Police officers will be deployed on this operation to keep Ariadne and members of the public safe.'

A smile hovered over Stanston's face as Wilberforce said a faint 'thank you'.

39

MANON MADE IT TO the house in Jericho by late afternoon, where she found roles reversed from her last visit. Tatiana was in the kitchen this time, making the supper.

Manon looked at a wild assemblage of pots and pans on the stove and in the sink, including frying pans, a chopping board covered with remnants of pastry, spoons and measuring cups and a half-empty glass of sherry. 'Gosh,' she said, putting down the bottle of wine she had bought on the way. 'What are you making?'

'A feast!' Tatiana declared. 'It was meant to be a surprise, but you have arrived early.' There was mock-reproach in her voice.

'Sorry. When I got to Marylebone, there was a train about to leave, so I took it.'

'No matter. I know it is a bit too soon according to the calendar, but I thought we could celebrate your country's birthday.'

'You mean the fourth of July?'

'I do. This means you should not feel homesick on the day.' Tatiana laughed. 'I hope I have got it right,' she said, looking with uncertainty at the cooker. 'Hot dogs, hamburgers, French fries – though I don't understand what is so French about them. There is corn too, but sadly it's from a tin. All followed by apple pie and ice cream.'

'The whole works,' said Manon appreciatively, though she was slightly dreading having to work her way through this *grande bouffe* of America, with not a green vegetable in sight.

But later, when Manon had consumed a hot dog with ketchup and mustard in a most unAmerican bun, a hamburger with chips and a side of buttered corn, and even managed a slice of pie with a dollop of ice cream, she put down her napkin and sighed contentedly. She tried not to think about the extra-long run she'd need to take once back in London to offset the enormous calorie count of this meal. 'An all-American feast done to perfection,' she said.

'Did I get it right then?'

Manon nodded vigorously. There was something touching about Tatiana's keenness, though Manon knew what lay behind it. And sure enough, a little later, Tatiana said, 'I don't suppose there's any news from the States about whether they'll have me?'

'I asked my boss, in fact, just last Friday. He's due to speak with them again next week, but he said you should feel encouraged – the people in Washington are very interested.'

'Really?'

'Yes, really,' said Manon, inwardly appalled by how easy it was proving to lie – though in fairness, she told herself, Wilberforce had seemed to think he could swing a visa, possibly even a Green Card, for the Russian. But she also remembered his strictures against letting Tatiana think it was a done deal, so she said nothing further.

'I am so pleased. And then even my father won't be able to reach me.' Tatiana seemed cheered by the prospect, but then a shadow of worry crossed her face. 'About tomorrow—' she started to say, then stopped.

Manon looked at her. 'Why don't we talk about it in the morning? I'll be up first thing. But don't be worried – I know it will all be OK.'

The morning began well enough; Manon had already made coffee and been out to buy some breakfast rolls when Tatiana appeared. She was wearing a long yellow nightshirt and slippers. Manon was surprised, since Tatiana was an early riser and always appeared dressed for the day. Now she looked pale, as if she'd had a sleepless night.

'Morning,' said Manon. 'Would you like some coffee?'

Tatiana shook her head. 'To tell you the truth, I am not feeling so good.' Usually her English pronunciation was near-flawless, but now it came out heavily accented, almost deliberately so.

'Why, what's wrong?'

'I don't know. I have fever, I am sure, and ache all over. I did not sleep,' she added.

'I'm so sorry.' Manon felt Tatiana's forehead; it seemed perfectly normal to her. 'Have you taken anything? I have some paracetamol.'

'You are very kind, but I have taken two an hour ago.'

'You might feel better if you get dressed and then have some breakfast. I think after you've seen this man, you should come straight back and get into bed. Forget about the seminar this week. What you need is rest.'

Tatiana shook her head. 'It is not good, Manon; I am really not too well. I don't think I should go out at all.'

'What, and miss your meeting?' Manon was horrified. It had never occurred to her that Tatiana might consider not seeing Robinson. It would be a disaster if she cancelled;

Manon knew, from what Wilberforce had implied on the phone, that some sort of plan was in place to monitor the meeting. People would be on their way now, if they had not already arrived.

Tatiana said, 'I can see the Russian Englishman another time. I will call him.'

'But he's probably en route, Tatiana. He'd allow a lot of time – traffic in London is terrible in the morning.'

Tatiana just shrugged. Manon's anxiety was growing. How could she explain to Wilberforce that Tatiana had copped out – and during the very time Manon was with her, supposedly keeping an eye on the woman?

What was this about anyway? She observed that Tatiana wouldn't catch her eye, and she didn't believe she had a fever. Was it conceivable that she had planned this sudden withdrawal and – Manon only reluctantly considered this – been working for the other side all along? Or had she simply changed her mind about helping the British and Americans? Given everything she knew about Tatiana, and what the woman had said, Manon found this impossible to believe. Unless…

Unless Tatiana was terrified. Scared of the Russians, scared of her father… possibly also scared of the British. And most of all, scared of this man and what he might do to her. And that was without even knowing that they suspected Robinson of having murdered Harry Bristow.

So how could she calm her down, enough to ensure the meet went ahead, the contact was made in front of whoever had come to observe it?

It would be fatal to let Tatiana go back to bed. Once there she would never re-emerge, not today at any rate. So objective number one had to be to get her dressed. But that wouldn't allay the Russian's worries; if anything, the prospect of putting on her clothes might simply make her more scared, since it would bring her one step closer to the dreaded rendezvous.

Manon decided to take a firm line. She said, 'Tatiana, it's really important that you see this man today. I can't begin to explain, but there's a lot depending on it, not just for my colleagues, but for others as well – including you. We both know this man is not what he's pretending to be, and I can tell you as a fact that he's a bad man. We need to do something about him. But it's not like in your country – we can't do anything to him until we've got some evidence. We're pretty sure that the meeting with you today will give us that.'

She wasn't sure that what she was saying was getting through to Tatiana, who still refused to meet Manon's gaze, and who looked as if her thoughts were miles away. In any case she was probably used to hearing this kind of stern sermonising from people in authority – her father or even the Russian government perhaps. Compared to them, Manon must sound polite and reasonable, but also weak and toothless and ultimately resistible. Trying to order this woman to do something would hit a brick wall; she would be all too accustomed to threats.

What else could Manon say? Her mind was racing, when suddenly she realised what might help to get Tatiana over to the University Parks in time for her assignation. Wilberforce would have her scalp if he knew what she was about to offer, but she saw no alternative.

'Tatiana, would it help if I came with you?'

There was a new spark in Tatiana's eyes, and her pallor seemed to lift. Manon went on, 'I wouldn't be there when you met him – if he saw us together it would probably scare him off. But you'd know I'd be nearby, and also that nothing could happen to you on your way there. And once you're in the Parks, you'll be fine – there are too many people around for him to do anything.'

Tatiana thought about it. Manon, who was beginning to worry about the time, risked a last push. 'What do you think? Shall I go with you – would that help?'

And slowly, gradually, Tatiana nodded. 'Yes,' she said quietly. 'That would help a lot. You are very kind, Manon. I will go and get dressed now.'

40

A FTER A WEEK OF glorious sunshine the wind had swung round to the north, and it had turned much colder. Manon was glad of the sweater she had pulled on at the last minute as they left the house. Tatiana too had dressed for the weather with a blue gilet over her jumper. Manon waited while Tatiana double-locked the front door, then they set out for the University Parks.

It was ten thirty, and Manon reckoned that Tatiana could reach the pavilion with time to spare – enough to choose a seat and be ready for Robinson's arrival, but not enough for her to have another attack of nerves.

They crossed Walton Street, its shops and cafés all open and busy, and walked along Observatory Street, its small houses freshly painted and done up as part of the gentrification of the neighbourhood. Manon had been astonished, looking through the *Oxford Times* property pages, to discover what they sold for. In fact it was just a narrow claustrophobic street and now it was making her feel nervous. There were one or two people around and she kept a sharp eye out for anyone following them, but no one seemed to be taking any interest. She was relieved when they emerged on to the junction with the much wider Woodstock Road, one of the city's main thoroughfares.

Tatiana was walking in silence, her face tense and her eyes looking straight ahead. Manon led the way as they zigzagged east to the artery of the Banbury Road, which took them towards the centre of town and one of the entrances to the Parks. So far so good, thought Manon, though in fact, unless Robinson knew where Tatiana lived, he would find it impossible to waylay her – he would have no idea which direction she would be coming from.

Manon glanced at her watch; there was ten minutes before the time of the assignation. She stopped just short of the park entrance. 'I think this is as far as I should go. You have your phone?'

'Of course,' said Tatiana. She seemed more alert now, probably realising she was on her own from this point.

'You can phone me if you need me,' said Manon. 'I'm going to the shops on South Parade, so I won't be far away – it's just up the road.'

'Thank you,' said Tatiana. It sounded mechanical; she was psyching herself up now as if for an ordeal.

'You'll be fine. Try and keep in the open. I'm sure he'll just give you a package and then clear off.'

Some sixty miles away, Wilberforce and Saunders were ensconced again in the ground-floor meeting room at Thames House. Stanston was there too with a couple of junior staff; his counter-intelligence head, Hugo Wilson, was over in the Met's operations room, where Commander Coates was running the show. Here in Thames House they were receiving the same audio, still pictures and slightly unreliable video feed from the scene as the operations room, but it had been made very clear to the Americans that they were observers not participants.

They had heard the teams in London report Rotation's departure from his flat on the South Bank. He was driving himself in a black BMW and making his way to the A40. A little later, the various teams in Oxford had reported in as they got into position – two near Tatiana's house, a couple at a café on her route, several in the Parks near the pavilion. The unwelcome news was that a cricket match was due to start at eleven o'clock and people were already gathering.

'Ariadne may have a problem finding a seat in front of the pavilion.' The voice from the Parks came through a box in the centre of the conference-room table very clearly. 'There's quite a crowd gathering. Extra chairs and benches have been put out in front of the pavilion and people are standing all round the boundary rope.'

'Make sure you have the walk down to the river and the bank itself covered,' ordered Commander Coates, over in the operations room.

A period of silence followed, with just the occasional exchange between the teams following Rotation as he drove towards Oxford. It seemed he was driving erratically, almost as though he was slightly drunk. Or possibly, trying to detect surveillance.

'I would think his nerves are shot,' observed Wilberforce to Saunders. 'Who wouldn't feel that way after all he's been through?'

Time passed. The group in Thames House helped them-selves to coffee and read the morning papers, which had been delivered to the conference room.

Then suddenly things started happening. Through the box came a report from the surveillance team that Rotation had arrived in Oxford. He was having trouble finding a parking place but had finally spotted one, and had got out of the car.

'He's on foot and we're with him. We're hanging back a bit but the street's quite crowded.'

Just after this came a report that Ariadne had left her house accompanied by another woman and that they were walking together towards Walton Street. A still photo flashed up on the screen that showed Tatiana and Manon moving side by side.

'That's Manon,' said Wilberforce. 'What the hell does she think she's doing?' He sat fuming as more audio reports came in about the progress of the two women.

'Pray God she's got the sense not to go into the Parks,' he muttered to Saunders, 'or the Russian won't show.'

The audio feed announced, 'They're at the gates now. They're talking... and now Ariadne's gone in on her own.'

'Thank God,' said Wilberforce.

Saunders smiled. 'You should have more faith in her common sense,' he said.

It was mid-morning before Yuri reported to Ivanov in London. He and his team had spent a second largely sleepless night in the white van, followed by an uncomfortable few hours waiting here, lying in the bracken and bushes near the little bridge that crossed this tributary of the Thames. They all wore combat fatigues to disguise their presence, but there were few people in the Parks – mainly dog walkers, who didn't come across the bridge to this side of the water. A yard or so along from Yuri, Mikhail was positioned, lying prone and hidden by dense greenery. In front of him, looking out over the river, they had cleared a hole in the shrubbery – one not more than six inches round, but enough to provide a clear view. And enough space for the rifle to sight its target.

Using his mobile phone, Yuri dialled the Resident's direct line and, avoiding the use of location names in case British intelligence managed to listen in, he said, 'We're in position on the far bank. Fairly well concealed. There are a couple of people strolling around opposite us on the other bank and there's a crowd up at the cricket ground. A match is due to start at eleven o'clock so I think Paris will come down here for his handover. There's a seat just opposite us on the bank; we've got clear sighting of that and of the footbridge over the river. It should be an easy shot. We'll use a silencer of course.'

'What about getaway?'

'Mikhail has the van on a small road behind us. Take us three minutes to get there.'

'Where's Alexei?'

'He's gone across the bridge to see if he can spot them.' He snuck a look out from his cover and saw his fellow Russian returning. 'Hang on,' he said. 'He's just coming.'

Yuri waited until Alexei had joined him, deep in the rough thicket of brush. The two were experienced field operatives and went way back, so Yuri knew Alexei shared his unease about all this – they'd had virtually no time to plan, and the setting was far from ideal.

Alexei spoke in a rushed whisper. 'I've spotted them. They're walking down the path that leads straight to the bridge. They'll be there in just a few minutes.'

Yuri relayed this to Ivanov. He could sense his superior's impatience, but Yuri couldn't afford to be distracted now. When Ivanov started to ask questions he said tersely, 'Later,' and ended the call.

Mikhail was in position on the far side of Alexei, and he craned his head sideways, looking at Yuri. Yuri nodded, and

Mikhail nodded back, then propped himself on both forearms before reaching for the Dragunov sniper's rifle. It was a heavy weapon, but Mikhail had forearms like a stevedore's, and he swung the gun like a little toothpick, then held it steady, ready to fire. All three of them waited, the only sound a bird somewhere behind them – that, and their own tense breathing.

When Peter Robinson reached the gate of the Parks he was surprised to find a small crowd of people there. They all seemed to be heading towards the cricket ground. He followed a group of young men wearing striped blazers and walked behind them until they came to the pavilion. He was puzzled, wondering why on earth the woman had chosen this place. She said she wanted somewhere quiet to meet. This made no sense. He stood with his back to the cricket ground and scanned the rows of seats outside the pavilion but could see no sign of Tatiana.

It was five minutes to eleven so perhaps she had not arrived yet. There was an empty seat at the end of the second row, so he sat down to wait and watch for her. He felt uncomfortable – somehow exposed even though he was in a crowd – checking all the time for anyone who seemed to be taking an interest in him. But he saw nothing suspicious. He slid a hand into the inside pocket of his jacket, where he'd concealed an A4 envelope, and was reassured when he felt the edge of the item he was looking for. But where was this bloody woman? It was still not quite eleven, he reminded himself. She wasn't late yet; he was early.

Then he saw her, coming around the boundary rope where some benches had been placed on the field's perimeter, making her way through a group of spectators with her head down.

She was carrying a briefcase. As she came closer she looked up briefly towards the pavilion, then she stopped, turned and faced the cricket pitch, standing behind the benches with her back to Robinson, staring out at the field. She was leaving it to him to spot her, thought Robinson. Well so be it; he had her in his sights now.

As he stood up to go and join her, the fielding side began to come out of the pavilion, running down the steps and on to the field to applause from the spectators. He had to wait until the pair of opening batsmen emerged, walking briskly down the centre aisle in pads and helmets and on to the outfield, heading for the crease.

All the time this was going on he was trying to keep his eye on Tatiana in case she moved from her position. But she stayed where she was.

Now, thought Robinson, while all eyes were on the game. He went out through the little fence and walked at an oblique angle to the spot where she stood. As he came up behind her, he spoke softly, almost directly into the back of her ear, 'I didn't know you were a cricket fan.'

If he'd surprised her, she didn't show it, and she continued looking at the outfield, saying simply, 'I'm not. I didn't know there was a match today.'

'In that case, maybe we should take a stroll. I gather it's very pretty by the river.'

'It is,' she said, nodding in agreement, and turning sharply she started walking briskly away. It was Robinson's turn to be surprised – by her abruptness. A few paces on, she turned back and stared at him for the first time. 'Well, are you coming then?'

He looked cautiously around him at the other spectators. None of them seemed to be taking any notice of either of them; they were too busy watching as one of the Oxford team ran up to bowl the first ball of the match. There was the sound of willow bat on leather ball, followed by clapping, and by the time he had caught up with her, there were four runs on the board.

A few other people were on the path as they walked towards the river.

'You said this would be a quiet place.' He was uneasy and irritated.

'I told you, I didn't know there would be a match,' she snapped back. 'There shouldn't be many people around on the riverbank. It's a good place to give me whatever it is I'm supposed to pass on.'

Excellent, thought Robinson. He wanted this over with. Happily, she looked to have no suspicion that this encounter might not be what it seemed. How naive she was, especially when you considered how her father made his living. He could almost feel sorry for her. But only almost.

A S MANON TURNED AWAY from the gates of the Parks, leaving Tatiana to go in by herself, she was in a dilemma. She knew what she should do: go back to the house and wait. But what she wanted to do was to enter the Parks and find a place where she could see what was going on, without being seen. She argued with herself as she strolled back the way they had come and then suddenly she made a decision and her pace increased to a fast walk once she'd turned around.

Norham Gardens was a pleasant, tree-lined street of large Victorian mansions that ended at the entrance to one of the colleges. As Manon approached, a group of students emerged, all wearing the formal black and white that indicated they were sitting their final exams. Good luck, she muttered to herself, thinking back to the anxiety of her own finals. Thank God those days were over and that she hadn't stayed on for postgraduate work. Life studying in a library could never have provided the excitement she was experiencing daily in this job.

She turned down a narrow path, walled on both sides, which led into the Parks from the north. Now that she was here, she had no plan for what to do next. She had felt an irresistible urge to be part of whatever was going on but she knew she had no actual part to play and shouldn't even be here at all. The most important thing was that she should not be seen by Peter Robinson.

She and Tatiana had agreed that if Robinson wasn't happy to give her the document while they sat in the pavilion, Tatiana would walk with him as far as the river, but would stay on the near side so she would never be out of sight of other people. Manon went towards the cricket ground, keeping among the trees. She was surprised to see the crowd of spectators and the game in full swing. Tatiana and Robinson would never be at the pavilion with all these people around, she thought.

But as she was wondering what to do next, she noticed among a few people on the path a couple moving slowly towards the Cherwell. The woman was the same height as Manon and wore a familiar-looking blue gilet; the man was tall and trim, and wore a suit. Bingo.

Tatiana was slightly ahead of Robinson as they walked towards the river when she suddenly turned and said, 'This is ridiculous. Why don't you just hand over whatever you have to give me and I'll be on my way? You said it was urgent; all this is just a waste of time.'

'One can't be too careful,' Robinson replied. 'Better to do the handover in a more private place.'

'You think we're being watched?' Tatiana asked scornfully. 'No one here gives a damn if you give me some papers.'

'We could be,' said Robinson, ignoring her scathing tone. 'You've no idea who might have been watching you.'

'What do you mean?' she asked. 'No one is watching me.'

'You wouldn't know if they were,' he said. 'And your father told me you're a student here – in International Relations.'

'So?'

She could see the River Cherwell ahead of them, and the little pedestrian bridge that crossed it. He was still talking. 'So don't you realise that the British authorities – and the Americans too – use this place as a recruiting ground? They are looking for young impressionable minds that are none-theless knowledgeable about current affairs. A perfect mix for an employee of the CIA or MI6. Everyone knows that some of the colleges are virtually annexes of the British Secret Service.' He looked at her with obvious contempt. 'If you don't know that, your father should have told you.'

'Well I didn't know that,' said Tatiana fiercely. 'And I don't care. I'm not part of your stupid secret world. I think this is all ridiculous. You might as well have posted the package to me instead of this elaborate charade. You've come all this way just to make an unnecessary drama and insult me. If you don't give me whatever it is now, I'm going home.'

They had come to the path along the riverbank. The pedes-trian bridge was just ahead, and Robinson kept walking towards it.

'Where are you going?' Tatiana demanded. She stopped. 'It's better if we go this way.' She pointed along the bank.

'No, I can see people up there,' he said.

'Yes, but there's a path before we get to them where no one will see us.'

Robinson walked back to Tatiana, shaking his head. 'No. Let's go over the bridge – there's nobody on the other side.'

'But—' she was starting to say, when he suddenly grabbed her arm.

'Come on,' he said, squeezing her upper arm so hard that she had to go with him. As she was half dragged on to the bridge she felt a rush of anger and decided she would not go across.

She was carrying her briefcase in her free arm, and swung it viciously, smashing it into his face. Staggered, he let go of her, and she ran down the slanted ramp and on to the path.

Robinson remained in the middle of the bridge, wiping blood from the cut made by the buckle of the briefcase. There was the sound of a faint *whoosh*, and he fell forward on to the handrail where he stood, propped up by the rail, with his head hanging down over the water and his arms swinging in the air.

Manon was about a hundred yards away, standing hidden in the trees. She saw Robinson and Tatiana pause at the bridge and then start to move slowly across it. She cursed, angry that Tatiana had not followed her instructions to stay on the near side. What had changed her mind? Had something gone wrong? Watching the couple, she began to wonder; Tatiana was moving very slowly and Robinson had his hand on her arm. Then she saw Tatiana's leather briefcase swing round and hit Robinson, and moments later Tatiana was running fast along the path towards her.

Manon moved out from the trees, shouting, 'Tatiana. I'm here. This way.'

As Tatiana arrived, Manon grabbed hold of her and pulled her back under the cover of the trees. 'I think he wants to kill me,' Tatiana gasped.

They looked back towards the river, expecting to see Robinson running towards them in pursuit, but instead they saw a small group of people on the bridge. They seemed to have come from nowhere. There were six or seven of them: men and women; some on their phones, some beside Robinson, who was still hanging over the rail; two others had crossed the bridge and could be seen on the other bank.

'What's happening?' Tatiana demanded. 'Who are those people? Where have they come from? What's wrong with the Russian Englishman?'

Then Manon's phone buzzed. She glanced at it. A text from Saunders.

Go back to the house immediately. Speak to no one.

'What's that?' asked Tatiana.

'Nothing important,' Manon said curtly. 'Now come on – let's get out of here before people start asking questions.'

In Thames House they all watched in stunned silence as Ariadne hit Rotation with her briefcase, broke free from his hold, and ran along the bank. Before he could chase after her, Rotation suddenly jerked grotesquely, and his body seemed to crumple before slumping over the balustrade of the bridge.

After that audio reports came through in quick succession. The fleeing Ariadne was met by the woman believed to be a friendly. Could London tell this other woman to take Ariadne and get the hell out of there before anyone started asking them questions? Then another surveillance team member reported from the bridge that Rotation was dead, apparently shot from the far bank. After this, two men from the same team stayed to guard the scene against inquisitive passers-by, while the others frantically searched the bushes on the far bank, looking for the marksman. They discovered a hiding place in the undergrowth, with enough flattened grass to suggest at least two men had been lying there; they also found, half-buried and overlooked in someone's haste to get away, a spent high-velocity rifle cartridge. But no shooter.

Soon the air ambulance and local uniformed police arrived, and a blanket news lockdown was imposed until a line for public consumption could be agreed. By this point, the observers in Thames House had seen and heard all they needed and the feed from Oxford was shut down.

'Well,' said Wilberforce, standing up and stretching. 'I'm taking bets on who shot him.'

'I suppose it could have been a business rival who hired a hit man,' commented Stanston, 'or some other enemy he'd made in the UK. But my money's on his own side – Ivanov and his merry men or some thug they've brought in to do the job.'

'I think that's most likely,' agreed Saunders. 'Though they needed a hell of a lot of inside information to pull this off. Otherwise, how did they know where Robinson would be today? And why would the Russians want to kill him after his success penetrating the UK?'

'They may have known he was blown,' said Wilberforce.

Stanston's eyes widened, and he nodded. He said, 'That's something for us all to worry about. God knows we've got plenty of questions to answer, though first things first – we need to square the media. I want to get to them before they get to us.'

In the house in Jericho, Manon and Tatiana spent the afternoon going over and over again the events in the Parks. Neither of them had any inclination to go to the seminar.

'What do you think really happened to Robinson?' asked Tatiana for the fourth or fifth time. 'Do you think he's dead? I hit him quite hard, but I'm sure it wasn't enough to kill him.'

'Well, he did look dead to me, hanging there on the handrail, though perhaps he was just unconscious. Maybe you knocked him out.'

'After I'd hit him I just ran, so I didn't see anything until I met you and we looked back. Thank God you were there – I can't thank you enough. I was so scared; I don't know what I would have done. I couldn't understand why he was trying to drag me over the bridge; I just knew I wasn't going to let him do that, or else die trying. I felt so angry, and I can't help wondering if he was trying to kill me.'

Manon was keeping an eye on the news, in between calls from both Saunders and Wilberforce, making sure that she and Tatiana were all right. She knew that if Robinson were dead, sooner or later something would need to be said publicly. After all, he was an MP. Then on the ten o'clock news came the announcement that Peter Robinson, MP for Liverpool North, had died of a suspected heart attack while walking in Oxford. There was a brief account of his background and that was all.

'So no one can blame you,' said Manon, thinking of how Tatiana's father might receive the news. 'And the press won't bother you. As far as they know, Robinson died from medical causes.'

'Thank goodness,' Tatiana replied. She tried and failed to suppress a big yawn. 'I think I'd better go to bed. At least I know now the man is dead.'

But Manon sat up a bit longer, wondering what the real story was.

I T WAS TWO DAYS before Manon discovered the truth. She had stayed on in Oxford the night after the events in the Parks and was there the following morning when a letter sent Special Delivery arrived for Tatiana from the American Embassy. Manon watched her face as she read it and saw her expression change from puzzlement to amazed delight.

'I can go to America,' Tatiana shouted, waving the letter in the air. 'They've offered me a job.'

'That's great,' said Manon, thinking, 'Well done, Wilberforce.' Tatiana held out the letter. 'Wow,' Manon said, once she'd digested it. 'Research post in the Library of Congress. That's fantastic. And they want you urgently.'

'Yes. They've even sent me a plane ticket.' Tatiana looked at it and her face changed again. 'But it's for tomorrow. In the evening. I can't possibly be ready in time.'

'Of course you can,' said Manon. 'I'll help you.'

Manon remained in Oxford another night, then went with Tatiana to London and saw her safely on to the Heathrow Express.

As she watched the train pull smoothly out of the station, Manon called Saunders.

'She's on her way to the airport,' she said. 'I don't think anything can happen to her now.'

'Well done,' he replied. 'See you back in the office.'

*

'If this were the army,' said Wilberforce, 'I'd have you up on a charge.'

'I understand, but—'

'Yes,' said Saunders, though not unsympathetically, 'we want to hear this "but" of yours. We did tell you to stay in the house.'

'I can explain.' And she described that morning in Jericho; how Tatiana suddenly panicked, threatening to pull out of the meeting; how Manon had wheedled and cajoled, with just a hint of threat, but had got nowhere, until suddenly she saw that only by actually going with her could she get her to the Parks.

'I can't fault you for that,' said Saunders. 'But when you'd got her there, why didn't you go back as instructed?'

'It's difficult to explain. I just had this feeling that when she got to the Parks she might turn tail and run. Avoid meeting him, and then come and tell me she had done the job. Which would mean that Robinson got away scot-free; we couldn't charge him with anything.

'I suppose I also felt that something might go wrong and I might be needed. I'm sorry. It sounds stupid now. But I did help, as it turned out,' she ended rather plaintively.

'Yes. That's true. I don't know where she might have gone if you hadn't been there to scoop her up.' Saunders looked at Wilberforce and went on, 'We took the decision not to tell you the details of the operation because we thought it might affect the way you were with Tatiana. That may have been a mistake. Perhaps you should have known the full picture.'

'Perhaps,' said Wilberforce, 'but we assumed you would obey orders and stay out of it. Take this as it's meant, Manon – informally, and with no repercussions – and remember, initiative is good but orders are there to be obeyed.'

She nodded, feeling chastened. Wilberforce continued, 'Now that's closed, we can move on. I expect you must be wondering what really happened.'

'I am. I heard on the news that he'd died of a heart attack.'

'Yes. That's the story the Brits put out. The actual story is – and this is for your ears only and that's an order – he was shot by his own side.'

'By the Russians? Why would they do that?'

'We're not sure. The British are working on it. But there's no doubt about it. The traffic cameras picked up their van in Oxford the day before. Then the camera at the gates of the Parks caught them going into the ground. They were holed up on the opposite bank just waiting for their chance, which came when your friend swiped him with her briefcase. Tough cookie, that one.'

'Gosh,' said Manon, almost speechless. 'Thank goodness they didn't shoot her by accident.'

'Yes. They had the good manners to wait till she was out of the way. But it wasn't only the gunman she escaped. Robinson had a knife in his pocket. It's pretty clear he intended to kill her.'

Wilberforce paused briefly. 'But now we want to talk to you about something else. You've only been in Dave's section for a short time, and we really threw you in at the deep end with this operation. Have you enjoyed it?'

'I have. Very much,' Manon said.

'Excellent. Would you be interested in more fieldwork?'

'Yes I would. Absolutely.'

'Good. I have to tell you, we both think –' and Wilberforce looked at Saunders, who nodded in agreement '– that you have a natural aptitude for operational work. I can get researchers and analysts any day of the week, but talented people in the field are far and few between. We'll make the shift gradually, assuming you want to do it at all, and you'll need to have training back at Langley.' He saw she was about to speak, but he held up a hand to stop her. 'Don't say anything now. I want you to sleep on it. And talk to Dave here. He's had a lot of operational experience, and will knock out any romantic visions of the sort of work you may have to do. Then come see me again, and tell us what you've decided.'

'I will,' said Manon, trying not to show her excitement. She could not conceive of anything that would make her say no to this offer. 'And thank you.'

'Well, you can thank me once you've got your beak wet a second time, and still like the taste of the water.'

The following day Manon and Louise were having lunch in their favourite restaurant – the same one where Manon had met Peter Robinson. This was the first time they had seen each other since the news of Peter Robinson's death had become public, though they had spoken on the phone.

'I'm glad he's dead,' said Louise bluntly. 'It's the best thing that could have happened. I used to think he was such a lovely man and I was so lucky to have found him, but I gradually began to grasp that he wasn't at all what he seemed to be. Then when poor Harry told me his story, I realised Peter was totally fake. Nothing about him was true. I must have been an idiot to have been taken in.'

'Don't blame yourself. He was a brilliant construction, designed to take in everyone.'

'It's very lucky for him, and everyone else, that he died when he did. I suppose otherwise he would have ended up in prison with a lot of scandal. As it is, he's a bit of a hero to people here. His constituency is holding a wake; they've invited me. I'm not going, needless to say.' She shook her head vigorously, as if ridding herself of a pest. 'But don't let's talk about him any more. I've got some news.'

'So have I,' said Manon. 'Is yours good news?' When Louise nodded, she said, 'Mine is too. Tell you what. I remember saying the champagne's on me the next time there was something to celebrate.' She waved at the waiter. 'And it looks like that's now.'

When the champagne was poured, Manon said, 'You go first.'

'Well. When things started going badly with Peter I decided I needed a complete change so I applied for something very different and I just heard yesterday that I've got it.'

'Oh fantastic. What is it?'

'I'm going to the Kennedy School of Government at Harvard to do a postgrad degree.'

Manon leapt up from her chair and gave Louise a hug. 'That's amazing – and just perfect because I'll be going back to the States too for a while. They've offered me an opportunity in a different branch of work which I'm thrilled about. So we'll be able to see each other over there – we won't be too far apart.'

'Let's drink to that.' Louise was smiling broadly. 'And I have a toast too. Let's drink to neither of us getting involved with politicians.'

They clinked their glasses. 'No politicians,' they said in unison.

A NOTE ON THE AUTHOR

Dame Stella Rimington joined the Security Service (MI5) in 1968. During her career she worked in all the main fields of the Service: counter-subversion, counter-espionage and counter-terrorism. She was appointed Director General in 1992, the first woman to hold the post. She has written her autobiography and ten Liz Carlyle novels. She lives in London and Norfolk.

A NOTE ON THE TYPE

The text of this book is set in Adobe Caslon, named after the English punch-cutter and type-founder William Caslon I (1692–1766). Caslon's rather old-fashioned types were modelled on seventeenth-century Dutch designs, but found wide acceptance throughout the English-speaking world for much of the eighteenth century until replaced by newer types towards the end of the century. Used in 1776 to print the Declaration of Independence, they were revived in the nineteenth century and have been popular ever since, particularly amongst fine printers. There are several digital versions, of which Carol Twombly's Adobe Caslon is one.